DIAL M FOR MEOW

a Bookshop Kitties Mystery

Ruth J. Hartman

DIAL M FOR MEOW

Cover design by Daniela Colleo
of www.StunningBookCovers.com

Published by Gemma Halliday Publishing

Many thanks go to my husband, Garry, for always encouraging me with my writing. And to my awesome agent, Dawn Dowdle, for believing in me and cheering me on. Also, to Gemma Halliday for not only publishing this book, but also for going the extra mile to make sure the book is the best it can be.

CHAPTER ONE

"If you keep pestering your sister like that, you'll be sorry."

Unblinking green eyes peered back at me from my car's passenger seat, holding nothing but feigned innocence. But his cute little mustache made it hard to be mad at him. My two cats, Milton and Pearl, were the lights of my life. It was no wonder they'd become the stars in my series of children's books.

Milton, a tuxedo cat, was classy in stark black and white fur, looking ready for a night out on the town, while Pearl, solid white with a fluffy tail that plumed like a huge feather, resembled a gorgeous Vegas showgirl ready to dance. They were siblings from a rescued litter of kittens a neighbor found in an alley two years ago. The woman had been sure I'd want to take them home with me. She'd been right.

The characters of Milton and Pearl in my books were furry sleuths, solving murders wherever their adventures took them. Sometimes, with the sly expressions my two cats wore and the way they seemed to communicate with each other with only stares, blinks, and purrs, I wondered if they really could solve murders if given the chance. I had no doubt they were smart enough. Definitely sneaky enough.

I glanced out the windshield at the road sign. "Just another ten miles until we'll be at Aunt Betty's bookstore. See? Didn't that nine-hour drive go fast?"

If cats could roll their eyes, my two might have wanted to do just that. How could I blame them? I needed a nap. And a snack. And something to drink. I definitely needed a shower. I was sure the cats would opt out of the shower but say yes to the rest.

"Okay, fine. It wasn't a fast trip, but you can't blame me

for rushing to Indiana from Philadelphia, can you? You heard on speakerphone how much Aunt Betty wants me to come and help in her bookshop."

Pearl blinked at me, her girly eyelashes giving her an exotic look. Milton flipped onto his back, pawing at air for lack of something better to do. I'd had them in their carriers until an hour ago then didn't have the heart to keep them cooped up any longer. So far, they'd been reasonably good, only wanting to sit on my lap a couple of times while I drove. My having fed them frequent pieces of dry cat food hadn't hurt either.

If we'd taken a plane flight to Green Meadow, Indiana, to see my Aunt Betty, it would have been quicker, but that took money. Unfortunately, I didn't have much. I clenched my fingers around the steering wheel, remembering the caught-red-handed expression on my ex-boyfriend's, Tony's, face when I confronted him about my savings account suddenly showing a balance of zero.

He'd also gotten ahold of my credit card and rung up a ton of purchases in my name. I was still fighting with the credit card company to convince them it hadn't been me doing the spending. I'd tried over the last few months not to panic that my money was running dry, but the more my overdue bills mounted up, the less calm I stayed.

I glanced at Milton and Pearl, now so serenely curled up in a purring ball together on the passenger seat. They depended on me for their safety, care, and kibble. No way I'd let them down and allow them to be hungry and homeless. This chance to work in Aunt Betty's bookstore might be my way to not do that.

"I don't know if I told you guys or not, but Aunt Betty has this great idea of me setting up a children's book section. You two could sit with the kids while they read."

Milton yawned, but Pearl gave a trill—her version of a happy meow.

I scratched her under the chin. "See? I knew it. You're going to love living with Aunt Betty. And a big bonus? She loves cats."

The kitties were sleepy again, so I didn't bother telling them about the special room I wanted to set up at the bookstore to promote their mystery series. At first I'd jumped at the lifeline my aunt had thrown me only as a way out of my financial distress. But now, her enthusiasm for me and the cats living with her had caught on.

When I spotted the exit sign for Green Meadow, I flipped on my turn signal. It'd been way too long since I visited. Though Aunt Betty and I talked on the phone and sent emails and texts, there was no replacement for spending time with a loved one.

I'd used the excuse of writing my latest book for not visiting before now, but I still should have found time to see Aunt Betty. She always encouraged me with my writing and said how proud she was of me.

Aunt Betty had jumped right in to help me after my dad spilled the beans about my boyfriend, but I was ashamed it was the reason I'd finally agreed to come. How had I been so stupid not to realize what Tony was up to? I'd thought he was the love of my life and had trusted him with everything I had.

Within a few minutes, I parked in front of the bookstore, the sign declaring *Words to Read By* swinging softly in the breeze from an overhead awning. I blew out a breath, so glad to finally be here after the long drive. My long dark hair, which had an adversity to humid weather, now sprang out in odd-shaped curls.

I got my phone from my purse in the back seat and sent a quick text to Aunt Betty that I'd arrived. She was probably waiting to hear from me and would text right back. I could picture her sitting at her bookstore counter, watching her phone screen for updates.

Several minutes later, I looked at the clock on my phone. She hadn't replied yet. Was she waiting on customers and couldn't get away? I craned my neck to see inside the large glass window, but it was dark inside. If the lights were out, did that mean the place was closed? It seemed too early for that.

After another couple of minutes, there was still no text from my aunt. Where was she?

Milton and Pearl, now antsy, mewed and pawed at the car door to get out. Not that I blamed them. I was ready too. My aunt might get a surprise when we entered if she hadn't seen my text yet. I hadn't told her what time to expect us, only that it would be today.

I glanced at my cats, sitting there with huge eyes and swishing tails. "Okay, you two. Time to get out."

Their duet of meows grew more insistent the longer it took me to undo my seat belt, get out, and close my door then run around to open theirs and fasten their leashes to their harnesses.

Finally, we were ready to roll.

I'd barely gotten the cats settled on the sidewalk and the passenger door closed when footsteps came from my left. "Christy Bailey? Is that you?"

I turned. Who was it? Sure, I'd met some people from town, but I hadn't been here in a while. Maybe someone who knew me from when I used to spend summers here. The late-afternoon sun was in my eyes, and I couldn't make out the woman's face. But her voice seemed familiar.

She edged closer. "It *is* you. Wow, it's been so long!" She flung her arms around me, encasing me in a tight clench, oblivious to the two cats at my feet. Pearl hissed when she was nearly stepped on.

I pulled back from her embrace. I took a closer look at her blonde hair, large blue eyes, and wide smile. A memory from a long time ago crossed my mind. "Janie Lambert?" I asked.

Her face lit up. "You remembered."

Ah yes. Now more was coming back to me. Janie had lived in Green Meadow when we were little. We used to play together in the bookstore when I came to visit Aunt Betty. But then her dad got a new job and they moved away. I hadn't heard from her since. I'd always wondered where she'd ended up.

"Gosh, it's been forever," Janie said. Her eyes crinkled when she smiled and glanced up at me. When we were young, we'd been the same height. I guess I'd kept sprouting, but she had already bloomed early

I laughed. "It has. I'm surprised to see you back here."

"I'm as surprised as anyone. Dad's job took us to California all those years ago. But later, after I went to college, the guy I married ended up getting a job near here. Weird, huh?" She pointed to her left. "I actually own that pastry shop three doors down. Dreamy Sweets."

"Wow, that's awesome. So, you're married?"

"Not anymore," she answered. Her face fell. "He turned out to be a lemon, unfortunately."

"Sounds like my ex-boyfriend. Maybe later on, you and I can swap stories of our sorry men."

Janie nodded then glanced at our feet. "Awww, who are these cuties?" Her eyes widened. "Oh, wait. Are they Milton and Pearl? From your books?"

I smiled. "Yep. Wow, you know about my books?"

"Of course. Everyone in town knows. Betty brags on you all the time." She crouched down and stuck out both hands, giving each cat a chance to sniff her fingers.

Pearl must have gotten over nearly being stepped on, because her purr and Milton's were both loud, trying to outdo each other, a cacophony of roaring motors.

I let out more length on the leashes so Janie could better address the kitties as they begged for attention. "I'm surprised Aunt Betty didn't mention you'd moved back," I said.

Janie stood then shrugged. "I haven't been running Dreamy Sweets for all that long. My ex and I lived about thirty minutes north of town. That is, until he up and left."

"I'm so sorry you went through that."

"It turned out for the best," she said. "He was a jerk. And I'm actually happier now. I'd wanted to work before, but he was so controlling he wouldn't allow it. Now that I run Dreamy Sweets, I'm having the time of my life. I'd love to catch up with you. It's so great to see you again." She glanced at the front of the bookstore and back, her eyebrows lowered. "Are you back in town to check on Betty?"

My heart lurched. "Check on her? Why, is something wrong?"

She shrugged. "I don't know. She's been acting differently lately. Nothing major, just hasn't seemed her usual upbeat self. When she didn't open the shop this afternoon, I thought she was out of town or something. But she doesn't travel much, as I'm sure you know. And she usually isn't sick, so it's weird when the bookstore is closed. I was actually on my way over to see if she'd opened up. Doesn't look like it though."

Alarm bells went off in my head. "Now you've got me worried too. Aunt Betty knew I was coming today. Where could she be?"

"Maybe that's why the shop is closed," said Janie. "Getting ready for you to visit."

I shook my head. "No. The bookstore is her first love. She'd only close if there was an emergency." And that word emergency took on a whole new meaning with someone my aunt's age. It was hard not to imagine the worst—falling and hitting her head or having a heart attack or stroke. I needed to get in the building. Right now. I glanced at the front door and back to Janie. "Would you mind holding the cats' leashes while I get the key from my purse?"

"Sure, no problem." She tilted her head. "You have a key?"

Janie obviously hadn't gotten over her habit of wanting to know everything about everyone.

"Yeah," I answered. "Never had to use it since she's always here, but she wanted me to have one just in case."

She bent to untangle the leash where Milton had circled around her leg. "In case of what?"

I shrugged, suddenly afraid I was going to find out the *of what*. And that I wouldn't like it.

With a step back, Janie urged the cats to follow. I stuck the large old-fashioned key into the lock below the stained-glass window. The ancient oak door gave the same shrill creak I remembered from my childhood, the noise so loud it used to make me jump when customers entered the building.

The place was dark, dust motes dancing in the afternoon light coming through a far window. After turning on the lights, I set my bag on the front counter and stepped farther into the room. "Aunt Betty? Are you here? It's Christy."

My heart thundered in my chest. I needed to calm down. How many times in my life had I jumped to conclusions, only to find out my fears were way off base and there was a reasonable explanation? Chances were she had just stepped out of the shop for a quick bite somewhere. Or had to run an errand. I took a deep breath and let it out slowly.

There. That helped.

The quiet was broken only by the cats' claws scraping across the wooden planks as Janie ushered them inside the building.

I stepped farther across the floor, relieved to see

everything seemed to be in its usual orderly fashion. My aunt was nothing if not tidy and fastidious. "Aunt Betty?" I called. "Where are you?"

After checking all the rooms and storage areas, I was convinced she wasn't anywhere in the bookshop. I crossed to the rear of the shop and opened the back door leading to an alley. I frowned. Aunt Betty usually kept the door locked. But this time, it wasn't. I peered outside. Her car was parked there, so she had to be around someplace. Time to check upstairs. I headed toward the staircase leading to her apartment.

Once I reached the stairs, I glanced down. Splotches of mud littered the surfaces, the majority on the bottom four steps. How odd. Aunt Betty was the type to clean up messes so fast, they'd barely had a chance to occur when she grabbed a broom.

As I climbed the steep staircase, a million memories raced across my mind of all the times I played on these steps or ran up and down them, laughing, loving being in the bookstore. The smell of book pages, the murmur of voices as my aunt spoke with her customers in the front room. I'd pretended it was my bookstore, that every book in the place belonged to me.

Thinking back, I couldn't remember a time when I didn't love to read. Aunt Betty had encouraged me in my quest to become an author. I sometimes thought it was as important to her as it was to me.

When I reached the top of the stairs, I headed down the hall toward the den. Maybe she was waiting for me and had dozed off in her favorite recliner.

Tiny soft-footed paws pattered on the stairs, followed by the trailing of leather leashes slapping against the steps. Janie must have released the cats once she had them inside the store. There were two things I remembered about Janie. She always wanted to be in the middle of everything, and I'd liked her very much. Nearly every day, she and I had played together in the store. It was strange I hadn't seen her for more than fifteen years. So much had changed in my life, as it obviously had for her.

When she first approached me on the sidewalk, I hadn't recognized her and had been startled a strange women would wrap me in a bear hug—something I didn't witness often on the sidewalks of Philadelphia. But when she gave me that familiar grin, her bottom teeth slightly crooked and dimples forming in her cheeks, I knew it was my friend from a lifetime ago.

Aunt Betty's den was the second room down on the left side of the hall. The door was open a few inches. I crept closer. "Aunt Betty? It's Christy." I gently pushed open the door partway, not wanting to startle her if she was taking a nap.

From behind, I saw the back of her gray-haired head as she lounged in her recliner. A book lay open on the floor next to the chair. Something marred the white pages in addition to the black ink of the words. Had she spilled something on the book? Just like with the mud on the stairway, the mess seemed out of place.

As I rounded the side of the chair, a couple of things came into view, though my mind couldn't quite grasp it. Whatever had spilled on the pages of the book looked like blood. And it wasn't my aunt in the chair, but another woman. A letter opener, plain and generic, like something from the general store, protruded from the woman's chest, and a large pool of dark red covered the front of her white summer sweater. Her eyes were open, mouth stuck in a permanent *O* of surprise and terror.

I fell to my knees and grasped the woman's wrist, knowing it was futile to check for a pulse, yet needing to do it. No evidence of a heartbeat fluttered beneath her pale skin. The woman wasn't napping. Or breathing. She was dead.

The door behind me creaked as it opened a little wider. Janie screamed. Both cats shrieked and scrambled in place before jetting from the room. Janie moved closer then let out a gasp. "Oh!" she said. "It's Nan Bittle. Is she…?"

I nodded but didn't turn to look at her as I tried to absorb that the person in front of me was dead. But where was my aunt?

I shot to my feet, sudden panic racing through my body. "Aunt Betty? Where are you?"

A yank to my arm had me facing Janie. "Look," she said, "over there."

A pair of pink sneakers were barely visible behind a couch in one corner. I rushed across the room, once again dropping to my knees. My hand shook as I took her pulse. She was breathing! I gently shook her shoulder. "Aunt Betty? Are you all right?"

Her eyes fluttered open, and she groaned. "Christy?"

"Yes, it's me. What"—I glanced over my shoulder and back—"happened up here?"

She sat up then winced when she reached up to touch the back of her graying head. "What happened?" Her eyes widened when she spotted the blood on her hands. "Oh no…"

I gazed into brown eyes the same shade and shape as mine. "We need to call the police. There's a…" I didn't want to say the words.

"A dead body," piped in Janie.

As my aunt's gaze swung slowly to the woman in the chair, her eyes widened.

I rubbed her shoulder. "How did you end up on the floor? And how did Nan end up no longer breathing?"

"I—" She shook her head. "Nan demanded to talk to me. Said it was important."

Janie moved closer. "Is that why your shop has been closed?"

"Yes," answered Aunt Betty. "She was so adamant we talk. I thought it best to close up so we wouldn't be interrupted."

I hated to bring up the obvious but forced the words out. "But she's…dead. How did—"

"—that happen?" Janie asked.

Aunt Betty glanced at Janie then me. "We argued. Over Wallace."

I lowered my eyebrows. "The man you've been seeing?"

"Yes," said Aunt Betty. "He and I have been together for several months. Nan was jealous. Wanted him for herself."

Janie now had her phone in her hand. "I'm going to call the police now, okay?"

I nodded. "Yes, thanks." But I wanted to hear from Aunt Betty what happened before the authorities got here. I squeezed her shoulder. "How did things end up so badly?"

"It all happened fast," Aunt Betty replied. "She was so angry. Threatening she'd spread lies around town about me, that I'd lose my bookstore if I didn't stop seeing Wallace. I couldn't believe she was saying those things. She knows—knew—how the bookstore is my life. How it has been since my husband died. How could she be so vengeful?"

A glance to the hallway showed Janie on the phone. It wouldn't take long for Green Meadow's police to show up. "Okay, so Nan was angry, and you argued. Then what?"

She blinked and looked at me. "That's just it. I don't remember."

CHAPTER TWO

As soon as Aunt Betty could stand without feeling woozy, she wanted to wash the blood from her hands. Much as I'd want to do the same thing in her place, I doubted it would make the police happy. "Maybe we should wait," I said.

"Why?"

"They'll want to see everything. As it was." Though the mysteries I wrote were for young readers, I'd still done enough research about crime scenes to know a little about the subject.

She grimaced, eyeing the dried, dark-red patches on her palms. "It's disgusting. I want it off."

"I know," I answered. "I would too. Just wait a little longer, okay?"

She gave a reluctant nod, clasping her hands together and looking anywhere but at them.

A knock at the front door had Janie dashing down the stairs. I'd thought about leaving it unlocked for the police, but that would be an open invitation for customers to enter, as well as nosy neighbors who might want to know why the police were paying the bookstore a visit.

Pearl and Milton trotted back into the room after their initial jolt from Janie's scream. With the shock of finding Nan dead and then Aunt Betty passed out in the corner, I'd forgotten to close the cats in a room somewhere. Their natural nosiness led them to Nan's body. Milton had his paws on Nan's knees. Not that she'd mind, poor woman, but I doubted the gift of cat hair on the body would please the police.

I rushed to the chair where Nan's body lay slouched against the back and then eyed my cat. "No, you don't!" I said as I lifted Milton, trying to ignore his growl of disappointment. I'd ruined his fun, after all. I'd no sooner pressed him beneath my arm when Pearl rose on her hind legs, stretching out her paw to take a swipe at Nan's hand.

With a sigh, I carted my wiggly bundles of fur into the hall and down two doors to the guest room where I stayed when visiting Aunt Betty. I placed them on the bed, giving a quick glance around to make sure nothing was disturbed. As far as I could tell, the altercation had only taken place in the den.

As I closed the door, I caught annoyed expressions from Milton and Pearl, pouting at not being included in whatever excitement was happening down the hall. Oh, the betrayal.

I headed back toward the den just as two men reached the top of the stairs. Janie was in their wake, peeking around them to make eye contact with me. Police, I assumed, though only one, a man who appeared to be in his fifties, was in uniform. His name tag said Officer Pike. The other, a man who looked to be in his thirties, wore a denim jacket over a white button-down shirt and jeans. Even though I'd visited Green Meadow over the years, thankfully I'd never had any reason to speak to the police.

Until now.

Butterflies bumped around in my stomach, causing an uncomfortable quiver in my midsection. What would happen when they saw the body? And Aunt Betty with blood on her hands? I darted into the den a few seconds before the men entered. The younger one eyed me strangely. But I needed to be at Aunt Betty's side when they questioned her. Being stuck in the hall while the action was going on inside the den wouldn't do. I frowned. That made me sound like Milton and Pearl.

Officer Pike stepped to the body and began his examination. No doubt he'd quickly deduce the woman wasn't breathing. Besides, a letter opener protruding from a person's chest wasn't conducive to a long, happy life.

Janie stepped close to me. "Did something else happen?"

"What do you mean?" I asked.

"You're frowning."

"Isn't it enough there's a dead body?"

She shrugged. "Well, I would think so but wanted to make sure you hadn't spotted a second one when you were down the hall."

"Second one?" said the younger policeman who was at our side in a flash. "What's going on?"

I eyed Janie, giving her my most annoyed glare, but either she didn't notice, or it didn't bother her that she might have caused additional trouble for Aunt Betty or me.

I crossed my arms and faced the man. "No, not a second one," I said. "Just a misunderstanding." Wanting to get things rolling, I stuck out my hand to the man. "I'm Christy Bailey, Betty Hollingworth's niece."

He shook my hand. "Detective Perry Combs."

A detective? But then, murder was a sticky business that might go beyond the small-town police's normal sphere.

"So, Miss Bailey."

"Christy, please."

He nodded. "Christy. I'll need to question everyone who's here."

Pearl raced in. How had she gotten out of the guest room? She pawed at his shoe.

The detective glanced down. "Well, I guess I meant to speak to everyone who wasn't a cat." The fact he didn't seem upset about Pearl eased my anxiety a fraction. Hopefully he'd be gentle with Aunt Betty when questioning her. He motioned Janie to a corner of the room. They spoke in muted tones. What would he ask her?

When Milton paused in the doorway, perusing the people standing there, I knew I'd better round up the cats, again, and find a more secure place for them to stay.

Janie appeared at my side soon after. The detective must not have had many questions for her. "I think your littles want to be in on things," she said. "Want me to take them down to the bookstore?"

"Yes, thanks," I answered. "That'd be great." The fact that Janie, who liked to always know what was going on, would risk missing something to take care of the cats impressed me.

She gathered both cats, who squirmed and kicked the whole way out of the room. Her footsteps clomped down the steps. Now, with the cats gone, maybe we could—

Within seconds, Janie was back. She hurried to me.

I lowered my eyebrows. "Um, I thought you were going to watch the cats."

"I put them in the bookstore and closed that door at the bottom of the stairs," said Janie. "I kept it unlocked so other police can get in and also unlocked the main door." She shrugged. "But I hurried back. Didn't want to miss anything here."

Ah, there was the Janie I knew and loved.

She grabbed my hand and tugged me close, something else I remembered from our childhood. However, clinging to a friend at age six was different than in a person's twenties.

Sitting in a chair across the room, my aunt looked beyond exhausted. I disentangled my hand from Janie's tentacles and hurried to Aunt Betty, taking a nearby seat. I put my arm around her shoulders and leaned in. "Are you holding up okay?"

She shrugged. "I can't even answer that. I'm just numb."

I sighed. Poor Aunt Betty. To not even remember what happened after the fight with her rival for Wallace's attention. I'd never met the man. Had he given Nan reason to think he might be interested in her too? I hoped not. The way my aunt wrote about him in her emails and texts, she was pretty smitten.

Detective Combs approached us and pulled up a chair in front of Aunt Betty. She eyed him suspiciously but relaxed her shoulders when he gave her a kind smile.

He took out a pad and pen. "Ms. Hollingsworth, as you can imagine, I have some questions for you."

"It's Mrs., and yes, of course," said Aunt Betty. She rubbed her hands together as if she wanted to get rid of the dried blood. "Can't I wash my hands? I really want to get this off."

He got Officer Pike's attention and waved him over. Once he reached the detective, they spoke for a minute and the officer went out into the hall. He returned with a camera and took several photos of her hands. Next, he took a small scraping of blood from beneath her fingernails. Then he gave Aunt Betty the green light to wash up.

She darted out of the room and across the hall. I could see her in the bathroom madly scrubbing her hands. I didn't blame her one bit. I didn't know how I would have handled having someone else's blood on my hands, especially for that long.

Janie stood just inside the doorway to the den, taking it

all in. Since she'd been unfortunate enough to discover the body along with me, I'd fill her in later on any details. Right now, however, my aunt needed me more.

When Aunt Betty returned, she carried the towel she'd used for drying her hands. She sat down and clung to the fabric like a security blanket.

Detective Combs glanced at something across the room. I followed his line of sight to notice Officer Pike had covered the body with a sheet and was on the phone. Green Meadow's tiny police force acted differently from Philadelphia's much larger one. Here, the police officers handled jobs that in a big city might have been fulfilled by a medical examiner.

The detective turned back to us and retrieved his pad and pen from where he'd stashed them while Aunt Betty cleaned up. "Now, let's start at the beginning. Tell me what happened here today between you and Nan Bittle."

Before speaking, Aunt Betty held out her slightly damp hand to me. I took it.

She inhaled, let it out, and then focused on the detective. "Nan called me," she said, "sounding desperate. Wanted to speak to me right away."

"Why was Nan so intent on speaking to you?" he asked.

"Wallace."

He raised his eyebrows. "Can you be more specific?"

"Wallace Wilkins. My…boyfriend."

Was the hesitation because she felt odd at her age calling him that or because there was something else going on with him? Maybe something to do with the murder?

Detective Combs nodded. "All right. So, you met with her. Then what happened?"

"It was all so upsetting."

He blinked then eyed the sheet-covered body.

She waved her free hand, her other still firmly clutching mine. "Oh, not that, of course," she said. "I mean, yes, that's upsetting. Quite more than upsetting."

I squeezed Aunt Betty's hand, hoping to convey my support. Who could blame her for being flustered? How many people were questioned by the police because a dead body had taken up residence in their den?

The detective leaned forward, his expression calm.

"Mrs. Hollingsworth, I know this is hard. I'm only trying to get the facts straight so we can proceed."

Proceed? I didn't like the sound of that. True, I understood the need for it, but still… What exactly did he have in mind for my aunt?

Aunt Betty cleared her throat then said, "What I meant was, when she came here, she was yelling at me. Threatening me."

"How did she threaten you?"

"She said if I didn't stop seeing Wallace, she'd put something terrible about me in her newspaper column. Something that would ruin me and my business forever. And no one would want to ever shop here again."

"Did she say what she'd print?" he asked.

Her face reddened. "I'd rather not say."

I eyed the detective, whose expression was troubled. A troubled officer of the law wasn't a good thing if someone I loved was the focus of his consternation.

I gently slipped my hand from Aunt Betty's and placed my arm around her shoulders. "Aunt Betty," I said, "I know this is hard. Maybe one of the hardest things you've ever done. But the detective might be better able to help you the more information he has to work with."

Her eyes watered and she blinked away tears. "I know. It's just…"

He gave her a kind smile. "I realize these questions seem intrusive and likely painful to answer," he said. "But your niece is right. The more facts I have, the quicker I can solve this case."

"Okay." Aunt Betty's voice came out as a whisper, as if she was afraid someone might overhear her next words. What could be so bad she didn't want to say it out loud? "You see, I've known Nan since we were young. We were never friends but went to school together."

I hadn't met Nan before. How was it possible Aunt Betty had always known her and they lived in the same small town? I opened my mouth to speak.

She held up her hand. "Christy, when you used to come and stay with me during those years, Nan lived someplace else. It's only been in the last year she moved back to Green

Meadow."

The suspense nearly did me in. Not in a nosy way, like my cats, where they almost lose their fur from the anticipation of something exciting about to happen. No, this was more like dread. That whatever Aunt Betty was going to say was something truly awful that might change her life forever once it came to light.

Detective Combs and I leaned closer to her at the same time. Across the room, Janie stood on her tiptoes, as if to get a better view of whatever was going on. The uniformed officer had stepped out into the hall, but I could hear his side of the conversation to another person on the phone.

My aunt sighed, as if giving voice to what she'd tell us next would wear her out.

Detective Combs said, "Go on."

"One day in Wallace's coffee shop, he and I were sitting in a booth together, having a chat and enjoying our drinks. I thought it would be like any other day. But that day, Wallace had a special smile. I teased him about it, asking him what was going on. He leaned closer but didn't keep his voice down at all. He told me he loved me."

The detective held up his hand. "I hardly see how that—"

I frowned at him. "Please," I said, "let her continue. If she thinks it's important enough to say, then we should listen."

His face reddened, but he gave a nod.

Aunt Betty shrugged. "Anyway," she went on, "I was pleased that he said it but surprised he'd choose a public venue to tell me something so important for the first time. It wasn't until I was ready to leave the coffee shop that I noticed a person sitting alone in a back booth, partially hidden by decorative ferns near the booth. It was Georgina Zann. The biggest gossip in Green Meadow."

I knew all about gossips. They were all the same, spreading news of a person's troubles to anyone who'd listen. I'd been subjected to smirks and stares after Tony had taken advantage of my trust in him and stolen my money, thanks to a gossipy neighbor who'd overheard my phone conversation to the police about what Tony had done. I patted Aunt Betty's hand in encouragement.

She went on. "Word soon got out what Wallace had said. Admittedly, it's not world news for most people. But when Nan found out through the busybody grapevine, she called then immediately ran to my bookstore, looking like a storm cloud ready to burst. Thankfully, it was near closing time, and we were alone. Nan was livid. Said she'd ruin me by printing something about me that would make people steer clear of Words to Read By."

"What might that have been?" Detective Combs asked.

She hesitated then said, "That I sell pornographic literature."

I gasped. "That's awful."

The detective watched her closely. "I assume it's not true."

"Of course not," she answered. "It's a family friendly shop. Lots of people bring in their children and grandchildren." Aunt Betty sat up straighter. "But that never mattered to Nan. All the way back in school, she had no qualms about lying to get her way, no matter what it concerned or who it might hurt."

"And this time getting her way was being with the man you're involved with?" he asked.

"That's right," she said. "She wanted him for herself. The fact that he'd made his feelings for me known upped the ante in her mind. That she had to work quickly to get him to change his feelings for me and turn to her. I guess she hadn't realized how often he and I were spending time together until then. It's not as if we made a big show of going out together. Usually we met at off hours at his coffee shop, or my apartment, or perhaps at the park for lunch."

Detective Combs made a few notations on his pad then said, "I understand it was traumatic for you being threatened like that. However, people lie about others all the time. And lies can be refuted. You could just say they weren't true."

Aunt Betty pressed her hand to her heart. "Even though it wouldn't be true, once people start passing around a rumor, the taint stays with you. It never quite goes away. You have to understand, Detective. Books are my life. Always have been. My heart would break if I had to give up my bookstore."

I nodded. "It's true," I added. "She's the reason I love books so much too."

"And"— my aunt gave a slight smile—"that love of books is the reason my niece is a successful book author."

His eyebrows rose. "Is that so?"

I shrugged, embarrassed the serious conversation had focused on me.

Aunt Betty glanced behind her and then back to the detective, as if afraid someone else might overhear. She gave a slight shudder and swallowed hard.

I frowned. "Aunt Betty, there's more to it, isn't there?"

She nodded, her eyes glistening.

Detective Combs eyed her. "If there's further information about this case, I need to hear it, now."

My aunt seemed to fold in upon herself and to have aged several years, worry lines deepening on her face, and then she replied, "Nan said..." Aunt Betty swallowed. "Nan said that she'd print those things about me. And if I still refused to give Wallace up after that, she'd...k-kill me." Her face went white.

Kill? I took in a huge gulp of air. It took me a few seconds to remember to let it back out. Poor woman. How scared she must have been. I wrapped my arm tight around her shoulder, hoping to convey love and support. She squeezed my other hand. "Thank you, love," she said. "I'm so glad you're here."

The detective tapped his notebook with his pen. "You do realize that Nan threatening to kill you only makes you a more likely suspect for her death."

A knock came from the door at the bottom of the stairs. Before I could stand, Janie slipped out of the doorway. Soon after, loud footsteps came up the steps. Two men with a stretcher entered the room, glanced around, and then carried the stretcher to the chair. They spoke with Officer Pike and within no time had Nan's body loaded and headed back out the doorway. A few seconds went by as the three of us stared at the now-empty space.

Unable to not know what the detective's thoughts were, I blurted out, "So, what happens next?"

He watched me for a second then addressed Aunt Betty. "First off, now that we have the reason Nan was here and threatened you, I need to know specifics about how she ended up in your den, dead because of a letter opener." He pointed down. "And you had blood on your hands."

Aunt Betty glanced at her hands, which began to shake.

I grabbed them between my own, stunned at how cold hers had gone. "Are you all right?"

She swallowed. "You see, Detective, I can't answer that."

"Why not?" he asked.

"Because I don't remember."

"You don't remember how she ended up stabbed?" he asked. "Or how you got blood on your palms."

"I have no recollection of any of it. It's a blank."

"I see." He narrowed his eyes with an expression I couldn't quite place. Annoyance? Irritation?

I edged forward in my chair then said, "Detective, when I arrived, my aunt was passed out cold in the corner."

"Is this true, Mrs. Hollingsworth?" the detective asked.

"It's true." She slipped her hands from mine, reaching up to the back of her head. "And I seem to have acquired a painful bump."

I glanced to where her fingers gently probed her scalp. "A big one," I gasped, reaching out to put a hand on her shoulder in support.

Detective Combs eyed the back of Betty's head. "Do you want to see a physician about that?"

She shook her head. "No. I'll be fine. I just want to get through all of this."

"It's possible you were struck with something that was already in the room," he said. "We haven't found any weapon besides the one used on Nan. The culprit might have taken the item with them when they fled. Can you tell if anything is missing from the room?"

I glanced around, my gaze stopping at a bookcase against one wall. "Hey, one of our bookends is missing."

The detective stood and went to check out the remaining one. He picked it up. "Something like this would definitely be heavy enough to have knocked out your aunt." He replaced it on the bookcase and walked back to us.

I edged closer to my aunt. "Since I know she didn't give herself that injury, that means someone else was here, right? They hit her on the head and knocked her out."

"We can't speculate about that yet, Christy," said the detective.

"But I'm telling you," I said. "She couldn't have done this. Someone else hit her on the head. The location of the injury wouldn't have been from her falling on the floor. Whoever it was also might have killed Nan."

His gaze lowered to the towel my aunt held. "But she had blood on her *hands.*"

"I don't know how they accomplished that," I answered. But whoever killed her did that too. Plus, there was mud on the bottom steps. Aunt Betty would never have left that there. And the back door wasn't locked when I checked the alleyway looking for her before I found her passed out up here. She always keeps it locked. The person responsible must have gotten in there and didn't lock it afterward."

The detective ignored me but faced Aunt Betty. "Thank you for being patient with my questions, Mrs. Hollingsworth. For now, you're not under arrest, but don't leave town. You are a person of interest."

My mouth dropped open as I watched him go. Did he even hear the evidence I gave to support my theory that another person killed Nan? Would he completely disregard my words?

Aunt Betty slumped against my side. "Christy, what am I going to do?"

CHAPTER THREE

Once the police had left with their required evidence, I got to work cleaning up the mess. There wasn't a professional cleaning service in town, so it was up to us to take care of it.

It was a good thing Aunt Betty was a clean freak, because she had an ample supply of disposable gloves and even some masks for the job. After I dug through my suitcase to see what I could wear, I borrowed a worn-out apron that covered me from chest to knees, slipped on a raggedy shirt I hardly wore anymore, and put on old tennis shoes I didn't care much about.

Aunt Betty wanted to help with the cleaning task, but I suggested she not be here while I did it. Since I didn't live here yet, I was somewhat removed from the situation and could rid the place of the unwanted items. For her, it might be hard to enter the den from now on, knowing what happened. If she had to clean it up herself, even worse.

She'd suffered enough trauma, both emotionally and physically. And she was a little dizzy from the bump on her head. Some distance from the scene of the crime might help her relax, as least for a while. But my aunt couldn't sit still and insisted on opening the bookstore. I waited until she'd headed downstairs before I got to work.

The chair, or what I now thought of as the death chair, wasn't as stained as I'd feared, and we could have it professionally cleaned if Aunt Betty wanted. However, she shuddered when I mentioned it. Though it was her favorite, the thought of ever using it again after Nan had met her demise there was unthinkable. Janie called someone we could hire to haul it away, so it disappeared within the hour.

Janie had her own business to run down the block but said she'd pop back in when she had a break, and her assistant could handle the customer flow. Knowing her, she'd buzz back down here as soon as she could to get the latest scoop.

That left throwing out the blood-splattered book—hard for a bibliophile to fathom trashing a book, but it had to be done—and cleaning the hardwood floor, which had minimal damage. I let out a breath once it was finished, glad my aunt hadn't been alone to have to deal with it. I tossed the gloves, apron, and cleaning clothes into a nearby trash can then closed the bag and set it in the corner to take to the dumpster later tonight.

Now to the task of finding out what really happened in this room. I knew in my heart Aunt Betty hadn't done this. So, who had and why? Was there someone living in Green Meadow who not only hated Nan enough to kill her but who hated Aunt Betty and framed her for the murder? It made sense it might be a person who knew both women, who had something to lose if they both kept on breathing. Had they planned on killing Aunt Betty too with the bump on her head or only knocking her out so she could take the fall for the murder?

I'd never met Wallace. He was in the middle of this mess, the object of two women's affection. Could he have had anything to do with the tragedy? Even though I wondered about it, I wouldn't press Aunt Betty for details about him unless she volunteered them.

Her past messages to me about him were glowing and happy. No way she'd think he was responsible for any of this. But I knew how love, or what a person mistook for love, could blind someone into believing the one they cared about could do no wrong. What if Wallace had pulled the wool over my aunt's eyes like Tony had done to me? I was firsthand proof of a woman who allowed her emotions to cloud her good judgment.

I headed down the hall. I'd put Milton and Pearl in the guest room while I worked. There'd been no need for little paws to help me deal with blood splatters. This time they hadn't managed to escape, and when I opened the door to grant them freedom, loud meows of complaint aimed squarely at me were quite testy and not at all complimentary.

The cats did as expected and entered the den, eyes wide, whiskers twitching, to check things out. But when they sniffed and pawed at things, it wasn't usual cat behavior, batting things around, playing with anything that looked like a toy, or attempting a nap where the chair had once stood. Instead, they stalked in tandem as they perused every square inch of the floor, reaching out tentative paws to touch surfaces, especially interested in where the blood-splattered book had lain, where the chair had been, and where Aunt Betty was when Janie had spotted her in the corner.

It seemed as if Milton and Pearl were prowling for clues, systematically checking spots and spaces in an organized manner, then sitting together for a moment, heads close together, purring in unison. I shook my head. No, how silly. I must be imagining things, stuck in my author state of mind, because how they acted now was shockingly like their namesakes in my mysteries. As if they'd read the stories and were acting them out. It might not have seemed so ludicrous if my cats could read. But, of course, they couldn't. At least I didn't think so.

My mind was playing tricks on me, and I was imagining things that weren't there. I rubbed my temples. Wow, I needed a change of pace and scenery more than I'd realized when Aunt Betty asked me to come here. I'd obviously immersed myself so deeply in the most recent book that I'd lost touch with common sense.

Time to do something productive to get my mind off this room and what had happened. I headed down the stairs, smiling as Milton and Pearl trotted after me. When Aunt Betty had invited me to come and stay and work in the bookstore, she'd also insisted my cats have the run of the place.

I'd happily oblige, as I loved having them around. Plus, with their feline antics, they'd be a great conversation piece for customers, as well as a helpful diversion for Aunt Betty. As soon as I opened the door at the bottom of the stairs, the cats hopped down the final step into the bookstore and took off at a trot. We'd have to put signs up on the inside and outside of the bookstore's main door, cautioning people to watch out for the kitties. My cats had never been outside, except on leashes, so I didn't expect them to try to dart out, but letting the customers know to watch out for them would be a good idea.

From inside the main room of the bookstore, several voices spoke at once. As I rounded the corner of a large display case to view the main checkout counter, I stopped, taking in the scene.

Three women and two men were gathered around the counter, though none of them were holding books or appeared to be making purchases. Were they here for a different reason? Had word leaked out already about Nan? I hurried across the room, taking a place behind the counter next to my aunt. I gave her a light nudge with my shoulder, pulling her attention from the cacophony of voices all asking questions at once. She looked shell-shocked. Maybe opening the bookstore so soon hadn't been the best idea.

When my aunt finally noticed me, she released a breath. "Thanks for coming down," she said.

I smiled. "Nowhere I'd rather be." And it was true. Though I hated the terrible circumstances I'd walked into when I arrived, it suddenly felt right to be here, with her. I shouldn't have waited so long to see my aunt, even though I had icky boyfriend problems to deal with that kept me away.

She glanced toward the stairway and whispered, "Is everything…"

"Everything is taken care of."

"Thank you," Aunt Betty replied then turned and gave her customers a tremulous smile. "Some of you might remember my brother's daughter, Christy Bailey. She used to spend summers here when she was small."

A woman a little older than me leaned closer and raised her eyebrows at me and said, "The children's book author?"

I twisted my hands together. "Yes, that's right." Even though my books sold well and I'd been to lots of book signings and conferences, my first preference was always to hide behind my computer and write the stories instead of talking about myself to people.

"Hi, I'm Lora Smith. My two daughters love Milton and Pearl."

I grinned, happy to talk about the cats. "Awww, that's sweet," I answered.

Pearl picked that moment to hop onto the counter then rubbed her white face against Aunt Betty's arm.

Lora gasped. "Hey, is that…"

I nodded. "Yep," I said. "This is Pearl. And…" I

glanced around, only seeing the tip of Milton's black tail sticking out from a shelf at the bottom of the counter. Squatting down, I reached in and gently tugged him out. He curled himself into my chest and purred as he kneaded the fabric of my shirt. "This is Milton."

"Oh!" Her eyes lit up. She reached into her shoulder bag, pulled out her cell phone, and held it out toward the cats. "Would you mind?"

"Of course not. I don't mind," I said. "They love photo ops. They're pretty, and they know it." I placed Milton next to Pearl. He immediately placed his paw on top of her head, holding her in place while he groomed her ear.

"Adorable," said Lora. For as long as she held her phone up and tapped her finger, she must have taken at least ten shots. Finally, she lowered her phone. "This is awesome. Thank you so much. My daughters will freak out when they see these."

Aunt Betty petted Milton's fur between his ears, but he had gone back to grooming his sister's face. Then my aunt ran her finger down his spine. "Better yet, Lora," she said, "bring in the girls sometime to meet the stars of the books."

"Wow, that would be amazing. I'd win parent of the year."

The other people standing around laughed.

A man held up his hand and said, "Having raised five daughters, that award would be priceless."

One of the women—a tall, thin brunette—tapped her short fingernail on the counter. "Hey, I want to get back to our conversation from before your daughter came down."

Aunt Betty's eyebrows lowered. "She's my niece."

The woman flipped her hand. "Whatever," she said.

I took a step back. Why was the lady so hostile?

The woman's brow furrowed as she said, "When I got to work this morning, Nan wasn't there. She's never missed a day at the paper since I've worked with her."

I held in a groan. Aunt Betty and I couldn't tell anyone what had happened upstairs. Not yet. Not until the detective said it was okay.

My aunt stood as tall as her short frame allowed. "Tina," she said, "why are you here asking about her?"

Whoa. Aunt Betty must be putting up a brave front,

trying to ready herself for an onslaught of people coming in to ask lots of questions. Usually, she was more easygoing. But this Tina woman seemed the type to get under a person's skin, and fast.

Lora leaned forward and said, "Annabelle Angstrom from the fruit market told me she saw two men carrying out a stretcher from this very building. And it had a sheet-covered body on it. I'm so glad it wasn't you, Betty!"

An older man, whom I remembered from years ago, named Hal Rogers dropped his mouth open. "A body?" he asked. "Who was it?"

Tina crossed her arms and said, "That's what I want to know. Seems too much of a coincidence I can't get ahold of Nan. She's not at work or home, and something happened here. And I happen to know she sometimes walks past this shop on her way to the office. I'm telling you, Nan never ever misses work." She turned and glanced around the room.

Was she hoping to see clues to give her some answers? Or did she want to check out our upstairs apartment? Nope, wasn't going to happen. Not only was it Aunt Betty's home, but it was now mine, as well as Milton and Pearl's. We'd protect our privacy as best we could.

No way I'd let on what happened upstairs. It was bad enough if people thought it happened in the bookstore.

Aunt Betty eyed the woman then said, "I can't help you with your questions, Tina. However, if you're interested in purchasing a book today, I'll be happy to be of service." She tapped her foot.

The woman let out a huff so loud Pearl puffed out her fur and hissed in return.

An older woman giggled from down the counter, earning a scowl from Tina, who pivoted and stomped from the bookstore.

"Thank goodness that Tina Jeffers is gone," Hal said. "Can't stand it when she gets all bossy."

"Me neither," said a small, spry, gray-haired woman around my aunt's age.

Aunt Betty angled her head toward the woman then said to me, "Christy, this is Rosey Davis. You've met before, but you were small."

Rosey blinked and eyed me. "Good to see you again. Although, it's sad it's during these circumstances. I have to admit, I was shocked when I heard about a body here in the bookstore."

I sighed and looked at my aunt. She'd wrapped her arms around her middle, obviously in self-protection mode from Tina's rude comments and the stress of having her life upended in such a terrible way. Better for me to nip this in the bud. "We aren't at liberty to discuss anything today besides book business. I'm really sorry."

Rosey squinted her eyes half closed and said, "Oh. Well… The way gossip flies around this town, there will be all sorts of stories, mostly wrong, that will make their way from one end to the other by tonight."

One of Aunt Betty's eyebrows rose, as if Rosey's comment had annoyed her as she said, "Yes, unfortunately they will."

Rosey studied Aunt Betty for a second then turned to me. "But now that I know you're here, Christy, I'll take a look at your books. My grandchildren have birthdays coming up, and they seem to read a lot of stories about cats for some reason."

I smiled. "Um, okay. Great." Even though Rosey's grandkids apparently liked cats, Rosey didn't appear to share their views.

Then I thought about all that had occurred since I'd entered the bookstore. Not one of those things had to do with completely unpacking my belongings, which included my supply of books. Aunt Betty stocked my mysteries, of course, but the brand-new ones were hot off the press. She'd asked me to bring some of my copies until she could order some for the store. "Let me run out to my car and get some," I said. "I only just arrived a while ago and haven't had a chance to unpack them." Walking into a murder scene had definitely derailed any previous plans.

I told the cats to behave while I was outside, earning chuckles from the customers. As I opened the door to step onto the sidewalk, a tall, thin man crashed into me.

He grabbed my shoulders and said, "Oh dear, are you all right?"

"Yes, I'm fine." I answered and refrained from shaking

my foot where he'd stomped on it.

"That's good," he said. "Would hate to knock someone over right after shopping in Betty's bookstore. Wouldn't be good for her business, now would it?"

"Well, I wasn't actually shopping. I—"

Footsteps came from behind me. Aunt Betty edged around me and flung herself into the man's arms. "Wallace," she exclaimed, "I'm so glad you're here."

Ah, the elusive boyfriend. The man of the hour who was the object of affection of two women, one now dead, the other made to look like the killer. I crossed my arms and waited until Aunt Betty had calmed and taken a step back. She wiped moisture from her eyes and turned toward me, her eyebrows raised, as if surprised to see me there. Was she so intent on seeing Wallace she hadn't noticed me standing beside him?

Wallace placed his hands on her shoulders. "Darling, what's wrong? Has something happened?" He must not have heard about the police being at the bookstore or carrying out a covered stretcher.

When Aunt Betty didn't speak right away, Wallace glanced at me and said, "Oh, wait. You're Christy, aren't you? I saw your picture in Betty's den one time." His left hand jerked, and he blinked several times.

Something about this guy bothered me. He seemed cagey, hyper, almost jittery, like he was on something. He definitely wasn't what I'd expected from Aunt Betty's loving words about him. My gut instinct was to not trust him. If Nan was so intent on having Wallace for herself and she was willing to blackmail Aunt Betty to get him, did that mean he'd at some point given her some reason to think he liked her too?

But was that a true reading of the man, or was I being overprotective of my aunt because of what had just happened? Wallace was definitely someone I'd keep my eye on. And even though I might have imagined how Milton and Pearl acted when checking out the room, maybe it wouldn't hurt to let them check him out too, just to be on the safe side.

CHAPTER FOUR

Nan's funeral took place three days later. Under the circumstances, Aunt Betty decided to steer clear of it, but I wanted to attend to see if I could pick up any useful clues about Nan's murderer. Janie had come with me but at the moment was speaking to a few people I didn't know. It would be nice once I'd been in town longer and knew more people from Green Meadow so I'd feel more comfortable. But starting out this way, with poor Aunt Betty embroiled in a murder investigation, wasn't the way I'd have chosen.

I spotted a few people who'd bad-mouthed Nan in the short time I'd been in town. I'd overheard them while they stood in line in our bookstore. Something about waiting to pay for a book seemed to loosen people's tongues. Theories about Nan's death and who might have killed her had bounced around from one customer to the next.

Now at the funeral home, did they actually care what had happened to Nan, or were they simply here now to satisfy their nosiness? For my part, I wasn't nosy so much as…well, I guess I was. But I was doing it for a good cause, to help out someone I loved. That made it acceptable, at least in my book.

Rosey entered the room. When she spotted me, she headed my way, her sensible soft-soled shoes making shushing sounds on the carpet. "Hello, Christy." She tilted her head toward the casket across the room. "The second time we've spoken since you've been back, and it's centered around something awful."

"True," I said. "I'll be so glad when all of this is over."

Rosey nodded. "Me too. This has every tongue in town wagging, that's for sure."

Was she more concerned about what people were

saying than the fact that a woman had been murdered?

She clasped her hands together in front of her then said, "Such a strange thing to happen, don't you think? I mean Betty finding a dead body in her apartment."

"Yes, very strange. And also upsetting, especially for Nan Bittle."

She waved her hand. "Oh, of course, that too," she replied.

Why was she even at the visitation, or as it was referred to here, the calling, if she didn't care about the person who'd died?

She peered over her shoulder and back then said, "Guess I should get in line and pay my respects to Nan, even though there doesn't seem to be any relatives to give my condolences to. Kind of defeats the purpose of even showing up. But if I don't show up to a fellow citizen's calling, I'll be the talk of Green Meadow."

I highly doubted missing one calling would amount to all of that, but I had to admit, life in a small town was way different than a big city. Eyes and ears were everywhere.

I should get in line too. Not so much for respect but to keep *my* eyes and ears open for any useful information.

Rosey stepped away, taking her place in the line of people to view the recently deceased. Normally, at least in a small town, the people who'd lost their loved one stood beside the body. Today, however, the line of mourners was only met with the somber expression and pose of Nan herself. Didn't she have anyone to stand by her to greet people as they walked by?

Not quite ready to be that close to Nan's body again, I took up what I hoped was an inconspicuous spot in a far corner. Far enough to be out of people's way, but close enough to hopefully hear conversations. An open doorway was to my left, leading out to a hallway. When I leaned a little to the side for a better view into the hall, I could just see the edge of a coatrack.

Footsteps approached from the hallway then stopped just beyond the coatrack. I could see the woman, maybe forties, bleached blonde hair, but she was partially turned away and couldn't see me. She was speaking on her phone, obviously excited, pacing back and forth, her shoulders stiff and bunched together. Waving her other hand around for emphasis, she said to her listener, "Can you believe it? The hag is finally gone."

I blinked. Even though I'd never met Nan, everything I knew about her was bad. Still, to talk about her while at the funeral home where her body lay prostrate in a coffin seemed a bit much. Was the blonde woman on the phone in the hallway because she assumed no one could overhear her crass comments? Well, she hadn't counted on me. If she had something to say that might help me find out who killed Nan, I was going to listen.

The woman laughed. "Thank goodness I won't have to deal with her anymore. What a pain in the neck."

My elbow bumped against the wall, creating a low thud. I held my breath, hoping she wouldn't hear me or turn and see me openly watching her. To be on the safe side, I tugged out my phone and pretended to be intently interested in what I was reading.

The noise from my elbow must not have been as loud as I thought, since she didn't turn in my direction. She took a step away but remained where I could still see her. Her free hand landed on her hip as she said, "What do you mean? Of course I'm at the funeral home."

Whomever she spoke to must be privy to this woman's private business. She was pretty blunt with her words about someone who'd just died.

With a chuckle, the woman said, "We must keep up appearances, mustn't we?" She let out a loud laugh then clamped her hand over her mouth as if remembering where she was. She whipped around to look through the doorway into the main room.

I jumped out of her line of sight, nearly stumbling against a tall arrangement of roses in the corner. Great. That sound was even louder than my elbow bump.

I'd no sooner composed myself and stepped farther back into the room, when the woman, no longer on her phone, moved briskly past me toward a grouping of empty chairs.

My heart raced. That was way too close. What if she'd seen me spying on her? I definitely needed more practice in the art of surveillance. I couldn't help but smile, thinking of Milton and Pearl, the very epitome of someone patient enough to sit, unmoving, while stalking a person, bug, or even their own shadows. Maybe I should spend more time observing their behavior. Too bad I couldn't have brought them with me today. No doubt they'd pick up information I might miss.

My next thoughts stopped me cold, as I imagined my two cats ready to take a nap. Seeing a rectangular wooden box with soft fabric inside. Jumping onto the casket, settling down for an impromptu snooze with—"No!"

"No?" replied a deep voice.

I gasped and turned, shocked to find a tall man staring down at me. Once I had a chance to calm down a little, my mind shifted from panic to surprise. Pleasant surprise. Because the guy was gorgeous. Dark-brown eyes, peering into mine. A lock of unruly brown hair hanging partway down on his forehead, and extra-long eyelashes. Then my heart pounded hard for an entirely different reason.

He angled his head toward me. "Are you all right?" he asked.

I blinked, trying to get my currently handsome-man-occupied brain to switch gears and allow me to say something coherent. "Um…I'm…um…fine…I think." Okay, not completely coherent, but better then stuttering, drooling, or gawking at him.

"Glad to hear it," he said. "When you yelped—"

"I yelped?"

"That's what I'd call it," he answered. "I guess we could use *yip* or *squeak*. Your choice. Although I think *yelp* sounds much more interesting." Two adorable dimples formed in his cheeks.

I smiled. So he also had a sense of humor. What a rare and amazing find. Most guys I met were one or the other. Or sadly, neither.

Leaning around him, I checked to see if the other funeral goers were staring at my outburst. No one pointed or looked in my direction. Either it wasn't as loud as I'd feared, or they hadn't found it all that interesting. Unlike this guy.

I focused on him again. "Thanks for checking on me to make sure I'm okay."

"No problem," he answered and shrugged his wide shoulders. "It's sort of my thing."

"Checking on people?"

"That and investigating loud exclamations." He grinned. "I don't think we've met before. Are you just in town for Nan's funeral?"

"No, not exactly," I answered. No sense in telling him the real reason I was people watching at the funeral. "My aunt, Betty Hollingsworth, owns a bookstore and—"

"Oh, Words to Read By. I love that place. And your aunt is one of my favorite people."

I smiled. "Mine too. She's done an amazing job. I'm here to help her run it."

"That's wonderful." His brows lowered as he said, "I'm sorry. I didn't get your name."

"Christy Bailey."

He stuck out his hand. "Nice to meet you. I'm—"

An older man rushed toward us, grabbed on to the handsome guy's arm, and hauled him to the other side of the room where a woman sat in a chair. I frowned. What was that about? Before I could find out more about what was going on across the room, the three of them hurried from the building. I sighed. Perfect. Well, at least he knew about the bookstore and seemed to like it. Maybe we'd cross paths again before too long. And if Aunt Betty was one of his favorite people, at least he had good taste.

"Hey, Christy."

I turned away from staring at the main doorway to see Janie. She might know who the guy was. "Did you happen to see that super-tall guy leaving with an older couple just now?" I asked. "He had legs for miles, wide shoulders, and the dreamiest dark eyes I've ever seen. Plus, he was nice, funny, and did I mention gorgeous?"

Janie frowned. "Sorry. Wish I had. Sounds like a keeper."

I sighed and said, "Yeah. I thought so too. Didn't even catch his name or anything about him."

She grabbed my hand and gave it a squeeze. "But I did see you watching Olive earlier."

I lowered my eyebrows. "Olive who?"

"The older blonde chick who'd been by the coatrack a few minutes ago. Olive Phipps," said Janie.

My eyes widened. "You saw that?" If Janie noticed me,

er, noticing the blonde woman, had other people seen my poor attempt at spying as well?

She waved her other hand. "I happened to be facing your direction just then. Don't worry. Most people were standing in line, faced away from you. I think you're safe."

"Good to know. Thanks. So anyway, who is Olive Phipps?"

"She's Nan's cousin," she said.

"Ah, now it makes more sense."

"What does?" Janie asked.

I leaned more toward Janie, which unfortunately gave her the opportunity to tug me even closer to her side. Needed to watch that. Otherwise, she'd be glued to my hip every time we were together. Didn't she realize adults who weren't in a romantic relationship didn't normally hang on each other? And did she do this to everyone or just me? I gently pried her hand from my arm and said, "What makes sense is, I heard—"

She brushed her blonde bangs away from her forehead. "*Over*heard."

"Okay, I was eavesdropping. Anyway, I heard Olive tell someone she was glad Nan was dead."

Janie's mouth dropped open. "Wow," she said. "So cold. And at the woman's funeral."

"That's what I thought too."

"I guess you and I have the unique memory of seeing Nan"—she glanced around and back—"of seeing her post-murder." She grimaced.

"Yeah, that was extra special, wasn't it?" I answered. "I hate that you had to witness that, but I'm glad you were there that day to help Aunt Betty and me."

She shrugged. "It was a strange day, for sure. But you and I got to reconnect. At least that's a positive."

"Definitely." With a glance at Nan's casket, I said, "Well, I should get in line."

She grabbed my arm again. "I'll go with you."

I refrained from sighing loudly at the way she clutched part of my body. Sure, she'd done it when we were kids, and at the time, I thought it was fun. Now, I'd love to say something to her about it, that it made me a little uncomfortable. But she was such a sweet person, and I was glad we were renewing our friendship. I didn't have it in me to say anything. Maybe later, if we got to know each other better as adults. For now, I'd endure my extra appendage by the name of Janie.

By the time we reached the casket, everyone else had paid their respects and moved on, either across the room to speak quietly to each other or having left the funeral home. As we stood side by side, looking at Nan's still form, I wondered what really happened to her. Who had done this and framed my aunt? There had to be a way to discover the real culprit's identity. Whoever it was must have hated her. That could be a long list of people, considering she hadn't been a nice person and no one I'd spoken to so far had even liked her.

I leaned toward Janie and said, "Okay, I think we can step away now."

"Right, just wanted to make sure you'd been here long enough to snoop."

My eyes widened. "Snoop?"

She winked and said, "Sure. You know? Check things out."

"You and I know that, but let's not let anyone else overhear, okay?"

For once, I was the one tugging Janie by the arm, gently propelling her to a couple of uncomfortable chairs placed against a far wall. We sat and watched our fellow mourners for a few minutes. Although to be fair, I shouldn't use the word mourner about myself. How many who'd been here could really claim the title themselves? How awful to be at the end of your life and no one seemed to be sorry or miss you.

Olive now stood beside the casket, a handkerchief dabbing her eyes. Who was she trying to fool? The conversation I'd overheard sounded anything but mournful or sad. Maybe the fact that she was here, seemingly in distress over her family member, was part of her ploy to make others believe her sincerity of having loved her cousin.

But I knew the truth.

After a couple more minutes of fake sniffling and dramatic boo-hooing, Olive left her cousin's side and strolled past us. She stopped just before she reached the doorway, retrieved her phone from her purse, and appeared to be texting someone. As she typed, her shoulders shook. Was she laughing?

I'd love to know what she'd texted and to whom. Maybe I could sneak over there and catch a glimpse. But before I could even rise from my chair, Janie whispered, "I'll go!" and hopped up. On her tiptoes, although the carpeted floor would have muffled her steps anyway, she crept up behind Olive, took a quick peek over the woman's hunched shoulder, and then backed away.

I waited, hands clenched together in my lap. Janie slunk back, still on her tiptoes, which seemed a little unnecessary now, but who was I to complain? Maybe she saw something useful.

She took her seat again and motioned me closer. At least this time she didn't grab my hand.

"Okay," she whispered, "I saw what she'd texted."

Silence went on for a full minute.

I blinked. "Care to share?"

Her eyes widened and she said, "Sorry, was trying to process what I read. It's so hateful. And kind of gross."

I nodded, hoping I'd hear the information before the funeral director closed up for the night and left us stranded with Nan's body.

Janie glanced around the mostly empty room then said, "Olive's message was, 'Ding Dong the witch is dead! Let's go bowling with her severed head!'"

Repulsed, my mouth dropped open.

"Wicked, right?" she asked.

"Ghastly. Did you happen to see who the text was to?"

She slumped her shoulders. "Sorry, no. Was so caught up in the message itself."

"No worries," I said. "Thanks for checking that out. It's a big help."

She grinned. "Believe me, after my hideous divorce and literal no-man's land of the dating world, helping you unearth a killer is the most exciting thing to happen to me in quite a while."

I shook my head. "Poor kid," I said. "Sounds like you and I both need excitement in our lives. Once we've figured out who killed Nan, we need to find some good men. Fast."

And I knew exactly who I'd be checking out first in the man department. If I could ever figure out who he was.

CHAPTER FIVE

The next morning, Aunt Betty had gone for a latte at Wallace's coffee shop, Perked Up. Since I was still acquainting myself with how the bookstore was set up, I spent the time walking around the store, checking out the book sections, displays, and general layout.

Milton and Pearl had gotten their breakfast upstairs then trotted down behind me when I opened up the bookstore. A rousing game of kitty tag took place throughout the store, and then they collapsed on a shelf beneath the counter, now both purring in their sleep, no doubt dreaming of fifty-pound mice and aquarium-size bowls of tuna.

My time alone was quiet and enjoyable. Until Olive Phipps entered the building. After overhearing her on the phone at the funeral home and learning from Janie what Olive's text had said, it took every ounce of politeness I had stored someplace deep inside to smile at her and say good morning.

Her own fake smile was enough to make my insides burn. I knew better than to trust her after her cruel words about her cousin. But Aunt Betty was counting on me to run the store as she would in her absence. And my aunt was nothing if not polite, even to rude customers. I needed to do the same.

Since I hadn't officially met her—I doubted eavesdropping on her conversation counted—I acted as if I'd never seen her before. "How can I help you today?"

With a frown, she marched closer. "I demand to see it," she said.

"Pardon me?"

"Right now," she insisted.

"I'm sorry. I don't quite understand."

She stepped to the opposite side of the counter, leaned

toward me, pointed her red-nailed, highly polished fingernail right at my nose, and then said, "I must see it. Don't make me call my attorney."

My entire body bristled with indignation, irritation, and intense dislike. "Ma'am, I—"

"Ma'am? Just how old do you think I am?"

I shrugged. What an awkward question for anyone to answer. There was never a good way to guess. Plus, this woman already seemed tightly wound. No use pushing her over the edge with what she might take as an insult if I guessed way wrong.

"Now you listen here, little girl," she said.

My eyes widened. Little girl? Just how young did she think *I* was? "Wait, I—"

"I don't have a lot of time, so stop messing around," she said. "Show me the place where my cousin Nan died. Right this minute."

My mouth dropped open, but I snapped it closed before saying something that wouldn't please Aunt Betty the least little bit. Instead, I took a steadying breath and let it out. "Ma'am—"

"My name is Olive Phipps. You may call me Ms. Phipps. But under no circumstances will you ever again refer to me as *ma'am*. Are we clear?" Her last three words were punctuated with foot stomps.

I bobbed my head in agreement, hoping to calm her down. Because any second, customers could walk through the doorway, and I'd rather not have this outrageous, rude woman's demands be what they'd hear. "Ma—er, Ms. Phipps," I said, "I'm afraid I can't accommodate you to show you where Nan died."

"And just why not? I have the right to mourn my cousin where she actually expired."

Expired? Her cousin hadn't been a quart of milk. "I'm sorry, but no."

Olive pounded the counter with her fist. "This is unacceptable!" she shouted. "Inexcusable. Unbelievable."

I wished Aunt Betty was here to help me deal with this lunatic, but at the same time, I was glad she wasn't. She wouldn't benefit from this crazy lady wanting to tramp up the stairs and view the spot where Nan had been killed. It was bad enough what my aunt had endured. Having it dredged up again—by someone I knew wasn't sincere in her motives—would only make things worse.

The door squeaked open, letting in bright sunlight, and a woman about Aunt Betty's age walked in. Even though I didn't want anyone else hearing hateful words from Olive, I was relieved to no longer be alone with her. Purposefully ignoring Olive, who still glared at me from across the counter, I leaned to one side to wave at the woman. "Welcome," I said. "Let me know if you need some help today."

Olive, obviously rebuffed, let out a huff.

Below me, something stirred. Were the cats waking up from their naps? I didn't want to take my attention completely away from Olive since I didn't trust her, so I refrained from glancing at the shelf below. But when a soft paw batted at my pant leg, I grinned.

Olive's eyes narrowed as she said, "You think refusing me my right as a family member to see where she took her final breath is funny?" Her voice rose with each word. And with each of her words, I cringed even more.

"Ms. Phipps, I'm sorry, but I do have customers to tend to. If you'd like me to perhaps show you some of our new book arrivals, I'd be more than happy to do that." I waited, letting the implication that it was all she'd get from me hang in the air between us.

Olive squared her shoulders. "Fine. I'll just have a look around on my own."

The apartment was off limits to customers. The door to the stairs was locked. The only place she could snoop around was right here in the bookstore. "Help yourself," I said.

"Trust me, I will." She pivoted and stomped away.

The second woman approached slowly, as if waiting for some wild beast to leap out and attack her. I couldn't blame her. Olive was scary.

I smiled wide, hoping to convey welcome and harmony in the bookstore. Since the stranger hadn't answered my first query, I tried again and said, "Hi there. Can I help you find something in particular?"

She watched as Olive skulked around the corner of a display of thrillers. She pointed toward the display. "Is…she all right?"

I blinked. Hmmm, how to answer that…

"Sometimes," she said, "Olive can be…er…" She lifted her shoulder in a shrug. "It's just, she seems awfully upset about something."

From what the woman said, Olive had a reputation for being difficult. I waved my hand in Olive's direction. "Who knows. Maybe she had a bad hair day or something."

She giggled. "Yes, hopefully this time that's all it is. Well, anyway, I was interested in seeing some of your books. Your Milton and Pearl stories."

"Great. They're right over here," I said as I pointed to my left and headed that way.

"I'm Annabelle Angstrom."

I stopped and smiled. I remembered hearing her name mentioned when several people were here right after Nan's murder. That she ran the local fruit market. "Nice to meet you. I'm Christy Bailey."

"Oh, I already know about you."

I raised my eyebrows. "Good, I hope?" I asked.

She nodded. "The best. Your aunt talks about you all the time. About your writing. And how excited she was that you were coming back to live here." She tilted her head. "By the way, where is Betty?"

"She's—"

The door opened again. This time Aunt Betty entered.

"There she is," I said as I waved. "Hope you had a good time."

Aunt Betty brushed back a gray curl of hair. "It was lovely. Just what I needed. Good food and pleasant conversation." She glanced to her right and smiled. "Oh, hi Annabelle. So nice to see you."

I showed Annabelle the kids' section, where Aunt Betty had insisted we showcase my books in a separate, larger display. I said, "We have the whole series, with just a few of the new release left. We'll have more of that one in soon."

She picked up a copy of the first book, *Cats and Capers*, and flipped through the pages. Every chapter began with an illustration of the two cats. "These are fabulous. I'll need the entire series for my grandson. He adores anything to do with cats."

"Wow, that's great." I collected the books for her and headed back to the counter. "How old is your grandson?"

"He's seven," she said. "That boy loves to read."

"Wonderful. I love hearing about little ones who catch the reading bug early."

"Me too. So many kids, and sadly adults, aren't interested in books. Only staring at their phones or TV screens."

"I agree," I answered. As I placed her books, and information on our store inside the bag, I smiled. "Thank you so much. I hope your grandson enjoys the books."

"No, thank *you*. He'll love them."

Aunt Betty walked across the store to the business office in back. Hopefully she'd stay there until Olive vacated the premises.

I glanced over my shoulder, making sure Olive hadn't caused mayhem or destroyed anything in the store. As angry as she'd acted, and after hearing what she was really like on her phone call, I wasn't inclined to trust her. At the moment, she stood in front of the Classics section. At least she wasn't yelling or demanding anything.

I focused on Annabelle and said, "I hear you run the fruit market."

She nodded. "Yes, have for years. My husband and I grow most of what we sell, but during winter months, we can order in from other states."

"I need to come and check it out sometime soon."

"Please do," she said. "If you prefer fresh produce, I think we can find something you'll like."

Rustling came from below me. First Pearl and then Milton climbed out of the same shelf. Being siblings, they often preferred sleeping together, even if the space was small. Maybe my cats didn't suffer from claustrophobia like I did. I tapped my fingers on the counter, the sound making their ears stand up straight and their whiskers twitch. Tails flipped to and fro right before they gracefully landed on the counter.

Annabelle grinned and said, "Well look at that." She glanced down at the sack I'd placed her new books in then back at the cats. "Are these the stars of the books?"

I laughed as Pearl stuck her fluffy white head into the

sack. "The very same."

Annabelle held out her hand toward Milton's silky black fur. "May I?"

"Of course."

When Annabelle's hand came in contact with Milton's fur, he closed his eyes and let out a booming, raspy purr. Annabelle giggled again, rubbing her fingers through his black and white tuxedo fur. "My," she said, "such a handsome fellow."

"Don't say it too loud, or he'll have an inflated ego and I'll be the one to have to deal with him."

Annabelle laughed.

Milton closed both eyes as he enjoyed his kitty massage. Having lots of extra people to give them affection would be good. I loved on them as much as I could, but these two required massive doses of human attention.

With a sigh, Annabelle said, "I'd love to have cats of my own, but my husband is allergic."

"Tell you what. Whenever you're close by, come in and visit them. They'll be spending the days in here with me and might get bored sometimes. They'd love seeing you."

"I can do that. Plus, as much as I love books, I'm in here a lot anyway."

"Perfect," I said.

Annabelle retrieved her purchase from the counter and waved first to me, next to the cats, and then left the store.

I let out a harrumph. That just left Olive. Why was she still here? I knew she supposedly wanted to pay her respects to her deceased cousin, but I didn't buy it. Not after hearing the awful sludge that came out of her mouth.

Even though I had lots of work to catch up on, I knew she wasn't here to shop. Time to nip this in the bud. I headed to the Classics section, where she stood, staring at the middle shelf. I made enough noise so I wouldn't startle her because I wasn't sure how she'd react, and I didn't love the idea of being yelled at.

But I remembered the text on her phone that she'd thought was funny. About Nan's head. And bowling. I shuddered. Even with plenty of firm footsteps to announce my coming, Olive hadn't turned around. With a sigh, I stepped up beside her and asked, "Is there anything I can help you with?"

She frowned and opened her mouth to speak.

I held up my hand to stop her. "Anything *besides* showing you where Nan *expired*?"

Her gaze slid to the door leading up to the stairs. Had she already tried it when I wasn't looking and discovered it was locked? I'd been occupied with Annabelle for a while. It was possible Olive had slipped past me to see for herself.

She turned to fully face me and crossed her arms. "You'll be sorry you didn't do what I wanted."

"Is that so?" I asked.

"That's so. I always get what I want. Even if I have to do things to get it that are…" She let what I took as a threat dangle in the air.

I moved closer and said, "Well, you're not going to get your way this time. And if there's nothing else I can help you with…" I tilted my head toward the front door. Polite but firm. No doubt she got the message that I wanted her to leave.

After glaring at me for twenty full seconds—I counted—Olive huffed out a loud breath and brushed past me. As she made her way to the door, Milton and Pearl batted at her shoes and hissed. She tried to kick them, but they were too quick and scurried back toward the counter.

I leaned against the shelves, so glad she'd finally left and that my cats hadn't been hurt. Also, that Aunt Betty didn't have to deal with the witch. Even though I didn't much like the role of bouncer, I'd do it in a heartbeat to save my aunt from any added stress.

Finally, I had time to get to the storeroom to unbox our newest shipments of books. Maybe Milton and Pearl's newest copies had arrived. As I headed toward the counter on my way to the storeroom, something brushed my ankle. Milton was at my feet, batting at something at the base of the counter.

"What'cha got there?" I bent down to see. It was the edge, barely visible, of a piece of paper. I gently nudged away Milton—and now Pearl, who'd trotted over to check things out—so I could get a better look.

Using my fingernails, which were badly in need of a manicure and wouldn't be helped by this, I scraped and tugged until the paper—a receipt, as it turned out—pulled loose from beneath the small space between the counter and floor. When I smoothed out the wrinkles and unbent a top corner, I could see printing at the top. It was from Petals and Stems. There was no name on it, so the person hadn't used a credit card to pay for their purchase. Should I return it to the florist or just give it a toss?

Before I could decide, Pearl pawed at it, trying to tug it from my grasp.

"Oh, no you don't, kitty. I need to—"

Milton gave a loud howl, causing me to jump. He did the same thing as Pearl, batting the paper in my hand. I stood, keeping the receipt out of their reach, even though they leaped into the air to try to steal it away. What was so special about a store receipt?

The cats sat and stared at me, identical round eyes sparkling like green marbles. Then they turned their attention to each other, pressing their heads close.

What was going on?

Was it the same as when they'd acted this way when snooping at the crime scene upstairs? The more I watched them, the more I thought yes, these cats were on to something. Had the killer dropped this receipt in the store and now my cats wanted me to know about the clue? And if they thought this receipt was important, then I did too. As soon as I could, I'd visit Petals and Stems to find out more.

CHAPTER SIX

A couple days later, Aunt Betty insisted I take a break at the lunch hour to get out of the shop for a bit. Aside from buying a sandwich somewhere, it was the perfect time to take the receipt to the floral shop. Milton and Pearl weren't thrilled when I left, but Aunt Betty assured me she'd be delighted with their company while I was out. As I stepped toward the door, I tried to ignore their mews of discontent. A mother's guilt never went away.

Petals and Stems was several blocks away, but it felt good to stretch my legs, plus the sun was warm on my back. Halfway to the shop, I noticed a few people walking their dogs. Mom-guilt hit me again. I had a stroller for the cats I hadn't unpacked from my car yet. When it was nice out, they loved being paraded around, the rays of sunshine warming their toes. On rainy days, not so much.

Oh, the whining and hissing when a few tiny drops touched their fur, even though the stroller was covered on top. Well, I just wouldn't tell them how nice it was today. But I'd have to get the stroller out soon. Because those cats were smart. They looked out the windows. Sunshine and no coats meant warm weather for kitties.

When I reached Petals and Stems, I grinned at the logo painted on the window, a cartoon rabbit sniffing a rose. And both were smiling.

A tinny bell sounded when I opened the door and stepped inside. The floor of the main room was covered with plants all the way around next to the walls, still leaving plenty of space for customers to enter and browse. The smell of roses, lilacs, and hyacinths was heavenly. A small water fountain surrounded by lustrous green ferns created an atmosphere of a tiny jungle near the middle of the room. The overall effect was relaxing, like a mini tropical vacation.

No one seemed to be around, but I stepped to the counter intending to wait. Maybe the employees were in one of the back rooms. If someone didn't come out in the next couple of minutes, I'd try again later. Even though Aunt Betty had shooed me from the bookstore for a while, I wouldn't take advantage of her kindness and be gone too long.

A rustling came from below, reminding me of Milton and Pearl. Did Petals and Stems have a cat? Personally, I thought every business should have at least one, but not everybody was a cat person.

I jumped when not a feline, but a woman's gray-haired head rose above the opposite edge of the counter. When the woman stood, a box of pink ribbons in her hand, I was surprised to see Rosey Davis.

When she spotted me, her thin gray eyebrows rose. "Oh. Hello," she said. "Sorry if I startled you. I was searching for something on the shelf below. I try not to jump out at people and be a Rosey-in-the-box, but sometimes it inadvertently happens."

"No, it's fine," I said. "I didn't know you worked here."

She nodded. "For a couple of decades, actually."

"Wow. It's really nice here. Do you own the shop?"

"Me?" she said. "No. That would be Essie." Her frown was so quick, I thought I imagined it.

"Oh, well, it's nice to see you." Maybe her boss wasn't a nice person. For me, I was grateful to have Aunt Betty as my boss. Not a sweeter or more thoughtful woman in the world.

Rosey set the box down on the counter. "What can I sell you today?" she asked. "A dozen roses? A bouquet of daisies? We also have miniature sunflowers, if you like that sort of thing."

I glanced where she pointed. The flowers were all indeed lovely. "I'll make a point to come back for flowers soon, but today, I wanted to show you this." I handed her the receipt.

She took it, reached for her glasses currently perched on her head, and squinted as she peered closer. "Oh, yes."

"Yes?" I asked. As much as I was glad she knew something about it, I was hoping for more than two words.

"Um, someone must have dropped it in the bookstore. I didn't know who…I mean, I thought maybe they would want it back." Even though I wanted to come right out and ask if she might remember whose it was, part of me wondered if that was okay. Sure, I wasn't asking for someone's medical records, but these days, people might take offense to a stranger poking into their financial business.

Rosey set the receipt on the counter. "That was from Olive Phipps."

Obviously Rosey had no qualms about sharing information. I assumed the receipt had been dropped there recently, but it could have been there for quite a while before the cats unearthed it from its hiding spot. "Wow," I said. "You have a good memory for what a customer bought."

"Not really. She comes in every week and buys turquoise roses. Very odd, I know. Not something that's a very popular item, so it sticks out."

Olive. Apparently Milton and Pearl had been right to want to show me what they'd found beneath the counter. Smart kitties. Not that it was a surprise to me. And if I ever forgot, they'd be sure to remind me.

I was ready to thank Rosey for the information and grab a bite before returning to the bookstore, but she leaned against the counter, motioning me closer with her hand. Was she afraid someone might overhear us? Maybe her boss, who she didn't seem particularly fond of, was in an adjacent room. I edged a step closer to the counter and waited.

She tapped the receipt with her fingernail then said, "You know, that Olive is a piece of work."

"Really?" If Rosey wanted to spill the beans on one of my suspects, I was all ears.

"Yep. I think she has one of those split personalities."

Wow. I'd only seen the bad side of her. Was there a good one? I crossed my arms over my chest and waited for more.

Rosey made a tsking sound as she said, "You never know what might pop out of that lady's mouth."

I nodded, hoping she'd add more but not wanting to appear too eager. I was still new in town, at least as an adult. No sense in getting the label of gossip during my first week here.

"In fact"—Rosey sighed heavily, causing the front of her buttoned sweater to bunch then straighten back out—"she's always had an eye for Wallace, I'm sorry to say."

My head jerked. "You mean Aunt Betty's Wallace?" I asked.

"That's right." Her mouth drooped down at the corners.

"First Nan threatens Aunt Betty about Wallace, and now I hear Olive wants him too?"

"Yes," said Rosey. "As cousins, Nan and Olive have always been competitors. For everything. It started when they were kids fighting over toys, progressed to teenagers competing in school for places in the choir, cheerleading squad, and student council, and then, as adults, to the affections of men."

"How sad. To go your whole life fighting over everything with a member of your own family."

Ignoring my comment, Rosey clasped her hands together on the counter then said, "Well, that Wallace…he's got a reputation of being a lady's man."

"Then it's not just one-sided that other women want him? He's interested in them too?"

"Yes. Isn't that awful? Especially for a man his age. I'd think he'd be embarrassed to act like some teenager running after any female who looks his way."

My heart sank. Was this what Aunt Betty had in store for herself? Loving a man who always had eyes for a woman besides her? It was a classic story of a person falling in love, only to have their heart stomped on and dragged through the mud. But classic story or not, this was my aunt. Even though I didn't like everything she'd said, Rosey wasn't shy about passing along useful information. If I listened closely enough, she might give me something I could use.

The bell on the door jingled. A man, maybe in his late forties, stepped inside. His shirt tail was hanging loose and wrinkled. His hair disheveled. And his shoes caked with mud. He looked like a bum. I'd hoped for more of a discussion with Rosey, but now that would have to wait. With a glance at a back room, I decided to go ahead and purchase something while I was here. No use getting Rosey in trouble with her boss if she walked in and found us chatting instead of Rosey doing her job.

Not really paying attention to what the man said to

Rosey, I stepped to the far wall, checking out some lovely bouquets with sprigs of lavender surrounding white lilies. Nope, that wouldn't work. Lilies were dangerous for cats. But what about the miniature sunflowers Rosey had mentioned? They wouldn't hurt the kitties and were bright and sunny. Might be just the thing to perk Aunt Betty up. We could set a vase of them on the front counter, welcoming customers when they entered the bookstore. Even though they weren't dangerous to cats, I'd still keep Milton and Pearl away from them. Flower petals weren't on their menu, as much as they might like them for a salad.

I selected a large bouquet in a brown vase, its color a shade darker than the center of the flowers. Aunt Betty was sure to love it. So did I. Just gazing at the cheery yellow petals, I felt a little better already. No wonder flower shops were so popular.

As I turned around to head back to the counter, I stopped. The man who'd come in obviously wasn't interested in flowers since he wasn't browsing and hadn't picked anything out. Nor did he seem to be placing an order for delivery. He had his hands on his hips, looking right at Rosey, who frowned. Did she need rescuing from an obnoxious customer? I knew a little about those. Olive was like ten obnoxious people all rolled into one. Was Rosey right about Olive's split personality? Or was Rosey the type to overexaggerate?

I hurried back across the room, stepping around the fountain, and placed my flowers on the far end of the counter. Maybe if the man saw Rosey had an actual paying customer, he'd get the hint and be on his way. But as I waited, it became obvious that wasn't going to work.

The man waved his arms then laughed too loud, the sound almost maniacal, sending a ripple of unease across my shoulders. What was with this guy? "It's like I was telling you the other day, Rosey, thank goodness that awful woman is gone."

Gone? I lowered my eyebrows. Did he mean Nan? What did he have against her? I waited, hoping he'd say more…

He didn't seem to have noticed me yet, as he rapped his fist against the counter and said, "Now my life can get back to where it should have been all those years ago. More than once, she disparaged my name publicly in her news articles, causing me no small amount of trouble. Now justice has been served. That woman was a menace. Someone doing her in was the best thing that could have happened to Green Meadow. And to me."

The guy sure didn't hold back. He must have despised her.

Rosey shook her head. "Listen, I know you're super happy about current circumstances with Nan being gone, but I really should get back to work." She pointed at my sunflowers on the counter.

He turned, noticing me for the first time "Who are *you?"* he asked. His gaze took me in from head to foot.

I jerked. How rude. "I'm—"

Rosey waved her hand to get his attention away from me. "That is Christy Bailey. She's Betty Hollingsworth's niece and is helping her in the bookstore." Rosey's words came out harsh, like she wanted to protect me from this man and his ranting and rudeness.

The man harrumphed then muttered, "Books. What a boring waste of time. You must be crazy to devote your time to something hardly anyone gives a rat's behind for."

Eyeing me with obvious distaste, he abruptly turned and marched toward the door, slamming it on the way out. The poor little bell on the door clanged loudly, as if injured.

Rapid footsteps came from the back room. A large, imposing woman with bright-red hair rushed toward us. "What's going on out here?" she demanded. "I'm on a business call. Can't you take care of the customers by yourself, Rosey?" Her cold blue eyes narrowed.

Rosey pressed her lips together, her mouth reminding me of a dam ready to burst open with the force of her words longing to escape. She swallowed once then answered, "I'm sorry about that, Essie. An unruly customer was making a scene."

Essie glared at me.

I took a step back, startled at her menacing expression. Part of me felt like a fly caught in the huge redheaded spider's web.

"No," said Rosey, "not her. She's buying some sunflowers." She pointed to the vase of flowers. "See?"

Essie's frown softened somewhat, but she still looked

annoyed. With another glance at me then focusing on Rosey, she huffed out, "Fine. Just try to keep it down out here, will you?"

"Of course." Rosey, looking prim, folded her hands together in front of her waist. The picture of subservience. Her smile looked fake, at least to me. Would her boss notice?

We waited until Essie had left us alone, and then Rosey shook her head. "Now you see why some people"—she tilted her head toward the back room—"aren't a thrill to work for."

"Yes, I sure do," I said as I tried to imagine working with someone so rude and scary every day. Nope. I'd hate it. "Hey, you said you'd worked here for decades, but she"—I pointed toward the back room—"looks to be in her thirties."

Rosey nodded. "That's right. She's thirty-two. And has only been here for a few months. Her father owns the shop. That's how she got the job. Believe me, getting sassed by someone young enough to be my daughter doesn't do much for my self-worth."

"Sure, I get it. She's not much older than me, and I wouldn't like it either."

Rosey glanced at the front door and back then grimaced. "So anyway, that man in here earlier was Burt Larsen. He's such a loon," she said.

"I noticed." I crossed my arms, still bristling about his book comment even more than the way he'd looked me up and down. I knew, of course, that not everyone liked to, or could, read. And that was fine. But why did he feel the need to put down something I obviously had an interest in? I mean, alligators weren't my thing, but if someone liked them…well, I wouldn't say nice things about them, but I wouldn't put the person down for liking them, either. Even though their cold eyes gave me the shivers and their huge mouths and sharp teeth looked evil enough to crush a Buick. A person's bones would be no match for—I gasped.

"Christy?" said Rosey, "what's the matter?"

Focus, Christy. Aunt Betty needs you to be sharp and figure out this mystery. "I uh… Just thinking about Burt. And what he said about books." Concentrating hard, I forced my body to relax.

She shook her head. "No one takes him seriously

anyway."

I was still ticked about his mini tirade as I asked, "What's that he was saying about 'Glad she was gone?'"

"Oh, that." She shrugged. "Just that he's relieved Nan isn't working at the *Green Meadow Gazette* any longer."

I was glad to have a subject besides horrid scaly reptiles to focus on. Maybe something would come up in talking to Rosey that would give me more information. "Why is that?"

She rang up the flowers, set them aside, and put her elbows on the counter, much as Burt had done, her eyes wide, ready to dish some gossip. "According to Burt, an article Nan printed in her column financially ruined him when she said that per a building inspector who refused to be named, the homes Burt was in charge of building were faulty and dangerous."

My mouth dropped open. "No wonder he couldn't stand her."

"Also, a month before that, Burt and Nan had a public argument out in front of Green Meadow's courthouse. Talk about everyone knowing his business."

I let my arms relax against my sides. "What was the argument about?"

"Again," said Rosey, "according to Burt, though I'm not sure I believe him, Nan told him she'd spoken to several homeowners who complained of problems in their homes he'd built and that she planned to write about it in her column."

"How did Burt respond to that?"

"With violence."

I gasped. Sure, I'd witnessed his displeasure and rudeness, but violence? That was a whole other level. An alligator in wrinkled clothing and messy hair.

She shrugged. "I didn't see or hear the argument myself," she said, "but from what I overheard from a checkout girl at the market, Burt reached out to put his hands around Nan's neck, but she was able to slip away before being hurt." Rosey shook her head. "I guess later on Burt, or someone, finally got the job done of getting rid of Nan. Permanently."

I shuddered, thinking of how Nan had looked when dead, slumped in Aunt Betty's chair. Even though she hadn't sounded like a person anyone had liked, having her life taken in that manner was atrocious.

The front door opened again, and a group of young women with babies in strollers entered. Chaos took over the small room as kids cried and moms tried to quiet them.

Rosey took a deep breath then let it out. Was she dreading having to deal with loud people, especially after Burt's annoying display? I didn't blame her. But the sooner I got out of her hair, the quicker she could see to the newest arrivals.

I picked up the vase of flowers and smiled. "Thanks for these."

"Yep. See you later," she answered.

As I stepped around the noise and commotion of the young families, I glanced at Rosey as I left the floral shop. That lady was a good source of information that might come in handy later on. For such a small town, Green Meadow sure did have its share of drama.

When I returned to the bookstore and opened the door, Aunt Betty was speaking to a man who had his back toward me. When he glanced over his shoulder at me, my heart sank. It was Detective Combs.

I caught Aunt Betty's frightened gaze as I hurried toward the counter. Setting the vase of flowers off to the side, I stepped around the counter to give my aunt some moral support. "Hello, Detective."

He gave a curt nod and said, "Miss Bailey—Christy."

I nodded back. "I assume you have further questions for my aunt?"

"Not so much questions as information."

Aunt Betty stiffened beside me. "And what might that be?" she asked.

He shifted his stance, causing his denim jacket to fall open, giving a clear view of his gun. "We've gotten the preliminary results from the murder weapon. Mrs. Hollingsworth's fingerprints were the only ones on it."

My aunt uttered a small gasp.

I frowned at the detective and said, "But—"

He held up his hand. "As I stated, hers are the *only* ones."

My heart thudded hard, wanting so bad for all of this to pass us by so my aunt could move on and not have to deal with any of this awfulness. "Well, couldn't whoever have killed Nan wore gloves? Maybe they put the letter opener in her hand to get her prints on the weapon."

He shrugged. "It's one explanation."

Aunt Betty cleared her throat and uttered, "The other being…"

Detective Combs crossed his arms over his chest. "I'm only passing along this information to let you know of our progress. But yes, it adds another question mark in your column, I'm afraid."

I stood up taller, trying to appear braver than I felt. "Is that all, Detective?"

"For now. Except…"

Aunt Betty blinked. "Except what?" she asked.

He tilted his head as he studied my aunt. "Are you certain you don't remember anything from the time surrounding the murder? Sometimes memories come back later, in pieces. Small details you might not have remembered before."

She shook her head. "No. Nothing."

"All right," he said. "That's it for now. I'll be in touch."

As we watched him walk out of the bookstore, I clenched my jaw. I had to find out who killed Nan. And quick.

CHAPTER SEVEN

Early the next morning, I went downstairs to the bookstore, surprised to see Aunt Betty already there. I rubbed her back. "Doing okay?"

"I'm all right. Just tired. I didn't sleep well."

"Did Pearl and Milton's nighttime crazies keep you awake?" I asked. "I kept them in my room, but they were so rambunctious, it was hard to keep them quiet."

She reached out to Milton, now stretched out on the counter, grooming his belly fur. "No, they didn't bother me in the least. It's all the…"

I gave her a brief hug. "Yeah," I said. "All the Nan stuff."

She nodded. "I try to stay positive. I really do. But then sometimes, when it's quiet and I'm not keeping busy, those worries crowd in again."

Time to try to lighten the somber mood if possible. "You said when it's quiet?" I asked. "Well, say the word and my two furry fanatics can bunk in your room. And trust me, it won't be quiet."

She gave a brief laugh. Not a belly laugh, like when we used to watch funny movies together when I was small, but at least she seemed a little bit cheered up.

Pearl jumped on the counter, gave a trilling meow, and made her way right to my aunt. The cat touched Aunt Betty's hand with her white paw then pressed her furry forehead against her arm.

Proud of my girl for helping my aunt, I ran my fingers through Pearl's fur, causing her to purr.

Aunt Betty sighed. "Christy, I'm so thankful you and your fur kids decided to come live with me. It's made all the difference in the world."

"I'm happy we're here too."

"I just wish your first day here hadn't been so traumatic," she said.

"It was, but obviously more for you than me."

Her smile fell again.

"Um, listen, I've been meaning to visit Dreamy Sweets but haven't had the chance," I said. "Since it's still too early for bookstore customers, mind if I run down there and get us some breakfast? My treat."

"That would be great, honey. Thanks."

"Any requests?"

"Everything Janie makes is delicious," Aunt Betty said as her mouth quirked up slightly on one side.

"Okay…but *your* favorite would be…"

"So glad you asked." She smiled "Janie's strawberry tarts are amazing."

"Then strawberry it is. Lucky for you, it's my favorite too." I winked and headed toward the door.

A duet of panicked meows followed me. I spun around, concerned one of the cats had gotten hurt. But they sat on the counter, side by side, with watery eyes and drooping whiskers.

"It's okay, guys. Mama will be right back."

Aunt Betty placed a hand on each cat's head, giving them some love. "Maybe Pearl and Milton heard us talking about the pastries and are putting in their order too?"

I chuckled. "As much as they'd love tuna-flavored"—both cats' ears perked up—"pastries, I doubt Janie has those. But..." I paused and held up one finger. "I happen to know there are t-r-e-a-t-s"—I really hoped they hadn't learned to spell—"in the back room in a cat-shaped cookie jar."

"Ah, I see," she said. "Then, bribery it will be." She moved her hands away from the cats. "Okay, kitties. Who wants treats?"

Milton and Pearl bolted off the counter, following her to the back room. They were in such a hurry, they passed her and beat her to the door. Too bad it was closed and they had to wait, pawing and meowing, for her to let them in. They sat by the door, pouting, until she reached them.

With the cats otherwise occupied, I slipped outside and

onto the sidewalk. On my walk to Dreamy Sweets, I waved at several people, some familiar, some new. A few of them might wonder about me. But then again, the way information flew around this town, most would already know who I was, what I was doing here, where I came from, and that my cats were named Milton and Pearl.

In a way it was comforting, becoming part of a close-knit community. On the other hand, with a murderer roaming the streets of Green Meadow, it was also disconcerting.

When I reached Dreamy Sweets and opened the door, the tantalizing aroma drew me in, as if my feet never touched the floor. As I stood in line, my stomach growled. An older man in front of me whipped around and stared at me.

I placed my hand on my tummy. "Uh, sorry."

His stare turned to a grin. "Understandable," he said. "I come here every single day for breakfast. It's that good."

I smiled, so happy for Janie that her business appeared to be successful.

When my turn in line came, I was disappointed not to see Janie at the counter. Maybe this girl was her assistant.

She blinked. "Hi, what can I get for you?" she asked.

"Four strawberry tarts, please. To go."

"Got it." As she rang up the order, I stood on my toes, hoping to see my friend. The girl noticed me checking things out. "Is there something else I can get for you?"

Realizing how it might have looked odd, me being nosy, I took a step back. "Oh, uh…I was hoping to see Janie today. Is she—"

"Christy!" yelled Janie when she spied me from the back of the kitchen area. She stepped out from behind a partition, dusted her hands off on a towel, and pushed at a swinging door that opened to the main room. As soon as she reached me, she grabbed my hand. How would that look to others? Curious, I watched the girl who'd taken my order. She rolled her eyes and shook her head. So maybe I wasn't the only one Janie did this to.

I gave Janie's hand a squeeze and tugged mine away. "Hey, wanted to check out your place." I glanced around. "It's great. And if the amazing aroma is any indication, I'm in for a treat with the pastries."

Janie grinned. "Aww, thanks," she said. She pointed to the counter. "Did Kiersten get you all taken care of?"

I waved to the girl, who rolled her eyes again. Wow, such a charmer.

Janie motioned me to follow her, and we took seats at a table near a back wall. "How are things going?" she asked. "Is Betty doing all right?"

"She's okay. A little down, as you can imagine."

"Sure. The whole thing is awful." Janie leaned closer. "Any more progress in the…you know."

I glanced around, but no one was close by. "Investigation?" I nodded.

She placed her elbows on the table and her chin on her fist. "What happened?"

I filled her in on Olive coming to the bookstore, demanding to see the place where her beloved family member died, about Milton and Pearl finding the receipt, and me taking the receipt to Petals and Stems.

"Oh wow," she said. "A lot has happened."

"Wait, there's more."

"Really?"

"While I was talking to Rosey, a guy came in, all rumpled looking, waving his arms and yelling like a lunatic," I said.

"Was it Burt Larsen?"

My mouth dropped open. "How could you know that just from what I said?"

She sighed. "Because he does it here too. And lots of other businesses from what I've heard."

"Well, he sure didn't think much of me when Rosey said I worked at the bookstore," I added. "Said I was crazy to spend my time with something no one cares about."

She made a face. "Don't worry about him. Nobody takes him seriously."

"That's what Rosey said."

"Smart woman," said Janie.

"Agreed."

A few people entered the shop, heading straight to the growing line at the counter. Janie shrugged and said, "Gotta go. Baking awaits." She stood then frowned. "Oh no. What's he doing here again so soon?"

I angled around in my seat to get a better view. It was a man, maybe in his forties, tall with muscular, broad shoulders. He stood at the end of the line, arms crossed, the deep creases in his forehead, an unwelcome addition to his frown.

Janie tapped her toe. "That man sucks the joy out of every room he enters. I was hoping I wouldn't have to listen to him drone on again today."

"What about?" I asked then stood when Kiersten called out my number.

"Wait, you'll see. If I know him, he'll give the same impassioned spiel he always does. It involves Nan."

Kiersten motioned impatiently to Janie.

"I need to go, but we'll talk later, okay?" said Janie.

"Sure."

Janie rushed off toward the swinging door. I stepped to the pickup side of the counter and grabbed the sack Kiersten held out to me. It was all I could do not to dive right in and grab one of the pastries. But I'd be good and wait. Aunt Betty deserved to be the first to take a bite.

Even though I wanted to rush back to the bookstore, I decided to stay a couple of minutes more. Maybe the guy would do his mouthing off again and I'd pick up something useful. I tried not to think about Milton and Pearl probably still waiting for me and not at all happy about it. I'd be there soon enough. I headed back to the same table and stood close by.

The man stepped to the order side of the counter, asked for strong black coffee, and then backed away. He glanced around the room, stopped when he spotted me, and headed in my direction.

Shoot. I'd hoped he'd tell his sad tale to the room in general, more like a broadcast. Not directly to me. Being a new town resident meant fertile listening ground for him. Someone to hear his story for the very first time.

Lucky me.

I plopped back down in my chair.

When he reached my table, he tugged out another chair and sat opposite me.

This was worse than I thought. He wanted to sit with me?

"I…uh…" I started to rise, but he held up his hand, palm out.

"Please sit," he said. "I have something important to say. And hear it you must."

I leaned to the left, allowing me a clear view of the counter. Janie peered out, mouthed *I'm sorry*, and then darted back inside the bakery area. The sack of pastries in my lap had cooled to lukewarm. I'd hoped for warm and scrumptious treats for Aunt Betty. Now, it might be cold and only sort of okay.

If he kept me here too long, I'd reorder some fresh ones. I didn't want to stay and listen to this guy, but Janie said I should, that it involved Nan. If sleuthing included buying more pastries, I'd gladly do it.

His hard-knuckled knock on the table startled me. I whipped back around and faced him.

His eyes narrowed. "Miss—"

"I'm Christy. Christy Bailey. I—"

He gave a curt nod. "You work at the bookstore."

"That's right."

"I'm Terrence O'Leary. I'm sure you've heard of me."

"Um…" I shrugged. Should I tell him the only thing I'd heard was just now and it wasn't complimentary? Probably not.

"Maybe I should take into account that you're new in town," he said. "Never fear, you and I shall be better acquainted after I fill you in on my tragic life."

How long was this going to take?

Terrence sat back in his chair, crossed one leg over the other, and gave a long, loud, heavy sigh. Just like the sound my cats gave when the food I served them was of the on-sale variety and not what their sensitive palates required.

Footsteps came from behind me. Had Janie come to rescue me? A hand stretched out toward Terrence, placing a cup of steaming coffee in front of him. I glanced up to see Kiersten smirking at my plight. She let out a distinct giggle as she walked away.

With resolve to stay and hear him out, I leaned back against my chair and waited.

Terrence shook his head and said, "As far back as I can remember, more than twenty years ago, I've longed for a better work environment. I kept thinking if I waited patiently, did my job diligently, I'd be properly rewarded."

I held in a sigh, resigned to the fact that the strawberry pastries were probably beyond hope. I'd order more after this ordeal with Terrence was through. Hopefully they didn't run out of strawberry before then. Another glance at the order counter showed Janie peeking out again. Why wasn't she coming over here to help speed things along? If she'd heard his story before, she'd know when he'd said the part she thought I needed to hear.

Terrence cleared his throat, drawing me back into the one-sided conversation. "Anyway," he said, "I worked and toiled for all those years, hoping, dreaming of the day I'd be taken seriously as a news reporter. But, of course, I was in competition with other people, most recently, Nan Bittle."

I shifted in my seat, aware of both my legs tingling, threatening to go to sleep.

He continued, "That woman took advantage of my kind nature, stealing away every benefit, promotion, raise, and accolade that rightfully should have been mine."

When he stared at me expectantly, I nodded, hoping that would appease him and he'd hurry up and finish.

He huffed out a breath and said, "Our boss assigned us stories to report on. But more than once I witnessed Nan rearranging the papers in our inbox slots so she'd get the stories she wanted. The more desirable ones. I told Nan I saw what she'd done, but she laughed in my face. When I accused, and rightly so, Nan of cheating to our supervisor, he called Nan in to see him. However, when they emerged, Nan wore a triumphant grin, and I knew she'd gotten her way."

My cell phone chirped, indicating a text. I wanted to check it but didn't know how Terrence would react. I hoped it wasn't Aunt Betty, worried that I'd been gone too long.

Terrence shook his head as he said, "And so I strove onward, working my fingers to the bone, hoping that someday, and soon, I'd get my deserved prize."

Then he stopped and stared at me. Was I supposed to finally say something? What did he expect?

He tilted his head and studied me. Finally, he held out his hands in a placating manner. "Well, don't you want to know what happened next?" he asked.

If it would get me out of here sooner, absolutely. "Er,

yes. What happened…next?"

"I'm so pleased you asked."

I longed to roll my eyes, even though seeing Kiersten do it more than once since I'd been here had annoyed me.

"Finally," he said, "one day in the not-so-distant past, I was given a gift. Nan Bittle, my nemesis, pain in my backside, was finally, irresolutely, and definitely without question, dead."

When he didn't go on, I nodded, hoping to encourage him. The pastry sack on my lap had now begun to leave a couple of greasy spots on the legs of my jeans. Those poor innocent strawberry edibles of delight. They never had a chance.

"When I learned of Nan's demise," he said, "I did a jig. An actual jig. Right there in the newspaper's main office. I got a few stares, but what did I care? I would finally get my due. I waited for my supervisor to tell me the good news, that I'd now get a promotion, a raise, the coveted office with an actual door that closed. With sadness, I must share with you, it didn't happen that way."

"It didn't?" I asked.

He shook his head. "A young woman, Nan's protégé, was given all that I'd been sure would come my way. I was cast aside, left bereft, having to once again scrounge for my livelihood."

"But don't you still work at the newspaper?"

"Yes," he said.

"Then, you still have your job, right? I mean, you're not really any worse off than you were before Nan died."

He stood. "Haven't you heard a word I've said?" With downcast eyes, he shook his head then walked across the room and out of the shop.

Glad the man had finally finished his tale, I stood, trying to ignore the not-so-attractive greasy spots on my pants. I turned to head back to the order counter, when Janie rushed toward me, a sack in her hand.

"Why didn't you warn me, Janie?"

Her face reddened. "I knew you needed to hear that about Nan. He's someone I think should be on your suspect list."

"Okay, but why didn't you help me out, sit with me or at least come to my rescue when you'd know I'd heard all I needed to hear?"

She shrugged. "My only excuse is I'm weak," she said.

"That's it?"

"Afraid so. I honestly thought if I had to sit and listen to him one more time, my head would explode." She grabbed my hand. "I am truly sorry though," she added.

I took in her hopeful expression, her wide, unblinking eyes, her shoulders, bunched together with tension. I squeezed her hand. "It's okay. Don't worry about it."

She let out a breath, smiled, and traded my old, cold sack for a new, fresh, warm one. "Peace offering?"

"Yes," I said. "Thanks." After she went back into the bakery area, I checked my phone. Oh no. The text had been from Aunt Betty wondering if I was okay. I hurried out the door.

CHAPTER EIGHT

Janie and I met for a work break one day at the local park. She brought along peanut butter cookies and cans of soda for our snack. As we sat enjoying the food and scenery of large maple trees, along with robins, cardinals, and tufted titmice that flitted around the area, I frowned.

"What's up, Christy?"

"Something's been bothering me."

"You mean besides the obvious murder taking place in your apartment?" she asked.

I gave a one-sided smirk. "Yeah. But it does have to do with that."

She set her cookie on a napkin and placed her elbows on the picnic table. "Okay. I'm listening."

"Well, the day of the murder, Nan called Aunt Betty, all upset, demanding to see her, right?"

"Yep."

"Obviously, my aunt didn't kill Nan," I said.

"True."

"So how did the person who did kill Nan know she'd be there? I mean, she worked at the newspaper office all day, and she and Aunt Betty weren't exactly on friendly terms."

"No," Janie said, "they weren't."

"Then, Nan going to see Aunt Betty would have been very unusual."

Janie nodded. "Right, so somehow, whoever the murderer is had to know where Nan would be at that particular time."

"Exactly."

"I'm guessing you have a plan. What do you want to do about it?" she asked.

"I thought I'd check out the newspaper office. Maybe ask some questions. See if her coworkers, um, former coworkers have any information that could be useful."

Janie popped up from her seat and placed the rest of the cookies in a sack.

"What are you doing?" I asked.

"Going with you."

I widened my eyes. "Now?"

"Sure. Why not. I don't want to miss out on what they might say. Plus, it's not often I get out of the bakery for a break with my friend, so let's go."

That was Janie. She definitely didn't want to miss out on anything. She grabbed the sack and drinks and powerwalked toward her vehicle. It all happened so fast, I just sat on the bench with my mouth open.

Janie, already in her van, rolled down the driver's side window. "Are you coming or not?" she shouted.

As if jolted, I hopped up and rushed to her van. "What about my vehicle? Shouldn't I drive too?"

"We'll come back for it later. Let's go!"

With the exception of Janie clutching on to me at various intervals whenever we were together, she was otherwise fairly mild-mannered. Except, apparently, for when she was at the wheel. Her tires squealed as she took a turn too fast. I grasped the door handle, not unlike how she sometimes did to my arm or hand. My fingernails dug into the handle as I held on for dear life. We raced through town, catching stares and a few glares from people walking along the sidewalks. One man yelled something not very nice, but under the circumstances, I couldn't blame him much.

I wanted to say something to Janie, ask her to not take turns on two wheels, stop running red lights, or maybe just to slow down so the scenery outside my window wasn't such a blur, but I was too stunned to use my voice.

Who would have guessed she'd be such a wild driver? What condition were her pastries in when she made deliveries? By the time she'd arrive, would they be nothing more than a bunch of crumbs, torn pieces of fruit, and smeared icing?

I was grateful when she halted in the newspaper parking area, even though the sudden braking of the van tossed us forward then back. It would have been much worse without seat belts. Catching my breath, I undid my belt, hoping it was safe to do so, that she wouldn't back up and start racing around again.

Janie put the van in park and turned off the ignition. She turned to me with a big grin. "Ready to go in?" she asked.

I swallowed hard, hoping my heart would stop hammering like a woodpecker on a tree. "Uh, sure." Next time, I'd offer to drive if we had to go someplace together.

We hopped out of the van and made our way to the front entrance. It was an old building that had been restored since I'd visited as a kid. Thankfully, they'd kept the original essence of the structure, updating it without modernizing too much. Huge white columns stood in front of the red brick exterior, with black wrought iron railings lining both sides of the steps leading to the door.

Janie had insisted on coming for this visit, but I wanted to be the one to ask the questions. I stepped slightly ahead of her as we ascended the stairs.

Two fortyish women, dressed in business casual attire, were exiting the building. I smiled and moved closer. "Hi," I said. "Do both of you work here?"

They nodded. The brunette fidgeted and checked her watch. But the redhead smiled and said, "Can I help you with something?"

"I'm trying to find out some information about one of your former coworkers."

"Who would that be?"

"Nan Bittle," I said.

The redhead shrugged. "Sorry, I didn't work directly with her. Just knew who she was."

I eyed the brunette, who was now tapping her foot rapidly on the floor, and said, "How about you? Did you work with Nan?"

She shook her head, causing her long brown ringlets to toss against her shoulders. "Nope. Didn't know her. She worked on the main floor, and we are on the third." She glanced at her coworker. "Can we go now?"

The redhead rolled her eyes at the brunette then said to me, "Sorry, um, we didn't really know her. Can't help you. But good luck."

They took off down the walk at a rapid pace, the brunette tugging her friend every bit as awkwardly as how Janie did to me.

As if hearing my thoughts, Janie snagged my hand and yanked it. "Come on. There must be somebody inside who can help."

We stepped inside, my eyes adjusting to the dimmer light from the small overhead chandelier-style fixtures. As we reached the front desk, I edged closer, getting the attention of Tina Jeffers, who I remembered from the day of the murder down in the bookstore.

She watched me warily before saying, "How can I help you?"

I opened my mouth to reply then was jerked slightly to the side as Janie clutched my arm. It was really hard not to roll my eyes, but I managed, barely. I tried again. "I'd like to speak to someone in charge, please."

She gave an exaggerated look left then right. "Well, as you can see, right now, I'm it. So I'll ask again, what can I do for you?"

A quick glance around showed she was telling the truth. Even if there were others around the building, no one else was presently at the counter. "Um, well…" I said.

Janie tugged on my arm again then whispered, "Ask about Nan."

As if I would have forgotten. "Yes, anyway, I had some questions about Nan Bittle."

Tina crossed her arms. "Yeah? Well, join the club."

My eyebrows rose. "Excuse me?"

"I'd like to know what happened too," she said. "I knew there was something fishy about her being away from work and ending up in that bookstore. Although, it did work out great for me, since I got Nan's old job."

My eyes widened. Getting Nan's coveted position at the paper would be a good motive for murder. Janie tugged on my sleeve. Was she thinking the same thing?

Tina pointed her stubby finger in my direction. "Hey, I remember you. From Words to Read By."

"Yes. That's right."

Janie gave an excited hop and said, "Christy works

there. With her aunt. Who owns it. And she's a famous author. Not Betty, but Christy."

Oh boy. I gave Janie a pained expression, hoping she'd give me a chance to speak for myself. Maybe coming together wasn't such a great idea after all, though I did appreciate her friendship and support.

Tina shrugged. "A famous"—she put the word in quotes—"author, huh? So what's that to me?"

Janie let out an annoyed squeak. Was she thinking of talking more? I made a little shake with my head, and she sighed then pressed her lips tightly together.

I gently removed the cute blonde's appendage from my arm and leaned on the chest-high counter to face Tina. I waved my hand and said, "I'm not here to talk about me." Janie shuffled beside me, but I ignored her. "I'm here to ask a few questions, if you have the time," I said.

With a shrug, Tina said, "Sure. Why not. I've finished my work for today. Just hanging around until time to clock out and collect my pay."

Wow, what a stellar employee. "Okay. Well, speaking of the workday hours, any idea why Nan might have left early the day she died?"

"Sure, that's easy. Everybody here knows that," she said.

Apparently not everyone, according to those we'd already questioned. "Is that so?"

"Yeah, along with anyone else who happened to be in the office that day for whatever reason. Customers and salespeople come and go all the time. It's like a revolving door."

I lowered my eyebrows. That hadn't exactly been my experience here today, with only Tina being here to speak to. "Oh, really?" I asked. "Was it broadcast on a loudspeaker or something where she'd be?" My voice was sarcastic. If Tina could exaggerate, then so could I.

"Exactly."

I jerked. "What? You mean it *was* broadcast?" Had Nan stood around with a bullhorn or something? Not likely. I doubted she'd want the whole world to know she was going to meet my aunt to discuss the man they both loved.

"In a manner of speaking," said Tina. "At least to those

on this floor."

Janie tugged on my arm again, whispering, "Ask her what she means."

I held in my sigh and focused on Tina again. "Could you possibly explain what you mean?"

Tina grinned. "What's it worth to you?"

"Worth?"

"You're a famous author, right?" said Tina. "Aren't you rich?"

At least she'd spared me the air quotes this time. "Definitely not famous or rich."

Next to me, Janie stomped her foot. It warmed my heart that she insisted I was famous, even though it wasn't true.

"If not money, then, what do I get out of it?" asked Tina.

Gee, what a peach of a girl. "How about helping your former coworker by giving details that might discover who killed her?"

She grimaced. "Is that all?"

"Shouldn't that be enough?" I asked. "The humanitarian thing to do?"

After drumming her fingers on the counter, as if thoroughly considering my question, she said, "Fine. What happened was this. Nan was on her office phone, hit the wrong button, and ended up on speaker phone. One of our interns stepped into the office to put something on her desk, and when he left, he didn't close the door. So basically the entire first floor heard her conversation—where she was going and when."

Aunt Betty would be mortified to learn that lots of people overheard her conversation. Although, comparing it with what she was going through now, it might not mean so much after all.

"Hey, wait a second," said Tina. "It was your aunt who Nan was talking to on the phone."

"Correct."

"Then don't you already know more about this than I might?"

I wasn't going to explain that my aunt couldn't remember what happened after Nan arrived. "I just wanted to know how the, um, a person might have known about Nan's plans that day."

"And isn't your aunt under suspicion for Nan's death?" she asked.

This conversation was going south, fast. "My aunt is innocent."

"Anybody who's ever committed murder could say that."

I blinked. Tina could fit that description as well, now that I knew she'd gotten Nan's job. "I think we're done here. Um, thanks for your information."

She crossed her arms. "And thank *you* for nothing. Famous author, my big foot." Her words came out snarky and rude.

Janie pulled me closer and started to speak.

I shook my head. "Time to go," I whispered.

At the very least, I now knew how the murderer knew where Nan would be and when, and that because of the speakerphone, that person could have been nearly anyone, which unfortunately didn't narrow down my list.

CHAPTER NINE

It was nearing closing time at the bookstore, and I'd just finished a display for the newest Milton and Pearl book when the front door opened. A man about Aunt Betty's age strolled in and checked out the books and the store in general. I made my way back to stand behind the counter. "Hi, how can I help you today?" I asked.

He reminded me of characters I'd seen on TV, of used car salesmen. Wide white smile, bright, multicolored blazer. And white belt and shoes. "Hello, young lady." His smile grew impossibly wider.

Something brushed my leg, and I glanced down. Pearl tapped me with her paw then meowed. Did she want to see who'd come for a visit? I was pretty sure my cats thought everyone always came to see them and the books in the store were just an added bonus. Who was I to disagree? I was their biggest fan, by far.

First Pearl, then Milton, crawled out from the shelf. A tiny scuffle ensued when Milton bopped his sister on the nose and she gave a loud hiss. I adored them, but why did they show off their sibling rivalry just as a customer walked in?

I crouched down and picked up one in each arm—not as easy as when they were kittens—and placed them on the counter. They immediately groomed each other as if their disagreement had never occurred.

He glanced down at the cats. "Well, now," he said. "What beautiful specimens of cat-hood."

I blinked. Cat-hood? "Thank you."

He placed his hands on his hips and turned from side to side, admiring the store. "This is a great place."

"Oh, thanks," I said. I hoped he'd say something else so

I could give an answer rather than "thank you." When he didn't comply, I smiled. "Is there a book I could help you find? We have some new thrillers just in that are wonderful."

He waved his hand. "No thanks. Not really in the market for books."

"Uh, okay." Then why was he here?

He angled his head a little to the side, fixated at something behind me. "Ah, there's the one I wanted to see. Hello, Betty."

My aunt stood a few feet behind me, as if frozen. She didn't appear to recognize the man. Should I be worried? I watched her, ready to come to her aid if need be.

The man's smile fell. "Betty, it's me, Dennis Paisley. Don't you recognize me?"

My aunt's brow furrowed then relaxed as she said, "Oh, of course! From school."

Dennis sighed. "Guess it's been a very long time, huh? I must have changed a lot. But you haven't, not a bit."

Her cheeks colored. "Well, thank you, but I'm afraid it's not accurate. You're being kind. And I apologize. I should have known you, but yes, it's been a very long time and I wasn't expecting to see you." She approached him and held out her hand for a shake.

"Come on now, two old friends?" he said. "We can do better than that." He wrapped her in a hug, his large frame dwarfing her tiny one. She looked decidedly uncomfortable and seemed relieved when released from his grasp.

She gave him a tremulous smile then stepped closer to me, wrapping her arm around my waist. "Dennis, this is my niece, Christy. She recently moved here to help me run the bookstore."

He nodded. "Nice to meet you."

I smiled. "Same here," I said.

Aunt Betty gave me a squeeze then moved away. "So, Dennis, what brings you to town after all this time? I don't think I've seen you since high school."

His face fell. "Actually, I came for Nan's funeral."

"Oh, yes. Of course," she said. "I'd forgotten that you and Nan…"

He ran his hand down his face. "Yes, we dated before I

married my now ex-wife. I was so sorry to hear about Nan's passing."

I hadn't remembered seeing Dennis at the funeral home, but then, it was during the calling and people came and went. I watched Aunt Betty. She'd been hesitant to give her old classmate a hug. Did she not trust him?

Dennis stuck his hands in his front pockets. "Listen, it really has been such a long time," he said, "I'd love to take you to dinner, Betty, to catch up. I won't take no for an answer."

Next to me, I could sense Aunt Betty's indecision. She obviously had qualms about being with Dennis. I gave a shrug. "Um, Aunt Betty, would you mind if I tagged along? I'd love hearing your old stories about growing up in Green Meadow."

She let out a breath. "Oh, yes, Christy, what a great idea. Don't you agree, Dennis?"

At first he didn't look pleased, but his smile rose, and he nodded. "Sure, the more the merrier. When might you two lovely ladies be available?"

Aunt Betty checked her watch. "Actually, we're getting ready to close."

"Then it's my lucky day," he said. "I'm ready whenever you are."

She and I exchanged glances. I picked up the cats. "I'll put these guys upstairs and fetch our purses, okay?"

"Yes, thanks, Christy." In her gaze, I took her "thanks" to include inviting myself along. She'd tell me her reasons later.

I hurried as much as a person could while lugging two fairly large complaining cats up a steep flight of stairs.

As I set Milton and Pearl on the floor of the living room, they gave me matching glares.

"Now come on," I said. "I don't really have a choice. Aunt Betty needs me. And you love her. Don't you want her to feel comfortable at dinner?"

The cats looked at each other. Milton let out a low growl, but Pearl gave a trill.

"Thank you. I knew you guys would understand. I promise you'll get extra treats when we get back."

I grabbed my purse then my aunt's from the top of a low bookcase in the hall. When I went back downstairs, my aunt and Dennis were standing by the main door. The store lights had been dimmed, and the sign had been flipped to closed.

Outside at the curb, Dennis opened the front door of his sedan for Aunt Betty, while I climbed into the back. He got in and started the engine. "So, I hear around town there's now a great seafood place," he said. "Sound like a good idea?"

Aunt Betty nodded, and I gave a thumbs-up to Dennis when he made eye contact in his rearview mirror.

He kept up a running commentary of what his life had been like since moving to Chicago decades ago. Aunt Betty interjected a few comments, but for the most part didn't have to add much. Dennis seemed capable of having a conversation all on his own.

Dennis parked his car near the front of the restaurant. When he opened Aunt Betty's door and assisted her out, he kept his hand on her elbow. Her frown told me she didn't like it one little bit. But I knew her. She was too polite to make a fuss about it.

I followed them to the door, which was opened by an employee who must have been a greeter.

I'd never been to Beneath the Sea. It hadn't existed when I'd visited as a little girl. The main room was large, with a high ceiling and beautiful ocean life murals painted on the walls. It wasn't crowded, so we didn't have to wait. Aunt Betty grabbed my hand and gave it a squeeze as we followed the waiter and Dennis to our table. Was she still nervous about being with Dennis, even with me along?

She quickly took a seat and motioned me next to her. Dennis's brow creased slightly when he had to sit opposite us, but he soon grinned and said, "Perfect. This way I can view two beautiful ladies at the same time."

My aunt gave a small smile, one I knew to be forced. I thanked him, even though his compliment didn't sound all that sincere. If Aunt Betty acted like she wasn't fond of him, and they hadn't talked or spoken in decades, why was he so intent on seeing her now? He could have attended the funeral then left town again.

Maybe he was doing more than going to a funeral. Were there other reasons to remain here? I leaned forward a little. "So, Dennis," I said, "do you still have family in Green Meadow?"

He ignored me and motioned to the waiter, who'd wandered away to seat someone else.

The waiter hurried back. "Yes, sir?"

"I'd like a double scotch on the rocks," said Dennis. "And keep them coming."

"Certainly, sir." The waiter left us again.

We'd barely sat down. He couldn't wait to order a drink? Dennis finally focused on me and said, "To answer your question, Christy, no, sadly, I have no family left here." He winked at Aunt Betty. "I do have friends, though."

Aunt Betty stiffened. The vibes coming off her were palpable. Why had she agreed to come if she disliked him so much?

Throughout our meal, Dennis repeatedly ordered more drinks. How much could one man hold? I didn't like the idea of him driving us home after this. What were the chances he'd let one of us drive instead?

Probably none.

His persona was headstrong and loud. Gone was his previous polite, if annoying, manner of speaking, the way he'd give us that cheesy grin and flowery compliments. With every sip of liquor, his facial expressions and tone came out gruffer and more rude.

Aunt Betty and I had long since finished our meals. Dennis had barely touched his, opting instead for a liquid supper. Several times, our waiter approached, asking if we needed anything. He kept his gaze on Dennis, obviously not trusting what the man might do next. Each time, Dennis shooed the waiter away.

Now exceedingly drunk, he waved his arms in the air, attracting the attention of every employee and diner in the room.

Aunt Betty frowned. "Dennis, maybe you should calm down."

"Why should I?" he asked. "When the love of my life is gone."

The love of his life? So now he was back to talking about Nan. I exchanged glances with Aunt Betty.

Her eyes widened as she faced Dennis again. "I really think you've had enough to drink."

He shook his head. "I assure you, I'm perfectly fine."

This was getting way out of hand. How could we extricate ourselves from this mess without causing even more bad attention sent our way?

Dennis knocked on the table with his fist, the light overhead gleaming from a thick gold ring with a huge red stone. Was it a class ring? He must really hold on to the good old days of school. I had a class ring but didn't even know where it was. Couldn't imagine wearing it every day now.

"I've never stopped loving Nan," said Dennis. "She and I kept up our friendship and corresponded regularly. Even when I married my wife and Nan married another man, she's always been the only woman for me." His eyes teared up. "At least, she was, until…"

I crossed my arms over my chest. "I'm sorry for your loss. Maybe it would be good if you talked to someone about it."

"What do you think I'm doing here with you?" he said as he eyed his nearly empty glass. "I've had so many emotions since I arrived in Green Meadow a week ago."

I frowned. A week ago? He came to town before Nan died? When I looked at my aunt, she shrugged. Had he been mistaken about when he arrived because he was drunk, or had he accidently let it slip that he'd been in the area sooner than he'd originally said?

A quick check around the room showed nearly everyone sneaking looks at our table. Dennis's loud voice had given the place an unpleasant show. Should we just get up and leave? While it was true we'd ridden here with Dennis, it was only a few blocks from the bookstore. We could simply walk home.

I bumped Aunt Betty's shoulder with mine and motioned my head toward the door. She nodded.

As I started to rise, large fingers clenched my wrist. Dennis's eyes, now bleary and red from the alcohol, peered up at me. "Don't. Please," he said.

"Hey, what are you doing?" I tried to tug away, but his grip was strong. Did he even realize how tightly he held me? Maybe it was because of all he'd had to drink.

"I've been kind enough to take you to dinner," he whined. "The least you can do is sit and listen. Please."

When I glanced over my shoulder, the waiter was speaking to an older man, possibly the manager. Hopefully, he'd come over and oust Dennis from the establishment. I turned back around, checking on Aunt Betty. Her face was pale, her eyes wide. Why did we have to agree to come with Dennis in the first place?

A rustling and footsteps came from behind us. "Do you ladies need some help?" asked a deep voice.

Finally, the manager.

At the sound of the man's voice, Dennis's fingers slid from my wrist. I rubbed it, embarrassed that Dennis made such a scene and had involved Aunt Betty and me as well. Would the whole town hear about it?

My aunt glanced over her shoulder and seemed to deflate as she said, "Oh, Micah. I'm glad you're here."

But when I made eye contact with the man, it wasn't the waiter my aunt had spoken to. Instead, it was the gorgeous funny guy from the funeral home. And now I knew his first name.

His eyes widened when he saw me. "Hi again."

"Hi."

Aunt Betty shifted beside me. "You've met?" she asked.

I shrugged. "Not officially."

Aunt Betty looked at Dennis then frowned. "I think it's time we left." She rose abruptly from her seat, gasping when Dennis tried to reach out for her hand.

Micah stepped closer to Dennis. "Hey, you've had a lot to drink," said Micah. "You need to let these nice women leave, and we'll have the manager call you a cab."

Dennis stood too fast, lost his balance, and plopped down on his seat. The manager finally showed up at our table, helping Dennis to his feet, keeping his hand on his arm clenched tight, much as Dennis had done to me.

Aunt Betty let out a sigh. "My goodness. What a fiasco."

I wrapped my arm around her waist. "Are you all right?" I asked.

"I'm fine, dear. But what about you? Your wrist… Are you hurt?"

Micah frowned. "Your wrist?" He gently took my hand

in his, the pressure so light I barely felt it. With care, he turned my hand slightly, his focus intense, his presence calming.

Aunt Betty patted Micah's shoulder. "Since you hadn't been properly introduced, Micah, this is my niece, Christy Bailey. Christy, this is Dr. Micah Remington. He's an ER doc at the local hospital."

That explained his exceptional bedside manner.

Micah seemed to barely have heard Aunt Betty's words, instead still concerned with my physical well-being. "I see some bruising starting to form on your skin," he said. "Looks like finger marks." His eyes narrowed as he turned to watch Dennis, now slumped awkwardly in a chair close to the entrance. "Did he do this to you?"

I slipped my hand from Micah's. "Yes, but I'm fine. Honestly. I really think it was because he'd had too much to drink. He might not have even realized what he was doing. He was saying crazy things, too."

He shook his head. "Well, at any rate, I don't think it's broken. But I'd put ice on it tonight to help with any swelling."

"Thank you," I said. "I will."

Micah glanced across the room. "Oh, um, I'd been in the process of paying for my meal when I saw you over here. Let me go give money to the waiter tapping his foot by my table."

As soon as he walked away, I leaned close to Aunt Betty. "Why did you agree to come out with Dennis?" I asked. "It was obvious you weren't comfortable."

"To be honest, he and I were friends when we were in high school. I remembered him as a kind of shy, nerdy kid who was nice to me. I thought…I thought maybe it would be nice to reconnect after all these years."

"But shortly after agreeing to come, I could tell you'd changed your mind but were probably too polite to say so. That's why I offered to tag along."

She nodded. "Yes, that's it exactly," said Aunt Betty. "And thank you so much for coming with me. I know the evening was horrible. And I feel terrible for what he did to your wrist."

"Don't worry about that. I'm fine. But what happened to change your mind about Dennis?"

"I thought that if Wallace heard I was with another man

at dinner, he might think I was on a date," answered Aunt Betty.

I could understand her not wanting to hurt Wallace's feelings if he got the wrong idea about her spending time with another man. But if he was as wonderful as she said, wouldn't he have understood her reason for coming, even if I hadn't offered to come along?

She patted my hand. "Christy, let's get out of here, all right? I think I've had enough for one night." She headed to the door.

Micah returned to stand beside me. "Are you all right, Christy?"

When he said my name, something warm and soothing flowed through me. Was that only his bedside manner, or more? "My wrist will be fine."

"I meant, you seem worried about your aunt."

Micah had the kindest, warmest brown eyes I'd ever seen. He and Aunt Betty knew each other, and she was relieved when he showed up to help us with Dennis. And I'd felt his gentle manner when he'd checked out my wrist. Maybe I could trust him with what was going on. I tipped my head toward the door. "Let's go outside and check on Aunt Betty, okay?"

He nodded. "Sure."

Unlike when Dennis had manhandled me—and yes, even though I'd downplayed it to Aunt Betty and Micah, my wrist was sore—when Micah put his hand lightly on my elbow as we walked out, I didn't mind, not the least little bit.

Micah drove us back to the bookstore. My aunt, tired from our not-fun dinner, excused herself to go up to the apartment. I wanted to get to know Micah better, along with seeing if maybe he had some ideas that could help Aunt Betty out of this mess.

I pointed to a bench located just outside the bookstore. We sat down and people-watched for a few minutes.

Finally, he turned to me. "Christy, I know we've only just met, but I can see how much you love your aunt."

"Yes, very much." Without warning, my eyes burned. I reached up and swiped away a tear from my cheek.

He gently took my free hand and held it. "Is there anything I can do?" he asked.

A sigh escaped my lips. "I just… My poor aunt. She's

been through so much. I just want to make it better for her."

"Yes, of course you do. I'd like to help too, if I can."

I faced him. His eyes, as he looked into mine, made me feel like he was truly interested. That he cared. His hand holding mine was firm and reassuring. Something about him inspired confidence and trust. Maybe it was to do with his profession—caring for injured patients—or maybe it was simply his nature, but either way, I wanted to trust him. "Thank you, Micah. I'd very much love your help."

CHAPTER TEN

After Micah left, I went upstairs to find Aunt Betty sitting in the front room with a frown on her face.

"What's up?" I asked. "Are you all right?"

Her eyes narrowed as if in thought as she cocked her head to the side. "You know what Dennis said about being in town earlier than we'd thought?"

I let out a breath. "Yeah, that was weird, wasn't it?"

"What if…" she said.

I tilted my head as I waited.

Aunt Betty's brow furrowed. "Why would Dennis have come to town before Nan's funeral? What purpose would he have had?"

"Are you thinking he let something slip to us?" I asked. "That because he'd been drinking, he might not have realized what he said?"

"Yes, I'm wondering that."

I crossed my arms. "Okay. Go on."

"Well, I think there has to be a reason," she said. "A very important reason Dennis came to town when he did."

I nodded. "As in, maybe he's the one who killed Nan?" I asked.

"Exactly." She rubbed the back of her head. "I've been thinking about our missing bookend."

My eyes widened. "What if Dennis was the one to use it on you? Do you think it's possible he might have hung on to it for some reason? It wasn't in our apartment, so it has to be somewhere."

"He might have thrown it out," said Aunt Betty.

"True. But he might not have. It's a long shot, but isn't it worth it to find out?"

"Yes. It's worth it," she answered.

"Okay. Then I need to somehow check out his hotel room when he's out."

"No, Christy. *We* need to check it out."

"But…"

"Christy, I'm not a fragile old lady. And this definitely involves me. I'm coming, and that's that."

When Aunt Betty set her mind to something, I knew from experience it didn't do any good to argue. I blew out a breath. "All right."

After calling the local hotel to see if Dennis would answer his phone, we were told by the concierge that Dennis was sitting in the hotel bar at the moment. Wow, how much liquor could one individual hold without passing out?

No time like the present. We headed to the hotel.

Once there, I peeked inside the bar area. Sure enough, Dennis sat slouched in a corner booth, half asleep, his fingers wrapped around a glass. I'd witnessed the man drink. I doubted he'd be leaving his barstool anytime soon.

Now to find out which room he was staying in.

We rounded the corner back to the front desk. A man maybe in his twenties, with black-framed glasses and a mustache that had only partially grown in, was behind the counter, looking at something on the computer. We needed a distraction to pull the guy away from the counter for a bit so I could hopefully check the computer to find which room Dennis was in. But how?

Behind us, the elevator pinged, and the door opened. A woman stood holding a little boy's hand. He glanced up at her. "Mommy, I bumped my leg. It hurts. Can we go back to our room?" She lifted her son's pant leg, sighed, and pressed the button to close the doors once more.

Glancing at Aunt Betty, I had an idea how to get the man's attention. In a whisper to my aunt, I said, "Pretend to fall, okay?"

She frowned then widened her eyes and nodded. As we approached the desk, I gave her a nod. She dipped down to her knees, though the man was still so involved in his computer perusing that he didn't seem to notice us.

"Oh, my leg!" wailed Aunt Betty from the floor.

I waved to the man and said, "Help! This woman is injured."

When he finally noticed us, his mouth dropped open. "Oh no! What happened?" He rounded the counter and approached us. When he was closer, I could read the name *Leonard* on his nametag. Looking at me, he said. "Is she with you?"

I shook my head. "No, we just happened to walk in together."

"Oooohhh," moaned Aunt Betty. "It's so painful."

He motioned to the desk. "Maybe I should call—"

I grabbed my phone from my purse. "I'll call, if you could…" Eyeing a seating area with a couple of couches across the lobby, I pointed. "Maybe you could help her to sit down over there?"

Aunt Betty nodded. "Oh, yes, please."

He helped her to stand and wrapped his arm around her. She kept up her limp, quite convincingly, the whole way to the couch.

I needed to get to the computer, so she'd need to keep him occupied. When she glanced at me, I wound my hand in a circle, hoping she'd understand to keep him talking for a bit.

As the man turned to come back toward me, my aunt said, "Um, listen… I'm a bit scared. Would you mind sitting with me until someone arrives to check out my leg?"

He did a good job of hiding his sigh, but I still noticed. No way did he want to sit with her when he was supposed to be working. But Aunt Betty widened her eyes, appearing the very essence of a sweet and innocent senior citizen. With a nod, he joined her on the couch.

I quickly stepped away. The way the furniture was arranged, if I was behind the desk, he wouldn't be able to see me from his place on the couch. When I finally got to the computer, I nudged the mouse with my knuckle. The screen jumped to life, showing a main page for the hotel. A couple of clicks had me into the guest area, where I finally discovered what I needed to know. I entered the last name Paisley. Dennis was on the second floor. Room 208. I clicked again on the tab for the main hotel site, hoping Leonard wouldn't notice that someone had used his computer.

Now that I had the information, it was time to rescue Aunt Betty. I rushed around the corner, headed toward the couch, as I waved my phone. I caught Leonard's gaze and said, "Good news, an ambulance will be here any minute. I'll stay with…er…"

Aunt Betty jerked. "Uh, Penny Smith."

I raised my eyebrows. Not bad for thinking on the fly. "Okay, Ms. Smith. I'll stay with you so this nice gentleman can get on with his workday."

The man shot up, seeming glad to be done with his current situation. "Right, glad to help," he said. "And good luck." He wasted no time getting back to his work site.

Aunt Betty and I walked through a back doorway that had a sign announcing *Stairs* and an arrow. We found the steps leading up and climbed to the second floor.

Since it was early evening, there wasn't a lot happening in the hallway. From my stays in hotels, it seemed like most of the work done by the housekeeping staff was earlier in the day. Still, since neither one of us knew how to pick a lock, we'd need somebody with a master key to let us in.

Voices came from down the hall. I angled to the side to see better. From the end of the long hallway, I saw two women in hotel uniforms talking together as they headed our way.

I eyed my aunt. "Okay, here's our chance," I said. "When they get closer, can you fake having a stomachache?"

She frowned. "I guess so. But how will that help us?"

"I'm hoping they might let us in if we say it's our room and we lost our key."

Aunt Betty grinned. "Yes, let's give it a try," she said. She wrapped her arms around her stomach, getting ready for her role as a sickly woman. One of the housekeepers stopped at a room down the way and knocked on the person's door. The second woman kept coming toward us, but she was focused on the cell phone in her hand.

I whispered to Aunt Betty, "Ready?"

"Ready."

When the woman was a few feet away, I waved to her. "Excuse me," I said. "Could you help us?"

She glanced at me then at Aunt Betty. "I can try. What do you need? More towels or bathroom tissue?"

"No, er… We've lost our room keys and need to get inside," I answered.

The woman glanced behind her at the room where her coworker had disappeared inside the other hotel room. "Um…maybe I should get my supervisor to…"

"Please," I said. "My mother is ill. She needs to get inside. Quickly."

With my last word, Aunt Betty covered her mouth with her hand and coughed, as if she was ready to lose the contents of her supper.

"Oh!" said the housekeeper. She grabbed a keyring from her pocket, opened the door, and nearly ran away, probably hoping she wouldn't have to be the one to clean up whatever mess my *mother* was about to make in our room.

We stepped inside and closed the door behind us. The room was a swirl of dirty clothes, trash, and pages of paper strewn about the room.

Aunt Betty wrinkled her nose. "Not much of a neatnik, is he?"

"Definitely not."

I pointed to the bed. "If you'd like to start searching for the bookend on this side of the room, I'll take the other," I said.

With a frown and a nod, Aunt Betty stepped over some dirty towels on the floor and headed toward the bed.

I eyed the room. "Gosh, I didn't think about it being so disgusting. Sure wish we'd brought some—"

My aunt reached into her pocket and produced two sets of disposable gloves. "Guess it pays to be a clean freak, huh?"

I smiled and said, "Yep, guess it does." I slipped on my gloves and got to work checking around my half of the room.

While searching for the bookend, I looked inside dresser drawers, the trash can, inside Dennis's suitcase, which sat on a nearby luggage rack, and then moved aside the jumble on top of the desk and table. A messy pile of papers sat on the desk, hanging precariously half off the edge. I grabbed the pile, shuffling the pages until they were aligned.

With the amount of liquor Dennis had consumed, and was evidently still drinking, hopefully he wouldn't notice if his room looked slightly neater than how he'd left it.

A glance toward the other side of the room showed

Aunt Betty on her knees, peeking beneath the bed. The disgusted expression on her face told me all I needed to know about the condition of things under there. I wiped some beads of sweat off with my wrist, not wanting to touch my face with my gloved hand. "I take it you're not finding the bookend, either."

"Nope," said Aunt Betty. "Just lots of dirty clothes, an empty gin bottle, and discarded candy bar wrappers." She pushed herself up from the floor, wincing when her knees popped.

I let out a sigh. "Okay, maybe we're not going to find what we came for."

"Let's keep looking a little while longer, and then we can go," she said. "All right?"

"Okay." We had to move fast, though. Even though Dennis would be drunk, there was a chance he might stagger back up to his room at any time. I bent over the desk, shuffling through the papers, even though I knew there was no way the thick bookend could be hiding there. But could there be something else? Maybe he had a—

I gasped.

Aunt Betty hurried to me. "What's wrong? Did you find the bookend?" she asked.

"No, but…"

She peered around me to see what I had in my hand. "Christy? What is it?"

I narrowed my eyes, attempting to read the words written on the fragile piece of stationary. "It's…" I shook my head." I can't believe I'm saying this, but it's a letter written to someone about a hidden treasure. And the place it mentions is yours."

"What place?" she asked.

"Your address."

"You mean the bookstore?"

"Yes," I said.

"A hidden treasure? That doesn't make any sense."

"No, it doesn't, but whoever wrote this letter seemed to think it did."

"So who sent the letter?" she asked.

I sorted through the pages of the letter until I found the final page. "You're not going to believe this."

"Why? Who was it?"

"John Dillinger," I said.

"The *gangster*?"

With a shrug, I answered, "I guess so." I thought for a minute. "Wait, didn't he live in Indiana at one point?"

She nodded. "You're right. He was actually born in Indianapolis."

"Still, to say there's money hidden someplace on your property?"

"I don't know what to think," said Aunt Betty. "Maybe it's some kind of joke or prank."

With a glance around the shambles of a room, I said, "I'm thinking maybe it's not a joke."

"Why is that?"

"There must be a reason Dennis would have something like this letter in his possession. Why else would he have it with him in his hotel room?"

"Maybe it's why he's in town," she said. "To try to find the supposed money."

"You might be on to something there." I read through the central part of the letter more closely. "According to this, Dillinger was on the lam and needed to hide the money for a while. He buried it beside an old tree. He was caught before he could go back for it, so it sat there for years. The old tree was cut down and a gazebo was erected over the site, so no one would've seen it."

"Wow, imagine that!" she exclaimed. "And that gazebo is still there, though much worse for wear. I never even use it. Was there anything with those papers besides the letter?"

"Let me check." I flipped through more papers that sat just beneath the letter. A crumpled, faded page that was larger than the other papers fell out onto the desk.

Aunt Betty picked it up. "It's a map."

I blinked. "Like a treasure map?" I asked.

"That's what we'll need to find out."

"Maybe there's more in the stack of papers to tell us something." I glanced at the door. "I'm starting to worry about Dennis coming back," I said.

"Why don't I go stand by the door? I'll keep it open a crack to listen for anyone coming down the hall."

"Good idea," I said.

As Aunt Betty scurried across the room, avoiding piles of discarded clothing, I sat down in the desk chair for a better look. After perusing through the stack of pages, I did come across something interesting. I slid out another paper, this one a printed-out email from none other than Nan to Dennis.

I read quickly through the message.

Dennis,

I know you're out of town on business but couldn't wait to see you to tell you this. You know how I love everything to do with the history of John Dillinger? Well, guess what? At an auction for items of his that the Indiana museums didn't have a use for, I came across an old box of very interesting information! John Dillinger himself wrote a letter to someone named Mr. Johnson, telling him about money hidden in Green Meadow! And there's a map. How lucky is that?

I'm going to check it out soon. How exciting! This could be our big break!

Nan

Wow, that might answer some questions about why Dennis was in town early. Had he come to town and murdered Nan to leave the way open for him to find Dillinger's money and keep it all for himself? Then stuck around to attend her funeral, acting like he'd just arrived, to cover his tracks?

Feeling the urgency to get us out of Dennis's room, I laid out all the pages of interest, took photos of them with my phone, and then shuffled them back into a messy pile, somewhat like he'd left it.

Hustling across the room, I touched Aunt Betty's arm. "I got some photos of those papers," I said. "We didn't find the bookend, but this might be even better. Let's get out of here."

CHAPTER ELEVEN

The next morning in the bookstore, Pearl and Milton were making a ruckus beside the counter. No customers were here yet, so I hustled over to see what mayhem they were up to. With my hands on my hips, I gave a mock glare. "And just what are you two doing?"

The cats froze. Milton sat on a low shelf, and Pearl's paw hung in midair, as if she'd been about to bat at something. Milton mewed, the sound sweet and innocent, though I knew differently. Pearl moved her paw to her mouth and licked her white fur. Both wore expressions of guilelessness.

"All right, listen. I know you're up to something or did something or found something. Which is it?"

With a small growl, Milton jumped down from the shelf and stood next to Pearl. He reached up and poked at a piece of paper sticking out of my to-do folder still on the shelf.

After nudging the cats aside, I picked up the folder to check out what they'd found. A folded piece of paper was the apparent prize. Milton's paw whipped out to snatch it, but I swiped it away before he could get it. Not an easy task, as their reflexes were quick. But living with felines for most of my life, I knew when they were on the prowl for an interesting object.

I opened the page, expecting it to be a packing slip for books or maybe an invoice from a sale. But my heart jumped when I read the words.

Stop snooping around for Nan's murderer. If you don't leave it alone, it's the end of the road for your precious cats!

A gasp escaped before I could hold it in.

Aunt Betty, who'd just entered the main area from the back room, stopped in her tracks. "Christy, what's wrong? Your face has gone pale." She hurried to me, placing her hand on my arm. She glanced down at the note in my hand, though it was faced away so she couldn't read the horrible words. "What's that?"

I didn't want to add to Aunt Betty's worries. Even though she was in on investigating Dennis's hotel room, my preference would have been to have done it myself. The less stress she experienced from the recent drama, the better. Folding it, I stuffed it into my pocket. "That? Oh nothing."

"But I heard you gasp," she said.

"I…the cats." I pointed down. "They were checking out something. I thought they had a mouse."

Her eyes widened. "Oh no. I detest mice."

"It's okay," I said. "I think maybe it was a shadow. A small shadow. You know, mouse shaped."

Aunt Betty's eyebrows lowered. "Are you getting enough rest? You don't seem yourself."

With a shrug, I forced a smile. "I'm fine. Really. I—"

The front door opened, and two older men walked in. Relieved I wouldn't have to continue fibbing to my aunt, even though it was for a good cause, I headed toward the counter to wait on the customers. Milton and Pearl trotted behind me. I waved to the men who'd come in. "Good morning," I said, "let me know if I can help you find something."

They nodded and headed toward the history section.

The cats hopped on top of the counter and made a beeline for my pants pocket, sniffing and meowing.

My eyes widened. "Stop that," I whispered. Thankfully, the customers were off browsing on their own. What were my crazy cats doing?

Aunt Betty joined me behind the counter, going through our inventory sheets for an upcoming order. "Do you think Milton and Pearl are acting strange?" she asked. Her eyebrows lowered as the cats were both now pawing at my pocket.

I laughed. "Um, maybe I spilled something on my jeans during breakfast? And they smell it?"

She crossed her arms. "Are you asking me or telling me?"

"Telling?" I asked. "Uh, I mean, telling."

She studied me for a few seconds. "I know you were deeply affected when you found me in that state and Nan, well, in *that* state. And who wouldn't be upset by all that? Maybe you need a vacation to take your mind off it. You have been through an awful lot since arriving here."

"Aunt Betty, I only just arrived in Green Meadow. I don't need a vacation. Thank you." I smiled. "But I'm okay. Really."

She glanced down at the cats. Pearl had her nose stuck inside my pocket as Milton paced on the counter behind her, like an expectant father whose wife was soon to have five kittens. Aunt Betty shrugged. "If you say so." Her phone buzzed, and she pulled it from her pocket. She smiled. "It's Wallace. I'll take this in the back."

As soon as Aunt Betty was in the back room, the front door opened again. I was glad to see it was Janie. She carried a large bouquet of sunflowers in a vase and set them on the counter. I set the cats on the floor, earning me flipped tails and paw stomps.

I eyed the flowers. "Oh, beautiful. For Aunt Betty?"

She nodded. "I'm so concerned about her. I know bringing these might not solve anything, but at least she'll know I'm thinking about her. Is she here?" She glanced around the bookstore.

"She is, but she just got a call from Wallace."

"Oh," she said. "Well, will you tell her I stopped by?"

"Sure. Hey, while I've got you here…"

"Yes?"

I checked behind me to make sure Aunt Betty was still otherwise occupied. "Milton and Pearl just found this right here under the counter. What do you make of it?" I handed her the note.

As she unfolded the page and read it, her eyes widened and her mouth dropped open. "I…" she said, as she shook her head. "That's horrible. Who would—"

"That's what I'd like to know. But one thing I noticed about the note, besides the awful words, was the slight coloring along that one edge? See?" I pointed to the paper. "It's turquoise. Kind of unusual. Well, maybe not, but after a conversation I had with Rosey about turquoise roses, I wondered if there could be a connection. Apparently Olive buys that exact color of flowers regularly."

Janie studied the paper again. "You're right. With the terrible meaning of the words, I hadn't noticed the edge." She ran her finger along the page. "Of course, it might not be connected." She frowned.

"But you think there's a chance it might?" I asked.

"Maybe. I've seen her use stationary before with turquoise flowers around the edge. She wrote down her food order recently then shoved the piece of paper at me. She marched outside to check her phone, like she didn't have time to stand around and wait. I felt like a peasant doing her bidding. And then there's that text I saw on her phone at the funeral home. Ghastly!"

"Definitely ghastly," I said. "How can a person even joke about something like that?"

"I think it takes a special kind of hatefulness to even think it." Janie set the paper on the counter between us. "I think Olive might be the guilty party for Nan's murder," she said. "She had a motive, and she's just plain mean enough to do it."

I shrugged. "True, but I'm still gathering evidence. There are several people who had motive and opportunity to do Nan in."

"Okay, so who do we have?" asked Janie.

"Olive, of course. And Burt Larsen. He drove Rosey crazy in Petals and Stems when he marched in and kept talking about Nan having ruined him financially by printing lies about his business."

Her brow furrowed. "You know, I actually remember reading at least one of those articles. She did really blast him. I could see why he might have motive to do Nan in. From what I heard, after he lost his business, his wife took their kids and left him. And there was something about his house… Like maybe he had to give it up because he couldn't afford it anymore."

"Wow, that's a lot for anyone to go through. Yep, definitely cause to do Nan some harm," I said.

She nodded. "Anyone else?"

"Well, after listening to Terrence in your shop"—I gave her a mock scowl, to which she bit her lip—"I think he should be added to the list. That guy, as you know, went on and on about how Nan had cheated her way to better writing gigs and, according to him, got all the positions and raises that should have gone to him."

Her cheeks turned pink. "Um, sorry about that. Again."

I grinned. "Teasing. You were right. I did need to hear what he had to say."

"The first time he came into Dreamy Sweets and started moaning about his tragic life," said Janie, "I tried to listen and be sympathetic. But it didn't end there. No, he kept showing up."

"Was it always the same speech?"

"Nearly word for word. By the time I'd heard it three times, I was ready to explode."

"Couldn't you have asked him to leave?" I asked.

"I did! But he kept returning. I threatened to have the police oust him, but he started crying. Crying! I couldn't stand it. Like I was telling a puppy it had to wait outside in the snow while I was warm and safe inside my building."

"Well, I hate to see anyone cry," I said. "Especially a man. Something about it is hard to take."

"Right? I know."

I reached below the counter for my purse to get my lip balm. Right inside was a wrapped mint I'd gotten with my meal at the restaurant. I made a face, remembering Dennis's atrocious behavior.

"What's wrong?" she asked.

"Well, Aunt Betty and I had a strange evening yesterday."

"How so?"

"We had dinner at Beneath the Sea with a man named Dennis Paisley," I said. "An old flame of Nan's. The whole evening was a disaster."

Her eyes widened. "That was you?"

"What was me?"

She waved her hand. "A customer came in earlier and said there'd been a loud scene at Beneath the Sea. That a man was raising his voice to two women. She didn't say who."

"Yep," I said. "That was us. I'm adding Dennis to the list too. He wailed the whole time about Nan being the love of his life, but something just doesn't ring true about that. I mean, he married someone else instead of her. Then he let it slip that he'd come to town the week before Nan died. Aunt Betty and I checked out his hotel room. Wait until you hear what we—"

Footsteps came from behind us. I turned as Aunt Betty approached. "My goodness. Look at those flowers," she said and winked at me. "Do you have a secret admirer?"

"Not me. Janie brought them for you."

Aunt Betty's face lit up. She walked around the counter and hugged Janie. "What a sweetheart you are. Thank you."

"I thought maybe these might cheer you up," said Janie.

"They do. You're so thoughtful."

Pearl mewed and sauntered over to Janie, who now leaned against the side of the counter. Janie grinned. "Hey, look at you, gorgeous girl."

Pearl stood on her hind legs then closed her eyes and rubbed her nose against Janie's outstretched hand.

Janie ran her hand over Pearl's fur. She eyed Aunt Betty. "I heard about what happened with Dennis last evening at the restaurant."

Aunt Betty clutched her hands together. "You did?"

I grimaced, wishing Janie hadn't spilled that bit of information. "I told her," I admitted. "I'm sorry if you'd wanted it kept private. I should have asked you first."

"No," said Aunt Betty, "there's no way it would stay private. It was a public place, after all."

Janie stopped petting Pearl, who'd curled up on the counter for a nap. "You're right. A customer heard about it and told me." She held up her hand. "Not who was involved but what happened. My guess is it will be all over town before you know it. I'm so sorry you had to endure that."

"Thank you, Janie," said Aunt Betty. "And thank you again for the flowers. They are breathtaking." She reached down, lightly trailing her finger over some of the petals.

Janie sighed. "I need to head back to the shop. Kiersten has kittens if I leave her for too long. Christy, call me later, fill me in some more." With a wave, she left.

Milton strutted to the counter, taking his place in the shelf beneath. Pearl opened her eyes and hurried to join her brother, the two of them creating a big lump of purring, sleepy fur. I watched them for a minute then pointed to Aunt Betty's phone, the top of which was visible from her pocket. "Is Wallace all right?" I asked. I didn't trust him, especially after what Rosey had said about him being a womanizer, but Aunt Betty seemed so sure of him. From her expression every time she even mentioned his name, she was in love. Didn't I owe it to her to find out what he was really like?

She nodded. "He's more than fine. Actually, the reason I came out here was to tell you that he'd like to spend some time with you. Get to know you better. How does that sound?"

While I wouldn't look forward to it, that truth would hurt my aunt terribly. And I'd do nearly anything to keep that from happening. "I think it's a great idea," I said. "But maybe not at Beneath the Sea. Bad memories." I grimaced.

"No, not there. I suggested he visit our apartment tomorrow night. I'll pick up some Italian food from A Taste of Rome. Their food is amazing."

"Sounds good."

Her eyes crinkled at the corners. "Perfect," she said. "I'll make a call now to place our order for tomorrow. From what I've heard, they fill up fast." She grabbed her phone again and walked across the room, stopping in a far corner beside our travel and history book sections behind a tall bookcase to make her call.

As soon as the two men who'd come in earlier exited the bookstore without making purchases, the door opened again. I sighed. It was Dennis.

His eyes were downcast as he headed toward the counter. "Um, listen. I don't remember much about last evening. I…guess I had a little too much to drink."

My eyebrows shot up. *A little?*

"The head waiter phoned me this morning, saying he found my wallet beneath the table where we'd sat," said Dennis. "When I went to get it, he told me how I'd acted." He clasped his hands together at his waist. "So, my AA sponsor said I need to make amends." He glanced around the room. "Is Betty here? I'd like to apologize."

I shook my head, glad she wasn't here to have to see Dennis again. "She's busy right now."

"All right. Then you'll have to do, I guess." He flung his hands out to the sides. "I officially apologize." He turned quickly and hurried out the door.

Wow, his apology didn't sound all that sincere, but in

any case, I was relieved he hadn't stayed long.

As I turned back to the counter, my foot kicked something on the floor. I bent down to see what it was.

It was Dennis's ring. Just as I was ready to flag him down to return it, something caught my eye. Around the stone in the ring was a brownish red stain. Was that blood? Blood might mean he'd been the one to kill Nan. I grabbed a tissue, wrapped the ring inside, and stuck it in my pocket until I could put it someplace safe. My suspect list was growing.

CHAPTER TWELVE

The next evening, I straightened the apartment while Aunt Betty left to pick up our supper order. As I put away stray books and papers strewn about the living room, I halted, once again picturing Nan's body in the now absent chair, her frozen expression of horror. At the memory, my heart pounded hard and my hands grew cold.

No, I had to pull myself together. My aunt was looking forward to tonight, wanting Wallace and me to become better acquainted. As distrusting as I felt toward him, would I be able to convincingly pull off the ruse? But I had to. For Aunt Betty.

Milton and Pearl bounded in from the hallway, apparent glee in their wide eyes. I'd offered to leave them in my room while Wallace was here, but Aunt Betty wouldn't hear of it. She wanted her guy to meet the whole family. The thought made me smile. While the cats were my family, I was glad she thought of them that way too.

As I picked up one final magazine lying open on the couch, I heard shuffling behind me. Pearl patted the space where the chair had been, as if reminding herself what used to sit there. Milton sat down in front of Pearl, right where the center of the chair would have been, and let out a howl.

I gasped. "Good grief, what's wrong?"

Pearl's fur puffed out, and she joined her brother in an eardrum-splitting duet. Thank goodness there weren't any customers downstairs to hear the kitty cacophony. With the screaming, they might think someone was being murdered up here. Again.

I grabbed a cat under each arm, supporting them with my hands on their bellies. Aunt Betty might want them around to meet Wallace, but I couldn't allow that unless they calmed down. As I rushed down the hall toward my room, I heard footsteps on the stairs. The moment I closed the door on two angry cats, Aunt Betty opened the door from the stairs.

Her eyes were wide as she stepped into the hall. "Christy, what was that awful noise?"

I pointed to my closed door. "Milton and Pearl…had a bit of a scuffle. I'm not sure if they'll be able to join us tonight."

Her face fell. "What a shame. I wanted Wallace to get to know them too. He likes cats."

With a shrug, I took the sack from her hands. "Maybe they can come out later. Hopefully," I said.

Were the cats trying to tell me something about the murder? Maybe some sort of kitty sense about Wallace coming over soon? I wasn't going to discount their input. The way they'd scouted around the room right after Nan's death and appeared to converse with each other still amazed me. They were definitely on to something.

I placed the food sack in the kitchen. Aunt Betty already had the table set for the three of us at the small table located by a tall, narrow window. When I returned, she was standing in the middle of the living room.

She glanced around the area. "Thanks for cleaning up."

"You're welcome," I said. My stomach fluttered with nerves. What would I say to someone I wasn't sure I could trust? "What time will Wallace get here?"

"Anytime. I got nervous waiting in line to pick up our food. I didn't want him to beat me home. I know you already met him briefly outside the café that first day, but I wanted to be here when you had a chance to actually meet and be introduced." She pointed to the hallway. "And I left the front door unlocked and asked him to lock it behind him after he comes in." She clasped her hands together nervously. "I really want this to go well. It's so important to me for you two to become friends."

I wasn't so sure that would happen, given the weird vibe I'd gotten from him, but I'd do my best not to rock the boat. I took her hands in mine. "Don't worry. I'm sure tonight will be great."

Aunt Betty glanced toward the hallway and back. "Listen," she said. "There's something you should know about

Wallace."

I frowned. Was she going to tell me why he seemed so jittery? So agitated and twitchy?

"What is it?"

She motioned me to follow her to the couch then patted the seat next to her. I sat and waited. Maybe whatever it was would relieve some of the tension I felt about her boyfriend.

"Before Wallace gets here," said Aunt Betty, "I wanted to share something with you that he told me. I trust you with it, but I won't be telling anyone else. It's...delicate."

Now she really had my attention. "Okay. I'm listening."

"You see, shortly before Nan was killed"—her glance quickly went to the spot where the chair had been and back—"she tried to set a trap for Wallace."

"A trap?" I asked.

Aunt Betty crossed her arms over her chest, as if trying to protect herself. "Yes. She asked him to stop by on some pretense, but he took it seriously enough to comply. She'd made up an excuse about his coffee shop, saying she'd heard some bad things about one of his employees and she wanted to write about it in her column. That's why he went that day."

"What happened?"

"When he got there and walked into her house, she shut the door behind him then offered him some pastries from Janie's shop. His favorite kind, chocolate éclair. Even though he didn't want to stay and talk to her, he'd been busy at his coffee shop during lunch and hadn't eaten. He thought having one pastry before he left wouldn't hurt."

"What happened next?" I asked.

"He began to feel a little woozy. He discovered later she'd tried to drug him. He's a tall enough man that he apparently hadn't eaten quite enough to do him much harm. But she ripped her blouse then pulled him on top of her on the couch."

"What?"

"It gets worse," she said. "Nan held on to him tight so he couldn't get away, but she screamed for him to leave her alone." Aunt Betty's cheeks turned red. "He was mortified. Nan was a tall woman, about the same height as Wallace. He said it took him a bit to finally push her away, especially since he was slightly dizzy."

"And then he left her house?"

Aunt Betty shook her head. "Not until Nan gave him an ultimatum. She pointed to something in the far corner. It was a video camera. The red light was on, indicating it was recording them."

"Oh no," I said.

"Nan told Wallace that if he didn't choose her over me, she'd edit the tape so the part with her ripping her blouse and pulling him on top of her wouldn't show, and then she'd put the tape onto the internet and spread the word around Green Meadow that Wallace had attacked her."

"Oh, Aunt Betty."

"It's awful, yes. Not only would it have affected his reputation, but his business and personal relationships too."

"And his relationship with you?"

"No, I love him too much to let that stand in my way. But it sure would have made things difficult, for both of us. Wallace said…"

"What?" I asked.

"He was so stressed. At the end of his rope. Nan had been after him for months, trying to get him to go out with her. Wallace told me the problems with Nan bothering him had to stop. For good."

For good? That had all kinds of terrible connotations. What if he was the actual murderer and Aunt Betty was in love with him? I opened my mouth to reply, but the door to the top of the stairs opened with a creak.

Aunt Betty's face radiated joy. "He's here!"

I wrapped my arms around my middle as I waited the few seconds it took Wallace to walk down the hall and turn the corner into the den.

He held Aunt Betty in a tight embrace. The way my aunt sighed and nearly melted in his arms made me feel like I should let them have their privacy.

If Wallace was guilty of murdering Nan, and with Aunt Betty being so smitten, would she even believe he'd done it if it were proven by the police?

Wallace focused on me and grinned. "Hello again," he said. "This time, I'll try not to knock you over."

I stood motionless as he embraced me. I did finally hug him back, but my arms and shoulders were stiff. His hands against my back trembled, and his right foot tapped against mine.

Watching us, my aunt clasped her hands together. "Isn't this wonderful?"

I stepped away from Wallace, forcing a smile. "Nice to see you again too."

Aunt Betty waved her hand in the direction of the kitchen. "Wallace, I picked up Italian for supper from A Taste of Rome."

"My favorite," he said.

"Everything's ready," said Aunt Betty. "Why don't you and Christy get better acquainted over our meal?"

Wallace motioned for me to precede him, but I shook my head and smiled. He took Aunt Betty's arm and escorted her down the hall and to the kitchen. I followed, watching closely. At first, I thought his hand on her arm was for her benefit. Now I wasn't sure. He stumbled, righted himself, and continued on. My aunt barely seemed to notice.

During the meal, which ordinarily I would have loved, I didn't say much, just replied when asked questions. I didn't need to make inquiries because Aunt Betty rattled on about Wallace, his coffee shop, and his cat.

Finished with his food, Wallace used a napkin to clean his hands. They trembled so badly, the napkin shook like in a strong breeze. Aunt Betty didn't even glance down, didn't seem to notice or care. What was going on with him, and why wasn't my aunt concerned?

Aunt Betty looked up at me. "Christy, do you suppose Milton and Pearl might be ready to come out of your room for a while? I've been telling Wallace all about them and would love for them to meet."

The way the cats had acted before Wallace got there, pawing and meowing where the chair had been, made me leery to set them free. But Aunt Betty had such hope in her eyes, as if it meant the world to her that I do just that. I smiled. "Sure. Just be warned that they were doing crazy kitty stuff before Wallace got here."

He chuckled. "Nothing to worry about there. King,

that's my cat, does strange things all the time."

Yeah, but did his cat seem to know something about a murder that occurred right where he lived? "Um, let me go get them," I said.

As I approached my room, they must have heard my footsteps. Clawing at wood and pitiful mews met me from the other side of the door. "Okay you guys, hold on. I'm letting you out." I turned the knob then immediately knelt, ready to catch them before they could dart past me. Pearl squeezed through the opening, but I latched on to her middle and gently pulled her onto my lap. Milton peered out at me, his green eyes huge, as if unsure of why I was sitting on the floor.

"Come on out, buddy. Mama wants to see you for a minute."

He crept out, sniffed my outstretched fingers, licked first my hands, then his sister's head.

"Good boy. Now, there's someone new here. He's Aunt Betty's…special friend. Please behave yourselves and be nice, okay?"

Pearl purred. Milton meowed.

"Excellent." I placed Pearl on the floor and stood. Patting my thigh, I said, "All right, let's go meet him."

They trotted down the hallway behind me, their tiny claws scuffing against the wood floor. When I turned the corner into the kitchen, it was empty.

"Christy?" called my aunt. "We're in the den now."

I switched direction, and the three of us went the short distance to the next room.

Wallace and Aunt Betty sat side by side on the couch. Unsure of what my cats might do, I watched and waited. Aunt Betty held out her hand, and both cats ran eagerly to her, tails held high with curls at the top like question marks, noses in the air, ears perked up.

When Wallace leaned down to try to touch them, he nearly tumbled from the couch. Aunt Betty's hand shot out to steady him. Once he seemed okay, he tried again. Milton and Pearl, now with wide eyes and puffy fur from his unexpected movement, stood rigid, not going near him.

The cats stared at Wallace's outstretched hand, jumping when his fingers twitched. I was just glad they hadn't batted at his hand, thinking he was trying to play with them. First Pearl, then Milton, cautiously sniffed his fingers. When he touched their heads, they both ducked down but held their ground.

Pearl turned and ran to me, winding around my legs. Milton followed, doing the same.

Wallace chuckled. "Hey, that's how King acts when he wants me to feed him." He pointed to the cats.

"Oh, of course," I said. "I forgot to give them their supper, and now it's past time. I'd better take care of that. Come on, guys." Glad to have an excuse to leave the room and also get my cats away from Wallace, I headed to the kitchen and fed them.

I went back to the den. Aunt Betty and Wallace were still sitting on the couch. She pointed to the recliner to her right, angled so I'd be able to see both of them. I sat down and crossed my legs, resisting the urge to wiggle my foot like I always did when anxious. I didn't want Aunt Betty to know my true feelings, but also didn't want to do something similar to Wallace's odd movements. "Milton and Pearl are happy now that their tummies are full," I said.

Aunt Betty smiled. "Great." She glanced at Wallace, and her smile fell. What was going on?

Wallace clasped his hands together and leaned a little toward Aunt Betty, but his gaze was on me. "Christy, Betty just explained that she filled you in on what happened with Nan—er, what she tried to…well…" His face reddened.

"Yes, she did," I said. "I hope you don't mind. I'll keep the information to myself, of course."

He nodded. "I appreciate that. It's so embarrassing. The whole thing." His hands, still clasped, tightened, the skin on his knuckles turning white. "Ever since that episode, I've had a hard time…that is…"

Aunt Betty touched his arm. "What he's trying to say is, he's had a difficulty controlling his temper."

His eyes watered, sadness etched on his features. Aunt Betty clung to his arm, offering support. Now I didn't know what to believe. He seemed sincere, but how did I know he wasn't just a good actor? What he'd said to my aunt about Nan needing to be stopped was a huge red flag.

I glanced to where Nan's body had been found. Had he

been angry enough to murder her to stop her from ruining his reputation and possibly causing Betty to break it off with him if she believed he'd done something wrong with Nan? And what about Aunt Betty? I'd found her in a heap, with a lump on her head. Had he tried to hurt her too to keep her quiet about the murder?

Or were his strange body jerks, whatever the cause, the reason she'd ended up knocked out? Maybe he hadn't meant to harm Aunt Betty. Perhaps he'd accidentally stumbled and struck her, causing her to fall and hit her head.

Then there were my cats' reaction to Wallace. Had they picked up on some bad vibe from Wallace and tried to duck away from his hand when he wanted to pet them, or had it simply been a normal cat reaction to a sudden jerky movement?

I was pulled in two different directions. For Aunt Betty's sake and safety, I needed to discover what was true and what was a lie.

CHAPTER THIRTEEN

I was pleased to discover Green Meadow still hosted its outdoor Strawberry Festival every year. As a kid, Janie and I'd had a blast racing around, checking out all the booths. The food booths were our favorite. Because of that, I'd always had an affinity for strawberries, no matter what shape, kind, or flavor. But the festival also was host to anyone in town who had wares to sell. Aunt Betty had made it fun when she let me assist her at the bookstore's booth, waiting on customers and counting out their change.

This year, Milton and Pearl were with us, lounging sleepily together in their stroller. Aunt Betty was especially excited about the display we had for Milton and Pearl's mystery series. She adjusted a few books on our main table. "What do you think?" she asked.

"I think it looks great. Thank you."

"For what?"

"For making such a fuss over my books," I said.

"Why wouldn't I?"

"You have all these other books by well-known authors who've written best sellers."

"But those people aren't my precious niece," said Aunt Betty. She kissed my cheek then stepped behind our table to tidy up some fliers about the store.

Honestly, I wasn't sure what I did to deserve her. And how her phone call to have me come work and live with her had come at exactly the right moment. I tried not to think about Tony much, but sometimes I couldn't help it. Being far away from him helped, though. At least I didn't have to see him any longer.

Maybe I needed to think about something more

pleasant. I glanced around, and my breath caught in my throat. Someone pleasant like *him.*

Micah was halfway down the walkway, stopping at every booth on his way, smiling and speaking to the vendors. He was a guy I couldn't wait to get to know better.

"What'cha lookin' at?" said my aunt.

I startled when Aunt Betty sidled up next to me. "Um…"

Her eyes widened. "You don't need to tell me. It's obvious."

"What is?" I asked.

"You're attracted to the good-looking doctor."

I shrugged and pointed toward him. "Well, who wouldn't think he was handsome? I mean, look at him."

She laughed. "True, but I know you. And you think there's more to him than just looks."

"Maybe." I grinned. "Would I be right?"

"Yes." she said. "There's much more to him, trust me."

Micah had made his way to the booth next to ours. After a minute of complimenting their wares, he turned, noticed me, and smiled.

He'd caught me staring at him. Perfect. My cheeks heated, probably an embarrassing red by now.

Aunt Betty dashed to the back of the booth. What was she doing? When I checked, she was straightening already aligned stacks of books, but the peek she gave me over her shoulder showed an impish grin.

The little matchmaker.

"Hi, Christy."

I jumped then faced Micah, who now stood right in front of our table. Would he think it odd that he'd startled me, when a few seconds before, we'd made eye contact? Like I would have been surprised to see him head to our table next? "Um, hey."

He glanced to his left and down, and his eyes widened. "Look at that," he said.

I frowned. "What?" Was there a giant spider on our table? Had a bee landed near my mug of coffee? I took a step back, hoping I wouldn't have to deal with bugs, since some of them—okay, mostly all of them—made me scream like a frightened kitten.

Micah pointed to Milton and Pearl. "They have their own stroller."

Was he making fun of them? Or of me, for pushing them around in there? "Well, they like it."

One side of his mouth rose. "I don't blame them. So would I."

"Yeah, wouldn't that be nice?" I asked. "To have the person who feeds you also chauffer you and your sibling around in cushy comfort so your feet, er, paws, don't have to even touch the ground."

"Are you offering?" He petted first Pearl, then Milton, earning him identical eye squints and twitching whiskers.

"Offering?"

"To do that for me," said Micah.

My mouth hung open.

"Kidding," he said.

"Oh sure. Of course." My face was so overheated, I wanted to fan it, but that might make matters worse.

Aunt Betty joined us. "Hi, Micah. Is it your day off from the hospital?"

"No, but I don't go in for a few hours. Thought I'd check out the offerings at the festival."

I eyed his empty hands. "Don't see any purchases." I tried to hold back a laugh, but it didn't work.

"Alas, my search has been fruitless," he said. "Until now."

"Ha-ha. Fruitless?"

He grinned.

"Okay," I said, "what did you find?"

He pointed toward the first book in Milton and Pearl's mysteries. "That."

Did he have children who'd like the book? Was he married and I just didn't know? "Sure, um, is this for your kids?"

"I don't have any of those," he answered.

Something in me loosened, relieved. But it still didn't tell me if he was single. I glanced at my aunt, who looked between us, her eyes twinkling. No, she wouldn't matchmake if he was. He must definitely be available. I tapped one of the books. "A niece? Nephew?"

"I have those. Two of each. But this purchase is for me."

"Oh," I said.

"Does that surprise you?"

I shrugged.

"I figure if I read the stories, it will help me get better acquainted with the person who penned the words," said Micah.

"Oh," I muttered.

Aunt Betty elbowed me. "Dear, I know you can say more than 'Oh.' I've heard you."

Totally embarrassed, I picked up the first book and put it in a bag.

"Sorry. Didn't make myself clear. I want the whole series," said Micah as he made a motion with his hand. "All of it."

When he said *all of it*, he hadn't been looking at the books. But straight at me.

"Uh…"

Aunt Betty shook her head. "That's better than just saying 'Oh,' but not by much."

Micah started to say something then frowned when his phone buzzed in his pocket. He answered, frowned some more, then ended the call. "Looks like I have to leave you lovely ladies after all. A triple-car pileup on the interstate is sending several to the ER."

I gasped. "Oh no."

"How awful, " said Aunt Betty.

Micah shook his head sadly then waved. He stopped a few feet away. "I'll come into the shop soon and get the books." He jogged off toward the parking area.

My heart ached, thinking about if it had been someone close to me who'd been injured. "Wow," I said. "How terrible for the poor people in the accident."

"And also for Micah and those who tend to them," said Aunt Betty. "It must be so hard."

"I can't imagine." I knew, of course, that he was a doctor at the ER, but after hearing of an actual case he'd soon be taking care of, my admiration for him grew. And the rest? The mild flirtation, the way his presence got me weak in the knees?

I'd have to think about that later. Because right now, I was staring at Olive, who was definitely glaring at Aunt Betty and me. Olive halted for a second, turned fully toward us, then hurried away. What was she doing?

I glanced next to me, but Aunt Betty was already engrossed in speaking to a man who'd walked over to check out the best sellers.

Why would Olive glare at us then leave? Was it supposed to be a threat? After overhearing her words about Nan at the funeral home, I wouldn't put it past her.

I put it out of my mind when a group of three women and several small children headed our way. All of them, but the kids especially, flocked around the cats, giving them pets and rubs. Milton and Pearl took it as their due as feline royalty, of which they were entitled.

One of them, Lora Smith, from my first day in the bookstore, held up her phone. Two pictures of my cats were featured on the screen. "Christy, look how cute they are. But why am I telling you? You get to see them every day."

I leaned closer to her phone. "Awww, I have to admit, they really are adorable."

The women laughed as they studied the books. Lora had already purchased the series but pointed them out to her friends. "See?" said Lora. "These are the ones I told you about. And they"—she pointed to the cats—"are the actual stars from the stories."

The kids took turns shaking hands—paws—with the cats, who thankfully were mellow enough not to mind. It didn't hurt that the stroller was partially in the sunlight, and the warmth made them sleepy and pliable.

A steady stream of customers, some who bought, others who browsed, and a third category who only wanted to love on Milton and Pearl, kept Aunt Betty and me occupied for the next couple of hours.

Aunt Betty stretched out her arms and straightened her back. "Say, Christy, why don't you take a walk around for a bit before it gets busy again?"

"I wouldn't want to leave you here by yourself."

She made a shooing motion to me with her hands.

"All right," I said. "I don't have to be told again. Can I

get you anything while I'm out?"

Aunt Betty leaned back in her chair, relaxing. "No thanks. Maybe I'll take a stroll around later when you get back."

"Great. Okay, I'll see you later." I grabbed my purse and phone. "Oh wait." I pointed to the cats. "What about…"

Aunt Betty waved her hand. "They'll be fine right here. I'll cat sit."

"Thanks."

I'd ambled down the corridor to see the booths and had only gone past three of them when I spotted Olive again. This time, she wasn't glaring at me or even noticing me at all. She had her phone to her ear and walked ahead of me, her back slightly hunched and shoulders curled, as if trying to shield her conversation from those around her.

Wanting to know what she was up to, I followed her but kept at a distance. There were lots of people wandering around, but if Olive turned around for some reason, she'd likely notice me.

When Olive darted behind an unoccupied vendor's tent, I hurried, trying to catch up. But when I was about to edge around the tent's corner, I heard her talking. She must have stopped here to finish her conversation.

Hoping not to look like a nut stalking Olive, which I most definitely was, I took out my own phone and held it to my ear as if listening to someone else.

Olive's voice was shrill as she said, "I'm tired of waiting. Sure. Nan's gone, but there's still the matter of my stupid uncle." She huffed out a breath as she listened then said, "Because he's not dead yet. And he needs to be!"

My eyes widened. What a witch Olive was.

A long silence followed. Had Olive ended her call? A sound like footsteps through the grass came from the other side of the tent. I took a chance and peeked around the edge of the tent then let out a breath when no one was there.

I stuffed my phone into my purse then clenched my teeth together in frustration. I didn't see where Olive had gone, so I turned and started toward a booth on the other side of the venue. Maybe checking out the booths and what they had to offer would calm me down before I headed back to Aunt Betty.

So many things to see. Booths with baked items, crafts,

clothing, honey, and marmalade. Even though I'd loved running around here as a kid, to see everything the vendors had for sale now was surprising.

I visited each one, complimenting the vendors, saying hello to ones I'd met and introducing myself to those I hadn't. Everyone was smiling and happy. But how could they not, on such a warm, bright day? My purchases of strawberry jam, handmade potholders in the shape of strawberries, and some cute little hand-sewn toys for the cats would delight the people and the felines in my family.

By the time I'd made rounds on the far side of the grassy corridor and had gone most of the way down the side where our booth sat, I approached the Petals and Stems booth. Rosey wasn't there, but her boss Essie sat behind a table filled with gorgeous fresh and silk flowers. Right as I was ready to step closer, a woman shoved in front of me, nearly causing me to stumble.

It was Olive.

I righted myself, made sure I hadn't dropped any of the sacks holding my purchases, and stood a few feet away from the booth while I waited to see what Olive was up to.

She spoke to Essie, asking about fresh flowers. I distinctly heard the word turquoise. Was she buying more of the specific color for some reason?

Tired of waiting and miffed at what she'd said about her uncle on the phone, I marched up to the booth and stood a couple feet to her right. She glanced toward me, stiffened, then presented me with a view of her back, obviously rebuffing me, or acting as if she hadn't recognized me.

When Essie came back to the table with a small bouquet of turquoise roses and held them out for Olive's inspection, Olive gave a curt nod.

"Great. Let me get this wrapped up for you," Essie said and took the flowers toward the back of the tent, where a small cash register was set up.

Olive had turned so I could see her profile but still hadn't faced me again. What was her deal?

I moved a little closer, hoping to force her to look in my direction. Not caring if I angered her, because I had to get to the bottom of who killed Nan, I said, "Wow, just noticed the pretty color of the flowers you ordered."

Her eyebrows lowered as she finally looked at me. "What about it?"

I shrugged. "They're unusual, that's all. I've never met someone who'd choose turquoise over say, pink, red, or white."

"Why do you care?"

"Just interested. Trying to get to know the people of Green Meadow better. Why did you pick that color?" I tilted my head, keeping my gaze steadily on her, hoping to unnerve her enough to talk to me.

Finally, with a huff, she crossed her arms. "Not that it's any of your business, but I buy that color for my grandmother, who lives in a nursing home. It's her favorite color."

I nodded. "That's very nice of you."

"Are you saying you're surprised that I could be nice?" asked Olive.

I held up my hand. "No, of course not."

When Essie returned, she held out the flowers to Olive, who gave her some money without even asking the price. She must buy those turquoise flowers quite often to know how much they were. Essie stepped aside to wait on another customer while Olive put her wallet back in her purse.

With the same glare she'd given me while on the phone earlier, Olive said, "Why are you bothering me?"

"I thought it was the other way around."

"What on earth are you babbling on about?"

I pointed to the grassy expanse in front of the booth. "When you stood out there in front of the Words to Read By booth," I said. "you stared at my aunt and me."

"You're lying."

"No," I said, "I saw you."

She grabbed her flowers from the table. "I don't have time to talk to the likes of you."

"Yet you had time to stare at my likes. Uh, the likes of me," I stammered.

Olive rolled her eyes and stepped away.

When I returned to the Words to Read By tent, Aunt Betty eyed the sacks in my hand. "Goodness, looks like you had a successful shopping experience."

"Very," I said. I opened the bags and showed her what

I'd found. Aside from the jam, potholders, and cat toys, I'd also purchased fresh cinnamon buns from the Dreamy Sweets booth, a gorgeous sea green scarf for Aunt Betty, and tiny hand-painted bookmarks for myself.

When I draped the scarf around her neck, she gasped in delight. "Oh, Christy. How lovely."

"I thought it would look nice on you. And I was right."

She kissed my cheek. "Thank you, love."

CHAPTER FOURTEEN

The following Monday, I packed up the cats, a small foldable table, and books from the Milton and Pearl series. We headed to the park to host a summer class for kids about reading. The cats were in their stroller, grooming each other's faces. Because they'd gained a little weight, it might be time for a stroller upgrade to accommodate their expanding girth. I glanced down at my own midsection. Not that I could criticize.

Janie, who had her assistant covering Dreamy Sweets in her absence, met me there, bringing along a bright-blue plastic tote filled with treats for the attendees. When she met me in the parking area, she immediately ran over and enveloped me in a huge hug, just like the day Milton, Pearl, and I arrived. She hadn't grabbed my hand or arm yet, but it probably wouldn't take her long. Janie seemed overly enthusiastic in the way she dealt with people, way more than me. Was it just her, or was it me too? Was I standoffish when it came to expressing my feelings?

For some reason that made me think of Micah. What sort of woman did he find attractive and interesting? Did he favor someone more like Janie, who threw caution to the wind and freely expressed her emotions? Or someone like me, who felt things deeply but wasn't always as demonstrative?

Janie smiled. "Great to see you. Thanks for inviting me."

I smirked. "Well, I knew if I invited you, there'd also be free snacks as part of the deal."

Her high-pitched giggle reminded me of when we were in fourth grade. "Ha-ha. You know you like having me around. Just like old times."

"Yep." I smiled. "You're right about that. I'm glad

you're here."

"Need help setting things up?" asked Janie.

"Sure. Thanks." We each got one of the cats out of the car. I handed her Pearl, as she also juggled Milton, but the cats were used to being carted around, so no problem. I retrieved their stroller from the trunk. They were particular about which blankets I put in for them to sit on and got fussy if I didn't place Pearl on the left side and Milton on the right. Who knew why? They were cats, and as far as cats were concerned, their wishes should be granted.

Aunt Betty had packed everything I needed for the presentation, so unloading and setting up the stacks of books, Janie's snacks, and pamphlets from the bookstore about the Milton and Pearl series was a snap.

Everything was in place, including the cats in their stroller, before the first people arrived. It was Rosey and who I assumed to be her grandchildren, a boy and girl both around seven or eight. Very cute.

I waved. "Hi there," I said. "Glad you could make it."

"Believe me, we won't be the only ones," said Rosey. "Those fliers Betty put out all over town will do the trick. Several folks read the one she put up in Petals and Stems and showed interest in attending."

"Great." I let out a breath, glad my fear of standing here with only the cats to talk to wouldn't happen. I didn't mind talking about my books and the cats. But it was so much different if I had to have the focus on me personally.

Rosey introduced the twins, Stu and Drusilla, who they called Dru, but they were totally absorbed in checking out the cats, who purred when the kids petted them—gently, thank goodness—between the ears.

Janie smiled at the twins. "Hey, in a little while I'll have snacks for everyone. Sound good?"

Both blond heads bobbed up and down.

Rosey tapped each of them on their shoulders. "Not yet. First, we have to listen to Christy talk about her books. " She glanced at me. "Right?"

Rosey's comment jabbed at me, like she'd have to endure drudgery if she had to sit and listen to me talk. But I put on a smile for the kids. "Yes," I said. "We'll have lots of fun, won't we?"

Stu jumped up and down, and Dru clapped. Stu poked his sister in the shoulder. She took off running, and the race was on.

Janie made her way to the other side of the table. She sorted through the pastries and cookies she'd brought. It was a wide assortment of chocolate chip cookies, peanut butter bars, strawberry tarts, and vanilla cupcakes with all ingredients listed prominently on the outside of the wrapping so adults could make sure nothing in the food would harm kids if they had any allergies.

While I talked with Rosey and Janie, I laughed, watching the twins chase each other around. I didn't have any siblings. How fun it must be to have a built-in playmate when a person is little. Glad I'd had Janie to play with, at least in the summers when I visited.

Within a few minutes, Rosey's prediction about other people came true. A dozen adults with at least twice that many children showed up and took seats on the log benches put there for any kind of presentation happening at the park. We'd placed our table facing the benches, a few feet away.

I went around and spoke to the adults—parents, grandparents, and in one case of three siblings, a great-grandmother—then pushed the kitty stroller out into the middle of the group for people from each generation to fawn over my cats. They stood and gathered around, some kids crouching down, reaching small fingers and hands toward the soft cats.

When I reminded them that these were the kitties the book characters were based on, many adults took pictures of their kids with the stars of the series. Thankfully, my cats were mellow and liked the attention. I shuddered to think what might happen if they were the sort to have continuous hissy fits or claw first and ask questions later.

When everyone had their fill of chattering, giving the cats attention, and taking advantage of the photo op, they settled down again on the log benches. I leaned back against the table and began my presentation.

A shuffle of rapid footsteps came from behind me. I turned. A small boy of about five was waving his arms. "Wait!" he yelled. "Wait for me!"

I grinned and motioned him and the man with him over. But when they got closer, I held in a groan. The man was Terrence O'Leary. Of the few people in town I didn't wish to see, he was definitely one. The minutes I had to sit and listen to his woeful tale in Dreamy Sweets was time I'd never get back.

Frowning, Terrence said, "Took too long to get him ready."

My smile was for the little boy when I said, "No problem at all. Have a seat. We only just started."

The boy laughed when he spotted some friends and maneuvered himself into the middle of a group of kids like a kitten spotting a pile of cats and jumping on top, because who could have too many felines? I waited for Terrence to sit as well, but he stepped away—choosing instead to lean against a nearby shady maple tree with his arms crossed—and he frowned at me.

Even though I loved talking about Milton and Pearl, a negative influence like Terrence could dampen my spirits. With the recent murder and the stress it put on Aunt Betty, it took all I had to come here and try to be upbeat.

Thankfully, the presentation went well. I gave Janie a quick hug, thanking her for her generosity and help. She waved as she hurried back to her van, needing to relieve her assistant during a normally busy time at Dreamy Sweets.

Now that the presentation was over, I had the opportunity to further my sleuthing about the murder. Terrence's grandson was taking turns with his friends going down the slide, which left Terrence still glowering beside his chosen tree. Wanting to find more clues about Nan's death and his possible involvement in it, I walked directly to him, intent on having a talk. As I got closer, he dropped his arms to his sides, stood up straight, and frowned even deeper than before. His wrinkles appeared to have acquired secondary wrinkles of their own.

He held out his hand, palm toward me. Apparently he was still miffed about what I'd said to him when he told me his woeful tale, when I'd mentioned that he was fortunate to still even have a job. "I wanted to thank you for bringing your…*grandson* out today," I said, lilting my voice in a questioning manner on the word *grandson*.

Terrence checked the kids on the slide and focused

again on me. "Clay's my grandson, all right," said Terrence. "My daughter works odd hours and doesn't always have time for him, so she brings him to me. Makes it difficult on days when I have to work too."

"Well, I'm glad Clay could come today. He seemed to enjoy it."

Terrence shrugged. "Apparently. Was that all you wished to say? To thank me? If so, you did your duty. You may go now."

It was my turn to cross my arms. I ignored his rudeness and pasted on a pleasant expression. "Actually, there was something else," I said.

His sigh was deep and dramatic. "I was afraid of that. It's the way with women. One more thing to say. Have to be right and get their way. Just like Nan."

My spine stiffened. How dare he talk about women that way? What a jerk. Even though I hadn't heard one single person describe Nan as having any positive qualities, it was still a shock to hear people treat her murder as if it was a nuisance to everyone else. Maybe the person guilty of murdering her would especially not care.

Terrence put his hands on his hips. "Listen," he said, "I'm weary of people grilling me about Nan's death, just because she and I were coworkers. I've even had a visit from the police at my place of employment, which was quite embarrassing. Apparently, the authorities got wind of me complaining about Nan and how she always got the promotions and raises that should have come to me. They indicated maybe it made me someone worth keeping an eye on."

With the way he'd droned on and on to me in Dreamy Sweets and apparently had done it countless times to others all over town, how could he really be surprised the police had heard about it too?

He watched me for a moment. "Someone must have tattled to them," he said as he tilted his head. "You wouldn't happen to know anything about that, would you?"

I was reminded what a large man he was. He totally dwarfed me and would most women. Nan had been tall, but I bet Terrence was even taller. It wouldn't be a stretch to imagine him easily killing her. I mirrored his earlier action and held up my hand. "No, I didn't tell the police what you said. Why would I?"

"Because I heard your aunt was arrested as a suspect," said Terrence.

"That's where you're wrong. Aunt Betty wasn't arrested," I said. But part of me shivered at the thought that it would take very little for the police to decide she was their main person of interest. "Besides, she's innocent, so it won't go any further than that."

His mouth rose in a smirk. "You don't think it would go further?" he asked. "Let me tell you, those policemen are on the warpath and are looking at everyone possible, no matter if they're innocent or not. They made that very clear when they questioned me. Practically threatened me with jail time if I didn't cooperate fully. And their insinuations of my supposed guilt were thinly veiled." He shrugged. "It's not my fault I have no alibi for that day except that I was home alone watching a documentary on TV with no one to corroborate my statement."

He didn't have an alibi? That was something to keep in mind. Plus, the way he described his treatment by the police didn't ring true. At least not the way they'd kindly and patiently treated Aunt Betty.

Terrence pointed his finger right at my face. I longed to back up but stood my ground. "Listen, you stay out of it. Leave me be. It's none of your affair. And you don't want to tangle with the likes of me. I'm warning you, stay out of this."

Warning me? Was he the one who left that threatening note in the pile of books the cats found?

Before I could reply, Clay ran over from the slide and tugged on his grandpa's hand. "Come on, let's go," said Clay. "I want to tell Mom about the books and the cool cats in their special chair."

Terrence frowned. "Now Clay, you know your mom said I had to keep you for another day, at least."

The boy's lower lip jutted out.

My heart went out to the little guy who had to deal with his mom's erratic schedule. He must get disappointed pretty often. I crouched down and patted him on the shoulder. "Hey, thanks for coming to the park today. Milton and Pearl told me they really had fun meeting you."

His eyes widened. "They did?"

Above me, Terrence gave a snort, but I ignored him.

I smiled at Clay. "Sure."

"I've never heard cats talk before," said Clay, his eyes wide.

"Well, you've heard them meow, right?"

He nodded.

I winked. "That's the way they talk."

His mouth dropped open. "Cool. Wow. Tell them I had fun with them too."

"I sure will, Clay."

Terrence frowned as his grandson tugged him across the grass toward the parking area. I sighed, thinking about Clay, but also wondering what Terrence's involvement in Nan's death might have been. The man certainly did have a strong motive for wanting Nan away from her job at the newspaper. According to what he'd previously said, she got everything that should have been his.

Across the playground, Rosey said something to her grandchildren then plodded across the grass toward me as the kids found a sandbox to play in. When she reached me, she pointed toward Terrence's retreating car as it pulled out of the parking lot. "I saw you talking to him. Didn't look like you were enjoying yourself."

"That guy…" I said.

"What about him?" She crossed her arms.

"He's kind of creepy. And always wears that scowl."

"Oh, that's nothing new," said Rosey. "He's been moody for as long as I've known him. Would just as soon bark at someone as attempt to be pleasant."

Having spent some time with Rosey, I could nearly say the same about her. She was the human version of a gray-haired, sensible-shoes-wearing porcupine.

"Did Terrence have anything else to say?" asked Rosey.

"He said the police had questioned him at work, causing him embarrassment."

Rosey harrumphed. "Well *poor* little man. Like he should get special treatment. I was questioned where I work too. They said they'd tried to find me at home, but you know what? I have a life. I'm not always at my house."

I nodded. "Oh," I added, "and Terrence complained that it wasn't his fault he didn't have an alibi. That he'd been at home alone when the murder happened."

Rosey tapped her chin with her finger. "No alibi? That's interesting."

I thought so too. I'd keep an eye on Terrence.

CHAPTER FIFTEEN

It was a sunny morning, so Aunt Betty suggested we set up a table of Milton and Pearl mysteries outside Words to Read By on the sidewalk. Lots of pedestrian traffic might turn up some new customers who didn't normally take time to step inside the shop. I'd just received my order of bookmarks to give to each customer who purchased a book. We figured the bookmarks might do double duty as an advertisement for people who didn't know about the children's series yet.

On one of my many trips carrying books out to the sidewalk table, Janie approached. With my armload of books, I was glad she hadn't grabbed my hand or arm.

She smiled. "I had a few minutes before having to be at work, so I thought I'd stop by. Wow, what's going on here?"

I laughed and placed the books next to another pile on the table. "One of Aunt Betty's brainstorms. We're going to set up an outdoor table to display the kitty mystery books."

She nodded. "Might get some new customers that way," said Janie. "I've done it before on occasion with some of my wrapped pastries. I picked out a selection from my shop, added ribbons and cute pictures to the front of the wrapping, and placed them on a decorative tray, along with some flowers from Petals and Stems. Worked like a charm. And for me, I had the added benefit of the yummy fresh-baked smell to lure people my way."

"You and Aunt Betty should be on a marketing team. You both think alike."

Janie winked. "I knew I liked that lady." She glanced behind the table and her eyebrows lowered. "Where are the cats? Will they be coming out with you?"

"Yeah," I said, "I'll get them as soon as I have things set

up. They'll like it out here since the sun is shining. Something about that warmth makes them nearly turn to a languid liquid state."

She grinned.

The door opened behind me. I turned. Aunt Betty stood there, her face flushed and eyes widened.

"Aunt Betty, what's wrong?"

"The kitties are really upset about something," she said. "I can't figure out what's going on. They don't appear to be injured. Can you come and see?"

With Janie on my heels, I rushed back inside. Milton sat on the counter, his back to me, his tail lashing. The way his head was bent down, he probably had something he'd captured in his jaws.

Please don't let it be a mouse.

Aunt Betty wrung her hands. "I'm sorry, Christy. I was hoping not to bother you while you set things up outside. But the cats…" She pointed toward Milton, who'd been joined by his sister on the counter.

At the sound of his name. Milton angled around just enough that I could see his face. A colorful piece of paper—no, one of my brand-new bookmarks—dangled from his mouth.

"Hey, Milton," I said. "Give me that."

He turned his head so I couldn't reach it.

"What gives? Don't be like that." Before I could snatch it away, Pearl was right up in Milton's face, sniffing the bookmark.

Pearl sat back on her haunches, stared at her brother's prey, and then reached out her paw and gave it a whack. She liked doing it so much, she did it again.

"Stop that, Pearl," I scolded. "You're really not helping." I picked her up, earning me a growl. I placed her on the floor, which then produced a narrow-eyed glare.

My next task would take a little more finesse. I slowly reached toward Milton, aiming for his mouth. Closer. Closer. At the last second, my sneaky cat whipped his head to the side, as I clutched only air.

Needing to get the bookmark away from him to see what the fuss was about, I tried again. But Milton was ahead of me and angled around the other direction.

The bookstore door opened, and an older man strolled in. Though concern about the cats still darkened her face, Aunt Betty stood up straight then forced a pleasant expression. She walked toward the man, asked him a couple of questions, and then led him past us toward the travel book section of the shop.

Once they were out of earshot, I faced Milton again. He hadn't budged and instead gave me a self-satisfied *mrrp* sound from deep in his throat.

"Now wait just a second, cat," I said. "I need you to hand over, er, mouth over…well, you know what I mean. Just give it here." I wrapped one arm around his tummy while I wrenched the bookmark out from between his teeth.

The bookmark tore, leaving me with only half. I'd gone way past using finesse and at that point didn't care. Gently prying, I finally dislodged the second half, which plopped on the top of the counter.

"Thanks a lot, Milton." I picked it up. After nudging him to the floor to join his still-miffed sister, I laid the piece out next to its other half.

Janie, who'd been watching from a few feet away, stepped closer. And gasped. "Look."

When I bent closer, I saw why she was so upset.

A smudged dark area covered Milton's face on the wet piece. But what was it? The second half told the ugly tale. Across Pearl's furry face was an angry black X.

My gasp outdid Janie's. It was as if someone had physically injured my cats. "How terrible!" I exclaimed.

Janie clutched my arm briefly. "Who would do this?"

I shook my head. "Whoever killed Nan has to be behind this. Has to be. I can't imagine all of it not being connected. That someone else would randomly deface the bookmarks."

"To do something like that, mark up your babies' sweet faces. I think it's from the murderer," she said. "And possibly someone who also didn't like cats."

She was right. Yes, it was probably the murderer. I should also be on the lookout for a feline hater. Just one more clue getting me closer to figuring out who the culprit really was.

Janie tapped her chin. "Come to think of it, something else happened lately that has to do with people not liking cats."

"Really?" I asked.

She nodded. "About two weeks ago, Patsy North, a new customer of mine, was in buying pastries, and she was so upset. Apparently, her neighbor had tried to run down Patsy's cat in the street. She said the way the car swerved toward the cat, it was intentional."

My eyes widened. "That's horrible."

"Very," said Janie.

"Was the cat okay?"

"Thankfully, the kitty wasn't hurt, was able to jump into their yard without getting hit."

"Thank goodness," I said.

"I know. Patsy thought about calling the police but admitted she was more than a little intimidated by her neighbor. I didn't think to ask where she lives, but I sure wouldn't want someone like that living close to me," Janie said.

A cold ripple of dread went across my shoulders. I was relieved my cats had no problem being indoor kitties, which drastically improved their lifespans. However, I knew some people couldn't have a cat indoors all the time, for various reasons. Every situation was different. "Why would the driver go so far as to try to murder an innocent feline?"

Janie crossed her arms over her chest. "According to Patsy, her cat had taken a nap on the neighbor's porch. There's an old chair there that gets a lot of sun."

Not that it was the cat's fault. They couldn't help it that they crave warmth. "And," I said, "because a cat wanted to get toasty, the mean neighbor wanted to…"

"That's right."

I grimaced. "What's with the crazy people in this town?"

My aunt, who'd still been with the customer near the back of the store, hurried over. "What's going on?" she said. "Did you find out why the cats were so stressed out?" Her gaze dropped to the defaced bookmarks. She didn't gasp, but her hand smacked over her mouth in shock.

I'd done my best to keep the most disturbing facts away from her, although there wasn't much more disturbing than waking up with a dead body and a bump on her head, but it had only been a matter of time until she witnessed something else. Like now.

She shook her head. "What…who…"

I sighed. "Aunt Betty, I think whoever killed Nan…"

Her gaze met mine. "You think that person did this too?"

"Yes," I admitted.

"Why would you think that?" my aunt asked.

Time to admit what had been going on. I gave her shoulders a squeeze then dropped my arm. "Well, you see—"

Janie sidled closer, grabbing Aunt Betty's arm like she usually did mine. My aunt didn't seem surprised by it, so Janie must do it often with her as well. "Betty, it's not the first thing that's happened."

Leave it to Janie to be helpful and tell my aunt. I couldn't blame her since I was about to do the same thing, but I'd rather it had come from me first. Janie let go of Aunt Betty's arm then gave me a sheepish smile. Maybe I'd been frowning, and Janie had figured it out.

Aunt Betty's eyebrows lowered when she eyed me. "Is this true, Christy? What's going on, and why didn't I know?"

"Listen, I wasn't trying to hide anything." My shoulders slumped. "Okay, maybe I was."

"Why would you do that?"

"I wanted to protect you," I said. "It's already so stressful. And I didn't want you to have to deal with it."

Aunt Betty stood up straight, narrowing her eyes. "Young lady, I'm not some fragile flower you have to hide things from. We've talked about this. You can tell me anything. I thought you'd know that by now."

Chastised, I hung my head. Whenever the words *young lady* came out, I was in trouble. Not that she scolded me all that often, but it still stung. Could I blame her? In her shoes, wouldn't I feel the same? "I'm sorry. I didn't mean to upset you further."

Wrapping her arms around me, Aunt Betty gave me a warm, long hug. "Now, don't think I don't appreciate what you tried to do, okay? Because I do. Thank you. Just don't keep things from me from now on, all right?"

I smiled. "All right."

Janie clapped. "Yay, everything's okay now."

In unison, Aunt Betty and I stared at her. I shook my

head. "Um, Janie, we still have to deal with the pesky murder thing."

She blinked. "Right. Yes. Of course."

Aunt Betty turned her attention back to me. "Does anyone else know what's been going on?"

My face reddened. "Um…"

Janie nodded. "Yes, Rosey does."

Aunt Betty's eyebrows rose. "She knows and I didn't?"

Uh-oh. I shrugged. "Sorry. Again."

Aunt Betty eyed me for a few seconds. "No, it's all right." She sighed. "It's just…Rosey is very nosey. Always has been."

"So you two aren't close?"

"We're more acquaintances than friends," Aunt Betty said. "Just be careful how much you tell her. She'll gladly spread the news everywhere."

As I watched Aunt Betty pick up Pearl and stroke her fur, I knew I should have been relieved that my aunt knew and understood. Still, until we, mostly me, figured out who killed Nan and was threatening us, I wouldn't feel safe. I wouldn't intentionally keep things from my aunt now, but that didn't mean I had to rush right over and tell her everything either. Sometimes a girl had to take care of her family.

Aunt Betty set down the cat and took the customer's money for his book.

"Thanks," he said. "I think I'm done shopping, but I'll check around a little more."

With the cats now calmed down from their furious fit of chewing and batting at the defaced bookmark, I rolled their stroller out from behind the counter and placed them inside. It was one of their happy places, and as soon as we got them situated to their satisfaction inside the cocoon of soft blankets, they let out a roaring duet of purrs.

Janie held the front door open so I could push the feline royalty out into the sun. They squinted against the rays, their chubby cheeks curved up in smiles.

"Well," said Janie, "I need to run to work. Let me know of any future developments with"—she glanced to the left then right—"you know."

"I will. Have a good day."

"You too." She patted Milton and Pearl on their heads then gave me a wave before practically skipping down the sidewalk.

The customer Aunt Betty had assisted earlier came outside, smiling as he held up his purchase so I could see. "Hey, thanks for the free bookmark. My granddaughter will love the cat pictures on the—" He glanced at the stroller and did a doubletake. "Hey are those the…"

"Yep," I answered. "This is Milton." I tapped his head. "And Pearl." I scratched her under the chin. "The inspiration for my children's series."

His eyes widened. "This is awesome."

"Oh, thanks." Maybe he was a cat lover and swooned every time he saw a feline. I certainly did.

"What I mean is, my granddaughter's birthday is coming up, and I had no clue what to get her. Now I do. She'd be thrilled with a set of mystery books about cats. I'll come back when I have a little more time to check out the series." He gave me a nod then headed across the street.

I knelt in front of the stroller and took a paw of each cat in my hands. "Hey you guys. Your bookmarks are making a difference already. Great job."

Milton's blink coincided with Pearl's yawn.

Aunt Betty squinted her eyes and smiled, much as the cats had done. She sighed. "A sunny day always brightens my outlook. How about you?"

I nodded, trying not to think about the defaced bookmarks and the probable tie to the murderer. "Yes," I said in agreement. "It's a gorgeous day."

A few people walked by and waved, and a few more stopped to peruse our book titles. One of the women bent over to get a closer view of the bookmark. She didn't look familiar. Maybe one of the new friends I was yet to meet.

I smiled. "Hi," I said. "Can I help you find something specific today?"

She straightened and grinned. "I was just admiring your adorable bookmarks. I love cats." When I pointed to the other end of the table where the kitties were snoozing in their stroller, her eyes lit up. "They're beautiful," she said. "May I pet them?"

"Please do," I answered. "They love attention. In fact,

they feel they deserve it."

She laughed and took a few steps toward the stroller. After a few seconds of giving Milton and Pearl chin scratches, the woman turned back toward us. "The all-white one reminds me of my Fluffy. But both of yours are gorgeous."

"Thank you. How old is your cat?" I asked.

Her shoulders drooped. "She's five. Thank goodness."

Thank goodness? Aunt Betty and I exchanged looks. My aunt, who didn't seem to know the woman either, frowned then said, "Is your cat ill?"

"No. But…" With a look behind her, as if afraid someone might overhear, she said, "Recently Fluffy was nearly run over in the street. Right in front of our house."

My mouth dropped open. "That's terrible. I'm so glad she's okay."

"You want to know the worst part?" asked the woman.

I shrugged, wondering if this was who we'd heard about from Janie but not wanting to appear too eager to hear gossip.

"The person responsible for my cat almost being hit was none other than my next-door neighbor," she said. "Gee, welcome to the neighborhood, huh? That Olive Phipps sure didn't put out the welcome mat for us. Just the opposite."

Olive?

I reached out and touched her arm. "I'm so sorry that happened to you and Fluffy. I just moved here recently too. Please know that not everyone in Green Meadow is like that." I wouldn't mention the recent murder. That piece of information wouldn't help her negative view of the town. Plus, if she hadn't already learned of the crime, she would soon enough.

"Thank you for saying that," she said. "It's stressful enough moving to a new place, and then having something like this happen on top of it…" The woman blinked. "Oh, I guess first I should introduce myself. I'm Patsy North. My husband and I moved to town a few weeks ago. I can tell you, it was quite a shock to have that happen to my cat right after we'd moved in. I don't normally let her out, but with the craziness of moving in, she slipped out the door a few times."

"It's nice to meet you. I'm Christy Bailey, and this is my aunt, Betty Hollingsworth."

"Nice to meet you too." She perused the books for a bit,

picked up a popular new best seller, and held it out toward us. "I'll take this one, please."

Aunt Betty, who'd brought out our portable cashbox and book of receipts, finished her order. Then, she picked up one each of the three bookmarks and said, "We're giving away a complimentary bookmark with every purchase. Which one would you like?"

Patsy grinned. "So hard to choose. Well, how about the cute one where they're playing with ribbons?"

"Perfect." Aunt Betty put everything in a bag and handed it to her. "So nice to meet you."

I waved as our new acquaintance turned to head past us on the sidewalk.

When I looked back at Aunt Betty, she was watching something to my left. Her face brightened. That could only mean one thing.

Sure enough, Wallace walked across the street. When he reached us, he gave Aunt Betty a hug.

After holding my aunt for a minute, Wallace finally seemed to notice me. "Hi, Christy."

"Hi."

"How's everything going today?" he asked me.

"Fine." My hope was that if I didn't engage in much conversation, he wouldn't stay long.

Aunt Betty made a little noise in her throat, which caught his attention.

"Isn't everything fine?"

With a shrug, she sighed. "Unfortunately, we've had some disruptive behavior today."

"Oh?" Wallace said.

She glanced at me then back to him. "It seems that Christy has discovered that some person has tampered with the new bookmarks she made."

His eyebrows lowered. "How so?"

"Well," she went on, "whoever the person was placed a black X mark over the cats' faces on the bookmark."

"I see. Anything else?" Did he not think that was important enough on its own?

Aunt Betty glanced at me again. "It seems a new woman in town has had her cat nearly run down by her neighbor, Olive Phipps."

"What? Olive?" He shook his head. "I can't…"

Was his shocked expression because someone he knew would do such a thing or because he was surprised someone else got the blame for what he might have done?

CHAPTER SIXTEEN

Our morning had been pleasantly steady. Enough customers to keep us hopping, but not enough to exhaust us. However, a little before noon, Aunt Betty and I were both ready for a break. We didn't often get to eat lunch together since there was usually someone browsing the books and at least one of us had to be around, but today, when the door opened and Janie popped in carrying a to-go bag from Thyme for a Treat, a local sandwich shop, I was the one who flung my arms around her for a change.

Janie laughed and said, "Walked by a bit ago and saw through the window you ladies were busy. Thought you might not have time to grab lunch." She shrugged and placed the sack on the counter.

"Bless you." Aunt Betty peered inside the opening and let out a happy sigh. "Club sandwiches. My favorite."

"I know." Janie winked.

While I was grateful Janie had done this thoughtful deed, it stung a little that she and my aunt might know more about each other, at least things from the last few years, than Aunt Betty and I might. I gave myself a mental shake. *No, Christy. Not good. Appreciate what you have.* And I did. So very much. Having Aunt Betty as my family and support system and Janie as my dear friend was way more than some people ever had. Besides, now that I lived here permanently, I'd have a chance to get to know both of them better as adults.

Then there was Micah. I didn't know him, really, but the little I'd been around him, there was a definite spark. At least on my end. Would I be fortunate enough he might feel it too? When would I have a chance to run into him again? It was a small town. Surely it would happen soon.

Needing to not concentrate on a scrumptious man but instead on yummy food, I followed Aunt Betty's example and checked inside the bag. "It looks delicious. But I only see two sandwiches. Aren't you joining us?" I asked.

She shook her head. "Can't. Need to get back to the shop. I have a large order of blueberry tarts to make for the bake sale at the elementary school. But you girls enjoy." She waved and headed briskly out the door, on to tackle flour, butter, and blueberry goodness.

Aunt Betty tilted her head. "That girl is a sweetheart."

"Totally agree," I said. After a glance around the room, seeing only two women who were busy browsing on their own, I pointed to the food. "Ready when you are."

"Better do it now. The way my stomach's been growling, I'm surprised Pearl and Milton didn't growl back."

I laughed. "It's been known to happen. Believe me." I got us each a hand wipe then placed the sandwiches on paper plates we kept below the counter for food emergencies, which included but weren't limited to brownies, cookies, pretzels, cake, pie… Hmm. Maybe I should check into eating some vegetables one of these days.

We actually got to eat our food with only one interruption. One of our browsers needed to check out with his purchase. The second customer had gotten a phone call, mouthed to us that she'd be back later, and rushed out the door.

By the time the door opened a few minutes later, we'd had the opportunity to each take a bathroom break, clean up our lunch disposables, and begin working on other mundane projects we did when we had a little downtime.

Since I'd never loved my particular mundane assignment, dusting, I was glad when another customer entered the bookstore. Until I realized who the customer was. Burt Larsen. The awful, disheveled man I'd encountered at Petals and Stems. I sighed and stuffed my dusting cloth on a back shelf, out of the way. I wiped my palms on the front of my jeans then rounded the short row of shelves to meet him by the counter. Aunt Betty was in the back room, paying some bills. No need to bother her with Burt. He was a pain in the backside for whoever was unlucky enough to deal with him. Apparently, today it was my turn.

He appeared more unkempt than when I'd first seen him. He'd obviously been a functioning member of society if he'd been a house builder before Nan supposedly ruined his business financially. Did the man decide bathing was no longer necessary? I tried to ignore the stench wafting off him. And the trail of mud his dirty shoes left on the floor would send Aunt Betty into orbit. After he left, I'd try to clean up the mess before she came out of the office.

Making eye contact, though I'd rather not, I forced a fake smile, hoping it looked somewhat believable. "Hi," I said, "How can I help you today?"

"I highly doubt you're the manager. I'll speak to him, but no one else," answered Burt.

The manager? My heart sank. Now I'd have to get Aunt Betty involved after all. "No, I'm afraid she's busy at the moment."

"She? Oh, is it that Betty lady?" He squinted as he looked at me. "Hey, I know you."

"Well, I wouldn't say *know*."

"Yeah," he said, "you were loitering in the flower shop the other day when I was in there."

"Loitering? I don't think so."

"Sure. You were in there bothering that snippy Rosey person. I could tell she didn't really want you to be in there."

My mouth dropped open, and I snapped it closed. What a creep. "Is there something I can help you with today?" I asked.

"Not if you aren't the manager."

"Could I ask what this is in reference to?"

"You could," he said. "But I wouldn't tell you."

I huffed out a breath. Such a cantankerous kook. The guy was tenacious. I'd give him that. Although I hated to bother Aunt Betty with this, from things I'd heard about him and how obnoxious he was, he might not leave until he spoke to her. And I wanted to get rid of him as soon as possible. "Fine. Let me get her."

He tapped his watch, which was so dirty I doubted he could see the face. "About time," he said.

I pivoted on my heel, practically marched to the back room, and entered. My face must have shown every negative emotion I felt, because Aunt Betty's eyes widened as she hopped up from her chair behind the desk and raced to me.

"Christy. What happened? Are you all right? Are Milton and Pearl—"

"They're fine. I'm fine."

"Then what's wrong?" she asked.

I pointed my thumb over my shoulder. "Burt Larsen is out there. Demanding to see the manager. I'm sorry. I was hoping not to bother you with this. With him."

"It's all right," she said. "I've heard what he's been up to, and I'm not surprised he's trying to pull the same stunt here." She huffed out a breath. "Let's get it over with and see what he wants."

I followed her out then closed the door behind us. Burt paced back and forth in front of the counter. My cats had woken from their naps and were now sitting facing him, their heads turning left to right and back again as they watched the frantic man with the waving hands who mumbled to himself. Milton and Pearl's body language wasn't tense, with hunched backs and lashing tails. Instead, their whiskers twitched in interest, and their eyes were bright.

Need some popcorn with the show, kitty cats?

The door opened, and two women I'd seen before in the bookstore entered.

I smiled and gave them a wave. "Hi ladies," I called. "Anything I can help you with?"

One of them smiled back. "Just browsing," she said. "Thank you, though."

Once the women had made their way back to the romance novel section, I turned back to our unwelcome visitor.

Aunt Betty, positioned behind the counter, had her hands clasped behind her back, like a general about to give bad news to her troops. "Christy informed me you'd like to speak to the manager. That would be me."

"Well, it took her long enough to fetch you," he said. "And you long enough to show up. Even though you're not a man, which I assumed the manager would be."

Eyes wide, Aunt Betty blinked. I was sure she'd love nothing better than to reprimand the jerk. But knowing her as I did, I doubted it would come out that way.

Moving her hands to her side, fingers relaxed, Aunt

Betty looked directly at Burt. "All that aside, Mr. Larsen," she said. "Here I am. And I'm a busy woman, so I would appreciate knowing what business you feel you need to discuss. Was there a problem with a book purchase? Do you wish to return something?"

"No. That's not it. Not even close."

"Very well, then. How can I help you?" she asked.

Burt took a step closer to Aunt Betty and me. I knew what to expect, as I'd experienced the less than lovely odor of him a few minutes earlier. But Aunt Betty hadn't. Her head jerked back. She blinked, scrunched her nose, and then crossed her arms over her chest.

He appeared not to notice her negative reaction. Instead, he pointed his grubby finger right at her. "I need a job."

Her eyebrows rose. "I see."

"Do you?" he asked. "Do you really see? I need a job, and I need it today."

"If you're insinuating that I'm to simply give you said job, you'd be mistaken," said my aunt.

His mouth dropped open, seemingly appalled that he'd been turned down. But from what I'd heard lately from people, the bookstore was way down on his list of businesses he'd thrust himself upon to procure employment. And since he hadn't yet landed a job, he'd gotten turned down from every other business so far.

"But I need a job. How am I to eat, to rent an apartment, to even take my next breath if I don't have a way to earn income?"

"I'm very sorry, Mr. Larsen," said Aunt Betty. "I wish I could help you. But the fact remains, I can't."

"You could if you really wanted to," he insisted.

"I beg your pardon?"

"If you were truly a kind person, someone who valued his, er, her fellow man, you'd grant me this wish right this second."

Aunt Betty sighed. "That's not possible."

"Whyever not?" asked Burt.

My aunt gave an eyeroll then gave herself a little shake, as if sorry she'd let her guard down in front of this man. "If you must know, I don't have the funds for another employee."

He lifted his chin in my direction. "What about her?" he asked. "Doesn't she work here?"

"Christy is my niece. She's—"

"Ah, nepotism. Such a marvelous quality in an employer."

My mouth fell open. "Now you wait just a second, Burt," I said.

"How do you know my name is Burt? We were never properly introduced."

"When I was talking to Rosey, she told me and—"

"Don't listen to a word that old crow utters," he said.

My mouth dropped open. He held up his hand. "I think we're getting away from the subject here. That I need a job. And you can give me one. As a matter of fact, I have a way to make that happen."

A shuffle came from behind us and to the right. Oh no, the two women who'd come into the shop earlier. They would have heard the whole wretched conversation. One of the ladies grimaced, as if sorry for us that we had to go through this with Burt. She shrugged, waved, and then departed the store with her friend.

Great. Now they'd tell everyone they saw what happened, making Words to Read By fodder for even more gossip.

As soon as they were gone, Burt said, "Seems we're all alone now, huh? Well, what I have to say is this. If you don't give me a job, and I mean right now, this very minute, I'll walk out that door and tell everyone I see, that you"—he pointed to Aunt Betty —"were the one who killed that lady in your upstairs apartment."

Aunt Betty's hand pressed against her chest as she gasped. "But it's not true!"

He shrugged. "What does that matter? Tell people something, and they're bound to believe it."

Was this guy for real? I couldn't take much more, and I knew Aunt Betty had reached the end of her rope. It had gone far enough. I leaned partway over the counter, even though that put my nose much too close to his unbathed unpleasantness. "Burt. Mr. Larsen," I said, "I think you need to leave. Now."

"And who's going to make me?" he scoffed. "You?"

"No, I'll call the police."

His eyes narrowed. "You wouldn't dare."

"I wouldn't? Watch me," I said. My hand shook a little as I reached for the phone. The door opened again.

And in walked Micah.

I nearly wilted against the counter. Because as much as I bluffed, would I have actually phoned the police and taken on more of Burt's wrath? The guy came across as so unhinged, I wasn't sure what he might do if I actually punched in the numbers and reported him. If he really was the murderer and had killed Nan and knocked out Aunt Betty, he was capable of so much more than spewing angry words.

Burt swiveled around to see who was behind him. "What's he doing here?" he asked.

I didn't know and didn't care. I was just glad that Micah how shown up when he did.

Micah approached, a frown marring his handsome face. "What's going on? Betty? Christy? Are you all right?"

I blew out a breath, thankful reinforcements had arrived. "We're fine. Just…"

Aunt Betty waved her hands and said, "This man…he's demanding I give him a job."

As Micah eyed Burt, I watched for signs he might be put off by the other man's attire and smell. But he didn't flinch, blink, or lean away. But then, working in the ER, he was surely used to that. And much worse.

Frowning, Micah said, "Burt? What's going on? You causing trouble here?"

Had Burt also gone to the hospital begging for a job?

Burt shrugged. "Just looking out for myself is all. A man's gotta eat, right?"

"Sure, a guy has to take care of himself. But not if it means upsetting some nice women who only want to run their bookstore in peace."

Burt waved us away with his hand. "These two. Not worth it. Just a couple of—"

"Stop right there," Micah said and stood taller. "I wouldn't finish that sentence if I were you."

Instead of questioning Micah's ability to force him to leave, as he'd tried with me, Burt stared up at Micah and his eyes widened. Had he just realized the younger, larger man could make things difficult for him if he continued his harassment? "All right," Burt said. "I get the drift. But…" He watched me then Aunt Betty. "Don't you forget what I said before. And I'll do it. Just try me."

When Micah took a step closer, Burt stepped back then rushed from the store. A hiss came from Pearl. I picked her up and smoothed her frenzied fur. "Guess Pearl gave her opinion of Burt Larsen."

Aunt Betty petted Pearl's head. "And I agree. Smart girl, Pearl."

Milton lashed his tail. Was that a belated reaction to Burt, or was he simply feeling left out when his sister got affection?

"May I?" Micah reached out toward Milton.

I nodded. "Yes, I'm sure he'd love it."

When Micah scooped up the cat, he purred. The cat not Micah, although it wouldn't bother me a bit to hear that noise from the handsome doctor. A sudden image of Micah curled up on a couch, purring, with me cuddled up next to him, made my knees weak and my face hot. I couldn't help watching Micah, the way he ran his hand over the cat's fur. His broad shoulders, brown hair, long eyelashes surrounding dark brown eyes, and full lips.

Aunt Betty nudged me with her elbow. "Why are you grinning like a lunatic?" she asked.

I jerked. "Um, what?"

When I dared a glance back at Micah, I wanted to slide beneath the counter and hide. His expression was a cross between triumph and glee.

Oh boy. Yeah, it seemed he was interested in me, which was great. But now that he'd figured out the direction of my thoughts, I wondered if I'd get teased. Of course I would be by my aunt. But the thought of getting razzed by the new object of my fascination made me nervous. Time to change the subject. "Thanks, Micah," I said. "I'm glad you came in right when you did."

His grin fell. "I am too. Looks like you were in for some unpleasant conversation with that guy."

"Too late," my aunt said as she sighed. "We already got

it. He's a real menace, isn't he?" She gave a sideways glance toward me.

Micah placed Milton, who flipped his tail in irritation, down on the counter. "Is there more going on than Burt begging for employment?"

Watching him then Aunt Betty, I got the feeling they knew each other fairly well. Would my aunt want Micah in on the latest developments about searching for the murderer? I'd already decided to trust Micah and accept any help he'd give but wasn't sure about how Aunt Betty might feel.

I waited, not wanting to get ahead of my aunt. At first, I'd tried to shield her from the mess that having Nan murdered in the apartment upstairs created, but now that Aunt Betty had made it clear she didn't want to be kept in the dark, I wanted to see if she intended to involve Micah too.

Micah crossed his arms, as if he wanted to know her intentions as well.

"You see," said Aunt Betty, "ever since Nan was killed, Christy and I, along with Janie Lambert, have been keeping an eye out for possible suspects. Burt Larsen is on our list. The police haven't charged me with the murder, yet, but…"

I grabbed her hand. "And they won't. I don't see how they could. You're innocent." Even though I longed for my words to be true, there was always the possibility the authorities would decide Aunt Betty was their favorite person to take the blame.

Aunt Betty winked at me. "So, Micah," she said, "as you can see, I have a very good support system with these girls."

"I'm concerned for you, Betty." He tilted his head. "And you as well, Christy."

I frowned. "Me? Why?"

"Because you live and work here too. Whoever is behind this may not differentiate since you're family. And from what I've heard, you arrived in town the day of the murder and found Nan dead and Betty knocked out in a corner, right?"

"Right," I said.

"That's why I'm concerned." His mouth lifted in a half smile. "I realize I'm not one of Betty's girls, but please consider me an ally in your suspect search too, okay?"

I glanced at Aunt Betty, who nodded. Her eyes were teary as she said, "Thank you, Micah."

CHAPTER SEVENTEEN

Wanting to cheer Aunt Betty up with everything going on, I headed to Petals and Stems to buy more sunflowers. She'd said the others had brightened her day, and I wanted to make that happen again. If I had to get her flowers every day to see her smile, I'd gladly do it. My plan was to put these flowers in the apartment. Aunt Betty had mentioned possibly updating the décor up there when I moved in, to make it more our apartment and not just hers. Flowers sounded like a great way to begin.

When I entered the store, I was surprised not to see Rosey. Was it her day off? Along with purchasing flowers, I was hoping she'd fill me in on any new developments she might have heard about. But I was here and could still buy my aunt something cheerful. The fact that it would brighten our apartment was a bonus.

Stomping footsteps came from the back area. Rosey's boss, Essie, approached. Her sour expression was enough to make me want to run away. Even on my worst day, I hoped I never came across as scary as an ax murderer.

I took a breath and let it out. "Hi," I said. "I'd like to buy some sunflowers."

Her frown deepened, creating an unattractive pattern across her brow. "All right." She crossed her arms and waited.

Wasn't she going to show me what they had? Tell me about specials? Recommend something I might like? These were all methods Aunt Betty and I used at the bookstore. Maybe Essie could use a few suggestions.

Her eyes narrowed as if she could read my thoughts. Well, no, maybe giving the woman suggestions wasn't my best idea.

But my stubborn streak kicked in. Having been around

cats all my life, I'd learned how to be patient. This lady had no idea who she was dealing with. If I could outwait Milton and Pearl when they lied and said it was time to eat when I'd just fed them, I could easily stand and watch Essie until she cracked.

Besides, I didn't particularly like her because of the way she treated Rosey. Even though Rosey was prickly, nosey, and blunt, didn't everyone deserve a fair working environment? I crossed my arms and kept constant eye contact with Essie. And was rewarded when she let out a sigh to rival Milton's when he didn't get as many treats as he thought Pearl had gotten.

Finally, Essie said, "You want sunflowers?"

"Yes, that's right."

"Why don't I show you what we have?"

Gee, there's a thought. "Thanks, that would be great," I said.

I couldn't help noticing her disgusted snort as she turned away from me to get some. Was she annoyed to have to deal with an actual customer since Rosey didn't seem to be around to take care of it?

When she returned, she had a lovely bouquet in her hand, slightly larger than the one I'd previously bought.

I smiled. "Those will be perfect."

She raised one eyebrow. Was she hoping I wouldn't like them? Had my use of the word perfect thrown her off? I held back my smirk.

As Essie placed the flowers in a vase and measured and cut a green ribbon to adorn it, she tilted her head. "You were here before," she said. "When Rosey waited on you."

I nodded.

"Do you know Rosey well?"

It seemed like an odd question, as if Essie was checking up on her employee, but I went with it. "She's an acquaintance of my aunt's," I said. "I'm getting to know her since I moved back to Green Meadow."

Essie shrugged. "So your aunt is…"

"Betty Hollingsworth."

"Oh. Yes. From the *bookstore*." She sounded like Aunt Betty's business was a toxic waste facility.

Determined not to let her comment faze me, I said, "Yes. I work at Words to Read By too."

She blinked. A sudden interest sparked in her eyes, and her mouth stretched into a wide grin. Taken aback at the change, it was all I could do to not take a step backward, out of her reach. What was her deal? First she sounded like books were trash. Next she gave me a frightening expression that I supposed was to pass for a smile.

After she'd finished tying the bow for the ribbon, she glanced at me. "So, the bookstore…"

Was that a statement? A question? What was I supposed to say to that? "Um…"

"How fascinating that you work with books," said Essie.

Now I was really confused. Did she hate books or love them? "Well, I happen to think they're fascinating, yes," I said. "I've always loved to read." Glancing at the bill she laid next to the vase, I got out my wallet to pay. "How about you?"

"What about me?"

"Do you like to read?" I asked.

Her head jerked as if the notion of perusing something someone else had written was as pleasant as leaping into a vat of angry bees. But she gave herself a little shake. "Uh, sure. Books. They're the best. Love them."

Sure you do. Time to make her spit out what this was all about. "What kind of books do you like to read?"

Her face reddened. "I… Well…" She shrugged. "All of them. I guess. Yes, all of them."

"Ah," I said. "Well, we have lots of 'all of them' at the bookstore. If you're ever in the mood for a new one to read."

"Okay." She glanced behind me. Was she expecting someone else to come inside? She leaned forward on the counter, placing her elbows on the top. "Say, I've heard some things. Uh, when customers come in and talk, that is."

"Really?" I asked. "What about?"

"Your…er…the place where…you know, it happened."

Now I got it. She was another Nosy Nellie who wanted the scoop on what occurred in our apartment. Although it was the last thing I wanted to discuss with this woman, if she spoke to lots of customers, or at least listened to them talk to each other about the latest gossip, because let's face it, she wasn't the best conversationalist, she might have some knowledge I could use.

After paying for the flowers, I returned my wallet to my purse. "What have you heard about what happened?" I asked.

She gave a one-shouldered shrug, suddenly seeming not to care either way. "This and that."

I held in a sigh. Did she think acting coy would make me drop my guard? Give her more juicy details? Wasn't going to happen. "Hmmm. This and that. Well…"

I let it hang there, letting her know I wouldn't just start talking, that she'd have to actually say what she'd heard before I'd confirm or deny. Not that any answer from me was guaranteed even then. But she wouldn't have to know that.

The longer I stood, silently refusing to say more, the quicker her face reddened. Finally she frowned and, not quite meeting my eye, said, "I heard, that is, Georgina Zann was in here yesterday and said that your aunt, um, Betty, was the one the police had their eye on."

Georgina Zann? The name was familiar. Wait, she was the one who had spread the word about Wallace telling Aunt Betty in his café that he loved her. The word that had gotten back to Nan, who had then tried to blackmail Wallace shortly before she died.

I eyed Essie, whose reddened face was morphing back to pale. "Did you believe Georgina when she said that about my aunt?" I asked.

Her mouth hung open. "I, um…"

Was she that surprised I'd wanted to know her opinion after dropping the statement in my lap? Or was she hoping I'd agree wholeheartedly that my aunt was a murderer and I gladly supported that action and shared an apartment with her. I definitely got why Rosey didn't like working for her. Aside from her rudeness and bossiness, she was nosey and insensitive. Hmmm. Hadn't I just described Rosey, as well?

"She also mentioned something about that man, Wallace," said Essie. "Like maybe he had something to do with it too."

I didn't answer her about Wallace, since I wasn't sure about him myself. I did, however, flinch at the memory of him explaining what happened when Nan tried to drug him, videotape their encounter, and blackmail him. Was it all Nan's evilness that made it happen, or had Wallace really led Nan on and two-timed my aunt?

Wallace was still on my suspect list, though my aunt adored him and got all starry eyed when she even spoke his name. Though part of me wanted to give in and simply be happy for her, the part of me that recently got betrayed and dumped by my former boyfriend wouldn't allow it.

Footsteps came from behind me. I turned and saw Rosey, whose expression was troubled when she spotted me. "Hi, Rosey," I said.

She approached but kept her gaze on her boss. "Essie? What's going on?"

Essie snapped out of her speechlessness after my questioning her. "What do you mean?"

Rosey's hand landed on her hip. "Are you giving Christy here a hard time about something?"

My eyes widened. Wow, I'd never heard her talk that way to Essie before. Trying to keep Rosey's job from being in jeopardy, even though she hated working for Essie, I grabbed the vase of sunflowers and held them up. "I was buying more of these. For my aunt."

Rosey let out a breath, seeming to relax. "Good."

Essie stood up taller, looking down her sharp nose at her employee. "Now that you're finally back, I'll get back to my important work in the back room." The frown she gave Rosey as she left made the hair on my arms stand up. Would she reprimand Rosey, or worse, after I left the shop?

"I'm so surprised to hear you talk that way to Essie since she seems the type to hold grudges," I said. "Are you all right?"

She grimaced. "It's just that Tina Jeffers, who works at the newspaper, got me all flustered. Sometimes the words out of her mouth are downright rude."

Pot calling the kettle black?

The only time I'd met Tina was the first day I'd arrived in the bookstore, right after finding Nan's dead body and Aunt Betty crumpled in a corner. She'd been pushy and demanding to Aunt Betty. I wasn't enamored of Tina's general demeanor either.

Although I kept in mind Aunt Betty's warning about

Rosey's nosiness and tendency to gossip, I still thought she might be a good source of information. "What did she say that was rude?" I asked.

"I was in the fruit market, having a perfectly nice conversation with Annabelle Angstrom, when Tina sauntered in. She browsed through some of the produce and didn't say anything, but when she spied me, she went berserk."

"How come?"

"I honestly don't know," said Rosey. "She lit into me, yelling about Betty, Nan, Wallace, and Nan's murder. How she'd known from that first day it must have been Nan's body the police carried out of the bookstore under that sheet and how Betty was guilty."

"But Wallace?" I asked. "Why talk that way to you, especially about him?"

"That was the only thing Tina got right, in my opinion," said Rosey. "That Wallace must have been in on the planning of the murder because of the two-timing he was doing with Nan. How he'd wanted both women but settled for one, allowing the other one to…"

My eyes widened.

Rosey held up her hand. "I'm not saying I believe Wallace was guilty of the murder—although since I don't trust him otherwise, I guess I'm not completely sure. Still, I do have to agree with Tina about the womanizing."

With a glance toward the office door, which was now closed, Rosey motioned me to follow her out a side door. It opened to a greenhouse area, lovely with intense colors of red, yellow, pink, and orange, all of the various fragrances blending together in a heavenly, calming scent.

She picked up a nearby hose, turned the water pressure to a drizzle, and began to lightly spray the flowers housed there. I pushed up my long sleeves, suddenly too warm in the toasty environment. I could imagine my dark hair curling at the ends, its normal response to humid temperatures. "I thought we could talk better out here, away from Essie's big, flappy ears," said Rosey.

"What if a customer comes into the store?" I'd hate for Rosey to get into even more trouble because of me.

"There's a bell that rings back here if the door is opened

out front," she said. "I would have come in to see you sooner, but I was taking my break at the fruit market. Sorry about Essie. She's a force to be reckoned with."

I waved my hand. "It's fine. She's direct. I'll give her that."

"You're being too nice," said Rosey. "Direct is not a strong enough adjective for the likes of her." She moved a few feet and watered some white azaleas. "What did she have to say for herself this time?"

I rubbed my hand across the back of my neck, wiping away perspiration. It made me wish I'd worn my hair in a ponytail today. "At first, she was blunt, not being helpful at all about my purchase. Honestly, I wanted to give her some etiquette lessons but figured she wouldn't take it well."

Rosey let out a snort. "Probably not. Then what happened?"

"When she realized who I was and where I lived and worked, she seemed to switch gears."

"Like a switch went on and her personality changed?" she asked.

I jerked. "How did you know?"

"I've witnessed her doing it before. Many times. That lady has a screw loose."

I shook my head. "Yeah, as she was talking, I was feeling even more sympathy for you, having to put up with her," I said.

Rosey shrugged, causing the hose to wobble a little. "Don't worry about me. I'm a tough old bird. You might want to watch your back, though."

I crossed my arms. "Why me?" I asked. "I'm okay. "

She glanced up from her work. "I realize you're new to town, at least as an adult who just moved here, but you need to know something. Not everyone living in Green Meadow is as sugary sweet as Betty. Don't trust every person who comes your way."

I blew out a breath, "Right. With a murderer on the loose and all."

"Exactly. And the really scary part is, we don't know who it is yet."

"But we will."

CHAPTER EIGHTEEN

On Sundays, the bookstore was closed. After attending morning worship at the tiny Baptist church in Green Meadow, Aunt Betty and I decided to put up some wall hangings and pictures we'd purchased together the week before. The fact that Aunt Betty wished to change the décor to include me, wanting to make the apartment ours instead of just hers, made me feel special and loved.

We retrieved the sack of purchases from the hall closet, ready to hang up or place our new finds. After carrying the last picture from the closet, I placed it carefully on the couch. I glanced around the room. "Okay, it's all here. Now where do we start?"

Aunt Betty grinned. "That's the fun part. Now it's like a reverse scavenger hunt, where we aren't trying to find things, but using things we've already found and placing them in their new home."

"I love it," I said. "You have such a way with words. Maybe you should be a writer too."

"No, I'll leave that to you. But I do love reading and running the bookstore. My dream come true."

As far back as I could remember, Aunt Betty had owned the bookshop. When I thought of her, the bookstore also appeared in my mind because they were connected. It obviously made her happy, which in turned thrilled me.

Something rattled. Pearl had jumped on the couch, her head now inside a sack of new book-themed knickknacks that would look great on our coffee table. I frowned, unless that was exactly where the cats were hoping the items would go so they could bat them onto the floor. Maybe one of the small shelves we'd bought would be better for those. Otherwise, I'd spend part of every day either picking up the tiny book art or crawling around the apartment trying to discover where my wily cats had hidden them.

So, a shelf it would have to be. A cat mom always had to think one step ahead. Sadly, I didn't always get there in time.

"Christy? Would you mind helping me move this table away from the wall? I think the new picture of the waterfall in the woods might look nice here. What do you think?"

I crossed the room and eyed the space. "Yeah, I think so too. Let me grab this end of the table." It was a little heavy, but we managed.

Aunt Betty stretched her arms and rubbed her shoulders. "I would have asked Wallace for help, but then I reconsidered."

"Oh?"

She shrugged. "Let me get the picture so we can hang it up." She walked away.

What was that about? Did she think Wallace couldn't physically help? Or wouldn't want to? Or was there something in my aunt, deep down, that had doubts about her boyfriend, as I did? I wanted to ask more about it, but I knew Aunt Betty. When she got a certain stiffness in her spine and stood at her tallest, there'd be no arguing with her. I knew from experience it wouldn't do any good to ask further questions.

Might as well get on with the decorating. Once I'd hung the picture and had Aunt Betty's approval that it was in the right place and level, we shoved the table back to the wall. Milton leaped onto the table to check out the picture, standing on his tiptoes and stretching out his paw toward his newest interest. "Milton, no, don't..."

Aunt Betty waved her hand. "It's okay, Christy. This is their new home too. They can check things out if they want."

I laughed. "Oh, they will. Cats are so nosy, it's like it's part of their DNA to want to know what's going on, who's doing what, and to touch everything they don't understand. Especially if it's shiny. Or moves."

"Well," she said, "I for one am enjoying getting to know your cats. They're gorgeous and fun and playful, something my home has been missing for far too long." My aunt had been widowed a very long time. I barely remembered my uncle, since he'd died when I was little. She really must have been lonely all those years.

Then along came Wallace. Had he taken advantage of her loneliness and wormed his way into her life?

We watched as Pearl now had half her body in the sack. I pointed toward her tail, which waved furiously with interest. "Even though we're all for them checking things out," I said, "I was thinking it might be a smart move on our part to place those small knickknacks on a shelf. A high one. So they don't end up as tiny hockey pucks."

She nodded. "You might have a point there. With that in mind, why don't you grab one of the new small shelves we bought, and we can hang it and fill it with Pearl's newest treasures."

"Sounds great." I bent over, rummaged through the large box, and drew out a wooden shelf designed to be placed in a corner. I held it up. "Where do you think it would look best?"

She turned in a slow circle then pointed to the corner of the same wall where the death chair had once stood. "I think right there would work." Against the wall was an antique chest of drawers, given to Aunt Betty by my grandmother way before I was born.

I gave a mock sigh. "Well great. More furniture to move. My poor aching back."

"Sorry, kid. Has to be done."

We grinned as we headed to the corner and edged the chest away from the wall far enough so I'd be able to move behind it and hang up the shelf. Pearl was still pawing at things inside the sack, but Milton had left his perch on the table and was now sitting on top of the chest.

I held up the shelf against the corner. "Would this work here?"

"A little higher," said Aunt Betty.

I raised it a few inches.

"Perfect," she said.

I affixed the shelf into the corner. "Hand me the bag with the things we picked out, and I'll set them on the shelf."

"You mean, hand you Pearl's new bag?"

"My cats are sucking you into their vortex, aren't they?" I asked. "Making you say things you never would have before."

"Who knows? Maybe being around them with their

energy, the way they play and run around, it will reinvigorate me in my old age."

"You're hardly old," I replied. "Besides, you have more energy than most people I know. Me included."

She shrugged but smiled.

Once she handed me the bag—and it indeed must have been Pearl's bag by now because my cat had a little fit when I wouldn't allow her to stick her head in it again—I placed, then replaced, then moved the items around until it looked the way Aunt Betty wanted.

She clapped. "Perfect. Thank you."

"Hey, gotta keep the talent happy, right?" I answered.

Aunt Betty's eyes widened. "I'm the talent? I don't think so. You're the famous writer, after all."

"Not famous. That'd be nice, though."

"I'm your aunt, and what I say goes. You're famous, like it or not."

I put my hands on the top of the chest. "Oh, I like it, all right."

"With the publicity you're getting for your Milton and Pearl series since you came to Green Meadow and with all the future events we have planned, you're a shoo-in." She winked.

"I like the way you think," I said.

Now that the shelf and its contents were in place, I took a step to the left, nearly losing my balance when I stepped on something hard.

Aunt Betty gasped. "Are you all right?"

"I'm fine." I glanced down but saw nothing. "Just thought I was stepping on a cat. Because you know, they're always where they're not supposed to be."

"What did you step on?"

"I'm not sure." Bending over in the tight space, I saw something brown next to the wall. No wonder I hadn't seen it at first. It was the same shade as the baseboards and had blended in.

She stood on tiptoes to see what I had. "What is it?" she asked.

I tried to pick it up, but as soon as Milton caught sight of it, he jumped from the chest, snatched it up into his mouth, and raced from the room. Pearl ran after him. Claws scraped against the hallway floor as they headed toward the room they shared with me.

"Hey, wait!" I yelled as I ran after them, skidding to a halt in front of my bedroom's open doorway. Both cats were on the bed, playing tug of war with what appeared to be a piece of leather. What in the world was it? Whatever it was, I needed to get it away from them. One, because I never knew if what they were chewing on might be dangerous, and two, I was as nosey as they were.

Stepping softly so they wouldn't startle and bolt, I crept close to the bed, leaned over, and snatched it away, not unlike how Milton had stolen it in the first place.

Aunt Betty appeared in the doorway. "What did he bring in here? I didn't get a chance to see before he disappeared."

I held it up. After a closer look, I saw what it was. "It's a bracelet. See?" I held it out to Aunt Betty.

She took it and frowned. "I've never seen this before. It's certainly not mine. What's it doing here?"

I held up my hand. "Not mine either. Could it be from someone who visited?"

"I can't imagine who."

"Maybe Nan's?" I asked.

She shook her head. "I don't think so. That strap is wide, very noticeable. I think I would have remembered it. Although, since I can't remember the day of the murder to know who the killer was…" She knocked her head with her fist, as if trying to loosen the lost memories.

"I can't imagine how frustrating it must be for you not to remember what happened that day after Nan confronted you."

"I just don't understand it," she said. "Maybe it was so terrible my mind repressed it somehow. Like my brain doesn't want me to remember. At least, that's what Wallace thinks."

Wallace was giving my aunt medical advice now? Was that to cover for his own guilt if he was the one who'd taken revenge on Nan and stabbed her? But I couldn't very well say what was on my mind without upsetting my aunt.

Even though we were getting along so well and the cats were settling in nicely, I didn't want to rock the boat. I hadn't lived here all that long. If I did or said something to annoy or hurt Aunt Betty, would we be able to get back the amazing relationship we shared now?

Her eyes widened as she studied the bracelet. She handed it back to me. "You don't suppose…"

"What?"

"Well, there was obviously someone here that day who might have had that bracelet on," she said.

With a nod, I said, "That it belongs to whoever murdered Nan?"

Aunt Betty shrugged. "It could belong to either a man or woman, from its design. So yes, it's possible."

"True. I've seen lots of different people wear leather bracelets in Philadelphia. Though none like this." As I held it closer, a white paw slowly rose into my line of vision. Pearl's wide green eyes sparkled as she focused on her latest prey.

I whipped to the side, taking it out of her reach. "No you don't, kitty cat." From my other side, something soft patted my arm holding the bracelet. Milton, green eyes matching his sister's, gave me a blink. "No, Milton, you don't get to play with it either."

Chastised, both cats sat back on their haunches, wearing frowns and sad eyes.

"Awww," said Aunt Betty. "They look so sad. Maybe I should get them some—"

I held up my hand. "Don't say the T-word. It will only encourage them."

Even though we hadn't said *treats* out loud, my smart kitties got the gist. They jumped to the floor and wound around first my legs, then Aunt Betty's. My aunt's smile told me she was pleased they included her in their ritual, that it made her feel like the cats accepted her as family now.

She bent down and rubbed their heads. "Don't listen to your mom, babies. Aunty Betty will get you some treats."

Pearl stood on her hind legs and pawed at Aunt Betty's leg, while Milton screeched out a rousing meow.

As my cats and their new favorite person left the room for a snack, I shook my head. How was I supposed to get the mom respect from my cats with Aunt Betty giving into them on a whim?

A smile crossed my lips. But how awesome they were

all bonding. And sooner than I'd hoped. I shrugged. Truth was, I spoiled those cats terribly. Why shouldn't Aunt Betty?

Once they'd headed down to the bookstore where I kept the treat jar, I took a minute to study the leather band further. There were embedded sparkles of red, blue, and green. Very tiny. I had to squint to see them. On closer inspection, the latch appeared to be broken. Had it occurred during a struggle? Like someone clawed the bracelet from the intruder's wrist?

Maybe I could check out some of the shops around that might sell these bracelets for further information.

CHAPTER NINETEEN

On my break the next day, I walked to the nearest jewelry store to check on possible leads for who might have lost the leather bracelet in our apartment. The first shop, one block over, yielded nothing. They didn't make anything with leather and suggested I try Sparkly Wearables for better luck.

I slipped back into the bookstore, made sure Aunt Betty and the cats could do without me for a bit, and walked the seven blocks to the other shop. I hadn't told Aunt Betty what I was up to. While it was true she knew about the bracelet and that it might belong to the murderer, I didn't want to get her hopes up in case I didn't discover anything useful.

Upon entering the store, I was met with new age music. The woman standing beside the counter wore a flowing multicolored gown that reached the floor. Her red-polished toes popped out from beneath the hem, and no shoes were visible.

I loved going barefoot as much as the next person, but it didn't seem all that professional in a business. Besides, it would give Pearl and Milton too many opportunities to pounce on my naked toes. I got enough of that every morning after my shower.

A timid mew came from below. Briefly, I panicked, thinking one of my cats had somehow gotten out and followed me. But I grinned when a small orange kitten peered out at me from around the feet of the woman. I'd been right. Cats and bare toes went together.

The woman smiled and said, "Good morning, new friend. How may I make your day brighter?"

I blinked. Wow, super friendly. Maybe if I sent some of our grumpier customers over here, she could make them nice. No, probably not.

I smiled back. "Hi, I have a question for you and

wondered if you could help."

"I will do my absolute best to be of good service to you."

"Uh, thanks," I replied. I got the leather bracelet from the outside pocket of my purse and held it out. "First of all, do you have anything like this for sale in your shop?"

She squinted and bent her head over the leather strap. "Yes, that's one of mine. Was that your only question?"

"Actually, I'm trying to find out who this one belongs to."

"Why is that?" she asked.

"I…well, I work in my aunt's bookstore Words to Read By, and…someone dropped this. We have no idea who it might belong to, so…"

"You want to return it. How wonderful. And thoughtful. Great job."

I bit my lip. If only she knew the real reason I needed to find the owner. "Thanks."

"Just by looking at this one, I can't tell you who it might belong to. I've created and sold several, so there's no way to know."

Rats. I'd hoped this would be easier. "What if you, uh, checked out your purchase receipts for the leather bracelets?"

Her eyebrows lowered.

This wasn't going well. "Then, we, I mean you'd know who bought them. Right?"

She blinked. "I suppose if I had a client who lost their item of valuable and coveted jewelry, I'd want them to have it back," she said.

It was working. I clasped my hands together in front of me. "Yes, I agree. So sad to lose something so precious, never to see it again."

She nodded gravely. "However…"

I didn't like the sound of that. Not one little bit.

"I couldn't actually share with you who the buyer was," she said. "That wouldn't be prudent."

Deflated, I dropped my hands to my sides. "I see."

She held up one finger. "Never fear, new friend. I might still be able to see that the bracelet gets to the rightful owner."

Holding in a sigh, I nodded. "Sure," I said. "That would

be great." Although, it wouldn't help me in my quest for only her to know with me left in the dark.

A mew came from my right. Somehow, the tiny kitten had managed to scale the side of the wooden display case and now sat on top of the counter, staring at me with overlarge accusing eyes.

Good grief. Judged by a tiny orange fluff ball. I gave the kitten a shrug, hoping he wouldn't judge me too harshly. I did, after all, need the information for a good cause—saving my aunt from possible prison time. The kitten would have to understand that. At least, I hoped so. Apparently, being a cat mom brought guilt, even if the cat wasn't mine.

The saleswoman stepped behind the counter, leaned forward on its edge, and handed me back the leather bracelet, which I stuck in my purse. "If you will indulge me," she said.

Indulge her how? I waited for more, but nothing happened. "What do you mean?"

She pointed to the opposite side of the room. "Do you see the display of ornamental winter scene wall hangings?"

"Oh, thanks, but I'm not really looking for those today."

"You don't understand," she said. "I need you to walk over there, study them closely, and don't turn around until I tell you it's permissible to do so."

The crazy woman was putting me into a corner? I opened my mouth to retort.

She held up her hand to stop my words. "I'm afraid that's the only way this will work," she said. "You stand over there, with your back turned, while I peruse my receipts. I know right where they are, since I keep receipts by object and not date. It won't take long, I assure you."

Seeing I had no choice but hoping somehow she'd slip up and mention the names out loud—maybe she was one of those people who mumbled aloud what they read—I slogged my way reluctantly to the other wall.

There was a reflection on the winter scenes. Would it be possible to see what she was doing behind me? I leaned so close to the picture, my nose nearly touched the surface. But all I could see was a blurry image of the woman's bright dress.

A light patting sound, like touching a cloth to bare floor, came from my left. I could still see the woman working behind me, so what was—

Mew.

For Pete's sake. Now the kitten was spying on me? Maybe if I petted him or picked him up, he'd forget to keep an eye on me. I bent down and reached out my fingers, but they touched only air. Much quicker than even my adult cats could move, the orange ball jumped back, with an expression that looked every bit like a smirk.

I loved cats so much—I really did. But if this little guy were mine, we'd have to have a heart to heart about what helped me out and what didn't. But then, he belonged to the lady in the tent dress, so I really had no say. Maybe he was like a shop watch cat, a miniature furry guard, on a mission to make sure no mayhem occurred on his watch.

Sighing, I stared back at the reflection of the snowy, cold scene and sulked. There had to be a way to find out who the bracelet belonged to. Otherwise, this was all a waste of time. I needed to get back to the bookstore soon and help out Aunt Betty. Who knew how busy it might be? I hated the thought of her being there alone and getting slammed with customers.

Come on, lady. You said this wouldn't take long.

A phone rang from somewhere in the back of the shop. Footsteps headed that direction then stopped. From behind me, the woman's voice said, "I need to answer that. Brutus, make sure the nice lady stays right there."

Brutus?

The shop owner rushed out of the room, leaving me with the inappropriately named cat. I turned and glanced down at him. At some point after he'd backed away from me, he must have sidled closer, because there he was, staring up at me from six inches behind my shoes.

Shoes? Maybe he didn't like people who wore them since his mistress didn't have any on. If I removed my shoes, would he like me better? Feeling silly, I decided it was worth a try. I bent down and slipped off my sneakers, leaving them beside me on the floor.

"There, Brutus. Does that help? Will you trust me now and not be a guard dog, er, cat?"

Brutus blinked but didn't move. Maybe this would work. I took one step away from the wall, and the orange kitten whapped my bare foot with his paw. Obviously the shoes weren't the issue.

While the lady was still in the back, it was my only chance to take a look at those receipts, which I could now see were lying right there, a few feet away from me on the counter. I had to get over there. But how?

Dejected, I stuck my hands in my pants pockets. My fingers brushed against something small and hard in my right pocket. I frowned. What was in there? Then, I remembered. Early this morning, I needed to bribe Milton and Pearl to the back of the store while Aunt Betty held open the door for a delivery man. It was the best way I could think of to keep them out of the way and also not give them a chance to dart outside. What I now had curled inside my fingers were kitty treats. *Please let this work.*

I could hear the woman talking in the back room. Who knew how long she'd remain? It was now or never.

Pulling my hand from my pocket, I bent down slowly. "Hey, Mr. Brutus. Are you hungry? Want a treat?"

The kitten's eyes opened wide. The word treat must be universal for hungry felines everywhere. I placed one piece of food at my feet, nearly laughing when he inhaled it and peered up hopefully for more.

"Do you like to chase things?" I tossed one away from me, into the corner. Brutus bounded after it, sliding across the floor and nearly colliding with a mannequin wearing a ruby red necklace. He gobbled it up and ran back to me.

"Good boy." Taking a chance, I ran my finger over his soft fur. He let out a purr.

"See?" I said, "You're not a big tough guy, are you? Just a sweet puffball."

His purr boomed out.

Now, to keep him occupied for long enough that I could snap pictures of the receipts with my phone. I doubted I had enough time to stand there and read them all. "Okay, kitty, you get all the rest of the treats, Sound good?"

His tiny tail wagged in anticipation as I gave the rest of the treats a toss, causing them to scatter across the floor. The scavenger hunt would hopefully occupy him for long enough.

The second he took off toward the treats, I slipped on

my shoes and ran toward the counter. I grabbed my phone from my pocket then spread out the receipts so each was visible. I took one big one of them all in case the lady came out and I had to hurry away. When she still hadn't returned, I took a separate picture of each paper. When I had them all, I rushed back to the spot, slipped the phone into my pocket, and faced the winter scenes again.

Twenty seconds later, slaps from her bare feet hit the floor as she approached from the back. Uh-oh. Where was Brutus? I darted a sideways glance to my right, where the cat had finished the treats and stared at me. How would I get him to come back as if he'd never left his guard duty? I dug into my pocket, hoping I'd missed a treat. My fingers grazed what felt like a smaller piece, like one that had broken off. It was better than nothing and would have to do.

I dropped it right behind me, smiling when tiny kitty paws padded back to me and slurped up the morsel.

Good boy.

She entered the room. "Excellent job, Brutus," she said. "Mommy is very proud of you for doing your job correctly. You'll get treats."

Brutus meowed and ran toward the counter.

I bit my lip so I wouldn't laugh.

A rustling came from the counter. Was she going through the receipts?

"All right, miss. You may turn around now."

When I did so, she waved the stack and said, "I've checked through them, and several were paid for by cash, so there's no way to know who it was. Some of the ones with credit card payments were from out of town, so it will be more difficult to return the bracelet, although I highly doubt they'd be the ones to have dropped it in your shop anyway, since they aren't from here. Two were from Green Meadow, but I'm not familiar with them. If it will help, I will keep their receipts to the side, and if they return here to replace their lost bracelet, I can tell them to contact you."

I faked a frown. "Well darn. Thanks anyway for trying. I do appreciate it." I checked my watch. "Goodness, I have to be going back to work." I stepped toward the counter. "Thanks again." I gave her a wave and then glanced down at the cat. "See ya, Brutus."

He yawned.

I left the jewelry store, walked a few feet away so I wouldn't be seen through her front window, and checked the pictures on my phone. Some were indeed cash, which wouldn't do me any good. And I wasn't focused on names I didn't recognize. It didn't make sense to me that this might have been a random attack from someone who wasn't local. But two names stuck out. One was Olive Phipps. The other was Tina Jeffers.

CHAPTER TWENTY

Aunt Betty normally took the bookstore's deposit to the bank, but Wallace had stopped by the store to see her, so I volunteered to go instead. Not only did I want to give her privacy, but I also still wasn't comfortable around the guy. Imagining Wallace being a womanizer made my heart ache for my sweet aunt.

When I entered the bank, the teller, who I vaguely remembered from when I was little, gave a big toothy smile. "Why, hello there," she said. "So nice to see you."

I smiled back, not sure if she knew who I was now or if she was that friendly to every customer. "Hi."

Her nametag said *Stella*. Oh right. She used to be in a card club with Aunt Betty that they'd go to on Thursday evenings, usually meeting in the bookstore after hours. If I remembered correctly, there was more chatting and laughing than card dealing.

Stella placed her hands, palms flat, on the marble surface of the counter. "How may I help you today, Christy?"

That answered my first question. "Hi, Stella. I have the bankroll for Words to Read By."

Her face fell. "But Betty always brings that. Just like clockwork. Has something happened to her? Is she ill? Had an accident?" She leaned closer, a horrified expression on her face. "Did the person who killed Nan finally get her too?"

Get her too? Horrified myself at the thought, I raised my hand to stop her tirade. "No, everything's fine. Really. She just got busy, and I offered to come today instead."

She nearly wilted with relief. "Thank goodness. You scared the life out of me."

Was she going to do this whenever I happened to be the

one to bring in our deposit? Because it would likely happen from time to time. "Sorry to frighten you. No, it's all good."

"Glad to hear it," said Stella. "You know, *she* was in here earlier."

"Who? Aunt Betty?" That didn't make sense. She would've told me if she'd already done the deposit.

Stella waved her hand. "No, silly. That other one."

"Which other one?"

"The lady who just got a new job," she said.

I thought for a second. "You mean Tina Jeffers?"

"That's right," she said. "And boy did she have something to say."

I waited, hoping she'd say more. Most people couldn't stand getting the silent treatment and filled in the gap. I'd discovered that with Tony when he was particularly argumentative and I'd lost the energy to converse with him.

Stella glanced around then back at me. "That woman marched straight up to my window, slapped her paycheck down on the counter, and practically crowed like an expectant rooster about her good fortune."

I bit my lip, trying not to laugh, certain roosters were never pregnant. Then picturing a rooster wearing a maternity smock, I sputtered out a laugh.

Stella raised her eyebrow at me then shrugged. "After that, Tina proceeded to tell me all about her new job at the newspaper. How she'd been the one chosen to take over Nan Bittle's column after Nan's grisly death." She grimaced. "But I guess I don't have to tell you about that, do I? Since you were the one who found her."

I checked behind me. A couple of people were standing a few feet away filling out their deposit slips, but they weren't looking our way, so maybe they hadn't overheard. "Yes," I said, "it's true I found her, unfortunately."

"Unfortunate that she was killed or that you found her?"

I shrugged. "Both." Neither option was enjoyable. "Did Tina have anything else to say?"

"Mainly that she was thrilled her payrate had increased so much with the job change and that she was glad Nan was dead," she said.

My eyes bugged out at the last part. "She actually said

she was glad about Nan being gone?"

"Yep. Heard it myself." She touched her earlobe then shook her head and frowned.

I thought back to the first day when Tina had been in the bookstore. She'd been upset at the thought that it might have been Nan who'd been killed in our apartment. But were her words true, or was she putting on an act if she'd been the one to do her in, wanting to get the coveted position at the paper?

Either way, her actions and words, at least according to Stella, kept her on my suspect list.

Switching gears, all business now, Stella's wide smile returned. "Now, let's get your deposit taken care of, shall we?"

"Uh, yes," I answered. "We shall."

She winked.

As she tapped away at her computer, I took the opportunity to glance around the room. Not much had changed since I used to tag along with Aunt Betty way back when. Same polished floors, same gray and white marble counters and tabletops, and same row of doors that I assumed to be offices off to my right.

There was definitely something soothing about familiarity. It made me feel even more at home in Green Meadow. Even with Stella's overreaction to my showing up instead of Aunt Betty.

A line had formed behind me as Stella and I conversed. How many had heard her talk about my aunt's supposed demise? News like that was exactly what we didn't need, causing even more gossip to spread around town. And from what I'd already learned, gossip traveled faster than Milton when he spotted a June bug.

Stella finished up my deposit, handed me the slip, and looked behind me at the queue forming in front of her window. She gave me a quick wave. "Bye now. Come again."

Oh sure, and cause you to have another meltdown in public? I don't think so.

I turned and walked away, glad to have that behind me. Next time I did this, I'd be sure not to get in her line. Maybe getting stuck in a slow line wasn't all bad if the person serving you didn't leap to terrible conclusions about your loved one.

As I tucked the paper into my purse and headed past the

row of offices, a voice caught my attention. It was Olive. Had to be. I'd spoken to her, or, er, eavesdropped on her enough in the past few days to recognize that raspy, insistent screech.

My first instinct was to walk on by. There were several people in the lobby now, and even though I wanted to listen—okay, eavesdrop—again, how would I do that without being noticed? With Stella passing gossip to me about Tina, what were the odds she told others, possibly everybody, who stood at her window? Me loitering around the lobby of the bank might become the next item for her to discuss.

But I felt I had to stick around, at least for a few minutes, even though I might be the focus of wagging tongues as a result. Anything that might help Aunt Betty out of this mess was worth it. What was Olive doing here, whining loudly to someone in one of those rooms?

Unable to squelch my curiosity any longer—Milton and Pearl would be proud—I sidestepped to pause outside the door, which was open a few inches. Olive was inside the room, but I couldn't see her. I needed a diversion so people wouldn't stare at me while I openly listened at the door. Something that would give me a valid excuse to be there for a little bit.

I glanced down at my shoes. One of the laces was untied. It must be serendipity. I was meant to crouch down and tie my shoe. Perfect excuse. Although, once I accomplished that, I couldn't very well just take a seat on the public building's floor and press my ear to the door. Now what? There had to be another reason for me to be over here, kneeling on the hard surface.

On impulse, I upended my purse and dumped the contents on the floor. Not something I'd ordinarily do, since I hated dirt and germs, but it was the only thing I could think of to keep me planted where I was for a while longer. I'd try to focus on the fact that people might not readily notice a woman who'd accidentally spilled her purse, instead of what ickiness might be lurking on the floor.

As slowly as I could manage, I grabbed the tossed items one by one, replacing them in my purse, so I'd be in motion in case anyone glanced over here, but not so fast that I'd have to stand up and leave right away.

From the open doorway came Olive's voice again. "But

you have to help me."

A man's voice replied, "I'm sorry, Miss Phipps. It's out of my control."

I tucked my wallet back into the bottom of my purse and slowly reached for my compact.

"But if you don't help me," said Olive, "I'll go bankrupt."

"Again, Miss Phipps, my hands are tied at this point."

I stretched out my hand to grab a pack of tissues that had flipped a few inches away.

A footstep—Olive's?—and then her wheedling voice. "Because of you, I'll be penniless. Homeless. Hungry and destitute. Do you want that on your conscience? Do you?" Another stomp. "I'll report your bank to the Better Business Bureau, the mayor…the…well, whoever else I can think of. And I'll take out an ad in the local paper telling every single person in Green Meadow what a terrible excuse for a human being you are!"

My sunglasses had slid across the floor and were lying facedown next to the baseboard. Inwardly groaning, I sighed when I saw they'd acquired a small scratch across the right lens during the initial purse dump. I picked them up and placed them in a side pocket where they normally lived. Maybe I could buff out the scratch later.

Footsteps came from within the office. I gasped. Was she coming out already? I stuffed a pen and small notebook into the back pocket of my purse. However, more steps sounded like she'd walked farther into the room, and I relaxed. I hadn't thought about what would happen if she walked out suddenly and caught me there. But I wanted to hear if she'd say anything more that could be useful.

A rapping sound, like a person knocking on a door, or maybe a wooden desk, came next. Olive screeched out the words. "How can you live with yourself, treating me this way?"

With Olive's voice getting louder, a couple of women in the line closest to me turned their heads. One caught my eye, and I shrugged then held up a container of breath mints and placed them in my purse. The lady's eyebrows lowered, as if confused, but when the teller motioned her forward to the window, she quit watching me.

From inside the room, the man cleared his throat. "Look, I've patiently listened to you…explain the ordeal you've endured."

"Do you think I get enjoyment having to beg you for money? I'm desperate! Soon to be without funds to even live. I'll die, and my rotting corpse will lie by the side of the road. It will be your fault for not helping me out today. Are you so heartless you won't even extend me a loan?"

"Miss Phipps, perhaps if your past behavior warranted it, I might be able to allow a small loan."

"Oh, then—"

"But I'm afraid you've missed so many payments, and were late on many more, that the bank can't in good conscience give you any more loans. I'm sorry."

"Are you really? Because you don't sound sorry. Not in the least."

"Ma'am, please."

"Don't call me *ma'am*."

I cringed, remembering her berating me for calling her that when I first met her. I could have told the guy Olive had a thing about that and being called *ma'am* sent her into orbit.

He exhaled loudly and said, "Miss Phipps, I'm afraid you need to leave now. I have clients with appointments who will be showing up soon. I'm afraid I can't spare you any more time."

"You're kicking me out?" she wailed. "Abandoning me to the elements out on the street?"

Silence. Had he rolled his eyes? Pointed to the door? Picked up his phone to call the authorities?

Whatever the case, footsteps approached the doorway. Panic shot through me. I didn't have enough time to grab the rest of my things and make it across the room and out the door before she'd step out.

I used my hand as a shovel, scooped the rest of my belongings into the open purse, and scrambled to stand, my legs having partially gone to sleep. I took a few steps to the left, away from the doorway, and darted into a utility closet.

The door slammed from the office, and I jumped. Loud stomps stormed away from the office and toward the exit, where another door slammed.

I released my held breath, opened the closet door…

And yelped.

A large woman in an equally large hot pink business suit stood staring down at me, meaty paws planted on her hips. And she wasn't amused. How had she snuck up on me? I peered down at her feet and saw the reason for her stealth. She wore bright-blue sneakers, the size of small boats.

"Miss, is there something I can help you with?"

I jumped again at the sound of her voice, sounding like a grating foghorn. "Uh, no, thank you."

"Do you have business at this bank?"

"I…" My hand indicated the teller area. "I just now made a deposit. Over there. With the tellers. One teller." I shrugged.

"Do you have business with the loan department?" she asked as she pointed above her head. And by golly, right there, was a sign announcing *Loans*.

Maybe I hadn't noticed the sign before because it was small. Or maybe because I'd been panicked and hadn't been thinking straight. Although I'd assumed it had something to do with that since Olive had been in there begging for one. "Um, no. I don't need a loan."

"Then what might I ask were you doing standing over here?"

"That's a very good question—" I glanced at her name tag that was partially hidden by her wide lapel. Only the letters *Dap* were visible. I took a stab at it. "—Dapper."

"That's Daphne, you idiot."

My mouth dropped open. Idiot? In my opinion, she looked more like a Dapper than a Daphne. I stood up straighter. "I'll have you know, I was standing over here because I dropped my purse and things scattered and I had to gather it all up before I could leave."

"You were just in that closet." She pointed behind me.

"I…uh… My tube of lip gloss rolled under the door. I had to get it."

She eyed me, then the teller area, and back to me. "If you were with the tellers and dropped your purse, how did things scatter all the way over here? Was there a sudden gust of wind that materialized within the confines of this building?"

"That's another very good question," I said.

She tilted her head. "Well?"

Now what? I needed to leave the bank, but this lady meant business.

My phone buzzed with a text from inside my purse. I fished it out and saw it was my aunt. Even though Aunt Betty might only want to know how much longer I'd be at the bank, I allowed a horrified expression to cross my face. "I have to go. An emergency. There's been a terrible accident." I raced across the floor, flung open the door, and squinted against the bright sunlight.

To my surprise, Olive hadn't yet left the parking area. Her back was to me as she leaned against the rear of her car. I slipped behind a column beneath an overhang beside the bank's front entrance to listen to her conversation.

Olive's shoulders were bunched in a knot, one hand holding a cell phone to her ear, her free hand clenched in a fist. "I'm telling you, I can't go on like this much longer. The bank turned me down flat." Olive listened for a few seconds then said, "Of course I begged. I practically groveled at the man's feet to give me some money. He said something about me not paying previous loans. Whatever. Oh, and get this. On top of everything, I lost my leather bracelet somewhere. Not sure where. I tried to get into the bookstore apartment to check for it, but that Christy Bailey was like a guard dog."

My eyes widened. Could it have been Olive's bracelet I found in the den?

"Why was I there in the first place?" she asked. "Because I need money and I need it now. I'd gotten so desperate, I was going from business to business with a sad tale about raising money for arts and crafts where Grandma lives in the nursing home." She paused. "No dice. Betty Hollingsworth didn't take the bait. Said she couldn't help me. Well, since the bank turned me down, I'll have to come up with some other way to get some cash."

She'd been to see Aunt Betty? Why hadn't my aunt mentioned that? And how had Olive wormed her way up to the apartment to possibly lose her bracelet, anyway?

Olive barked out a laugh and said, "At any rate, now that Nan's gone, all I need to get my inheritance is for Uncle

Hoover to kick the bucket. What? Yeah, he's old but hanging on. But I think I'm just the girl to do something about that."

She rounded to the driver's side of her car and got in. I stayed where I was until she'd left the parking lot.

As I hurried to my vehicle and slipped inside, I tried to calm down after being caught somewhere in the bank where I shouldn't have been. But since hearing Olive's remarks about her bracelet and laughing about doing her uncle in, she rose even higher on my suspect list.

CHAPTER TWENTY-ONE

The following afternoon, I'd just rung up a customer in the bookstore and waved to them as they left, when my cell phone rang. I picked it up from the counter but didn't recognize the number. I pressed the button. "Hello?" I said.

"Is this Christy Bailey?"

"Yes, this is Christy."

"This is Edie Pratt. A nurse at Green Meadow Hospital."

The hospital? My heart dropped to my toes. I slumped against the counter. "Is it Aunt Betty? Is she…"

"Your aunt is here with me at the ER. She'd like you to come right away."

"Of course, but—"

Two loud clatters from the other end made me jump. Then the line went dead. What was happening?

A quick glance around the store showed no customers. Milton and Pearl were perched by my feet, eyes wide and staring as if they knew something bad might be happening. I stuck my phone in my pocket and grabbed my purse from under the counter. Crouching down, I gave each cat a head rub. "Guys, listen, something's going on with Aunt Betty, and I have to go. Be good, okay?"

Mournful howls followed me to the door as the cats scurried behind me. I turned the knob. "I'll be back as soon as I can, all right?"

Milton turned his head away from me, and Pearl licked her front paw. It was the best I could hope for under the circumstances since they were miffed I was leaving.

I turned the sign to *Closed*, slipped outside, and locked the door. I rushed to my car, parked partway down the block, and then raced toward the middle of town.

As I gunned the motor and drove as fast as my old car would allow, my mind raced even faster. Why was Aunt Betty in the ER? Had she fallen while shopping and hurt herself? Or had some medical emergency?

A truck honked loudly as I passed him on Main Street. It wasn't something I'd normally do, but I had to get to Aunt Betty. What if something ghastly happened and she was taking her final breaths? My heart pounded hard, and my hands were slick against the steering wheel.

"Hold on, Aunt Betty. I'm almost there."

I reached the hospital parking lot, barely slowing down as I navigated the turn. My tires squealed. My car lurched as I stopped in the parking space. I jumped out, but the car was still running. I let out a groan, got back in to turn the ignition off and grab the keys, then slammed the door and ran to the building.

The few seconds it took for the automatic doors to open nearly did me in. "Hurry up!" I shouted.

They slid open, and I rushed toward the check-in desk, where a woman was on the phone. I ground my teeth together as I waited. She didn't look up. I waved my hand close to her face. She finally glanced at me but wasn't smiling. Holding up one finger in the *give me a second* gesture, she went on with her conversation, which seemed to be about what she planned to prepare for dinner that night.

What?

The lady needed to talk to me. Right. Now. Knowing it would make the woman mad but beyond caring, I leaned closer and yelled, "Hey! I need help!"

With an eyeroll, she put the caller on hold and studied me with annoyance. "What can I do for you?"

"What you can do is tell me where Betty Hollingsworth is."

She sighed as she jiggled her computer mouse to bring the screen to life. "Let's see." She squinted at the screen as if she needed reading glasses.

I leaned to the left and saw a pair on the desk. Pointing to them, I said, "Maybe it would go quicker if you wore those."

She frowned. "No. I'm fine. Now, what was the name again?"

When my hands formed into fists, I placed my hands behind my back, not wanting her to see just how volatile I was. "Betty Hollingsworth."

"Fine." She tapped some keys. "Here we are. She's in cubicle C."

Nothing more was forthcoming. Was I supposed to guess? "Where the heck is cubicle C?"

Her chair squeaked at she angled around and pointed to a doorway in a row of rooms behind her. "Right back there."

I blinked. "You mean all this time she's been so close and you didn't tell me?"

Her eyebrows lowered. "Miss, I didn't know till right this minute who you were looking for."

"But…I…"

She pressed a button on her phone and said to the other person on the line, "Now where were we? Oh yes, I was thinking roast beef for tonight."

Giving myself a shake, I rushed around the desk and bolted to cubicle C. A purple and green–striped curtain was drawn across the doorway. Afraid of what I might find on the other side, I gingerly moved the fabric to the right.

Aunt Betty reclined against a white pillow on a hospital bed. When she spotted me, her eyes widened and she held out her hand. "Christy, thank goodness you're here."

In my haste to reach her, I stumbled but caught myself before falling.

From behind me, something rustled. A tall woman in lavender scrubs shook her head. "Glad you didn't fall too," she said. "Don't need two of you."

"Two?" I eyed my aunt. "You fell?"

Aunt Betty took my hand. "Yes, but I'm going to be fine."

"I had no idea what happened. I raced to get here. Then a lady out front was too busy on the phone talking about her dinner plans to tell me where you were, and…"

The woman, whose name tag said *Edie Pratt, RN*, stepped forward and said, "Oh yes, Gabby at the front desk has a habit of using the phone for her own use way too much. I'll have to say something to her. Again. And the clatter you heard? That was my fault. I was using the phone to call you, and it slipped from my hands to the side table. By the time I picked it up, you weren't there."

Edie rolled a chair closer and pointed until I sat. Then she walked back to a computer that was on a mobile cart, where she tapped the keys.

I let out a sigh, relieved Aunt Betty wasn't bleeding, in a coma, or worse. "Okay, sorry I was so upset."

"You have every right to be," said my aunt. "In your shoes, I'd be the same way if it was you."

The smile I gave her wasn't much, but it was all I could muster. I looked her over. There was a bandage on her left arm I hadn't noticed before. "Is it broken?"

She shook her head. "No, dear. Just badly bruised."

"Are you hurt anyplace else?"

The sheet rustled as she moved her leg beneath it. "Abrasions on my knees, but I've been assured they and my arm will heal in time on their own."

Tears pricked my eyes. "I was so afraid," I said. "I didn't know what happened to you."

"It's all right, love. Now that you're here, everything will be fine."

Footsteps sounded in the hall and halted. The curtain pushed all the way open. And there stood Micah.

He'd been on his way to speak to the nurse but stopped when his gaze met mine. "Hi, Christy. Glad you're here. Betty was asking for you earlier."

I swallowed hard. "Um, yes. I'm glad I'm here too." It sounded lame to me. Had it to him? "Aunt Betty told me about her injuries." I frowned and faced her as I said, "but I still don't know what happened that ended you up here in the first place."

He crossed the room and stood on the opposite side of the bed. When he took Aunt Betty's hand gently, she let out a sigh, as if his presence and touch comforted her. "Apparently," he said, "your aunt fell off of a curb into the street."

"What?"

"She narrowly avoided being struck by a car."

I eyed my aunt closely. "A car? Did you lose your balance?" I asked. Would my aunt need some sort of cane or device now, to help her not fall? I'd have to keep a closer eye on her in case she needed help.

She huffed out a breath. "No, I didn't lose my balance. I…" She turned her head and glanced at the nurse, who still busily tapped away at the computer keys. Did my aunt have something to tell me she didn't want the other woman to overhear?

I leaned closer to her and whispered, "Is there something else you need to say?"

She nodded then pointed her thumb toward the nurse.

"Okay." I glanced at Micah, who raised his eyebrows.

He released Aunt Betty's hand and stepped toward the nurse. "Mrs. Pratt," said Micah, "I think Mrs. Hollingsworth needs a little private time with her niece. Perhaps you could finish that out in in the lounge area?"

"Of course." The nurse smiled and pushed the cart toward the doorway. "I'll be back in a bit."

"Thanks." Next, he tilted his head as he eyed us. "Betty, I can leave too if you want to speak to Christy privately."

She shook her head. "No, I want you to hear this too, Micah."

She waited a moment before speaking again. "I'm pretty sure—no, definitely sure—someone pushed me from the curb," she said. "Micah wasn't kidding when he told you I narrowly missed getting hit by a vehicle. When I looked up and saw that front fender coming right for my head, I closed my eyes and prayed. Looking back, maybe I could have rolled out of the way, but I guess I was in shock."

"I'm sure it happened really fast," I agreed. "No time to think about what to do. Thank goodness it wasn't worse."

"Amen to that," said Micah. "You were very lucky, Betty. I'd hate to think how it might have turned out differently."

She nodded. "I know. And I'm grateful. Still shaken up though." She held up her left hand, which trembled.

I rubbed her shoulder. "Of course you are. I would be if it had happened to me. But how can you be sure it wasn't an accident? Were there lots of people waiting to cross the street? Maybe someone accidentally got pushed themselves with people rushing to get across the street. They could have gotten knocked into you."

"There were several waiting, yes," she said. "But I felt

the definite press of two hands on my upper back. And when they shoved, I fell to my knees in the street. It was awful. And right before they pushed me, the person whispered my name."

Micah took her hand again. "I'm so sorry you had to endure that, Betty. But I'm happy to say you'll recover fully." He smiled. "But"—his smile fell—"since you're sure you were pushed, we need to call the police to come talk to you."

She grimaced. "Do we *have* to?" Her expression reminded me so much of Milton when he didn't get the treats he wanted that I nearly laughed.

"Yes," said Micah, "we do. Don't you think they should know about this?"

"I suppose."

While we waited for the police to arrive, Micah left to check on other patients, but the nurse got Aunt Betty ready to be discharged. I was so grateful her injuries were minor. It could have been so much worse.

Voices came from out in the hall. Detective Combs and Officer Pike rounded the corner and entered.

Aunt Betty, who was now perched on the edge of her bed, stiffened when she saw them. I stepped closer to her, taking a seat in the chair situated next to the bed. She reached out to me, and I grabbed her hand.

The nurse picked up her paperwork and excused herself to go out into the hall.

Detective Combs eyed Betty's bandaged arm. "I'm sorry to hear you've been injured, Mrs. Hollingworth."

"Thank you."

The detective flipped open a small notebook and skimmed over its top page. "Why don't you tell me what happened to bring us here today?"

After giving my hand a squeeze, my aunt released me then placed both hands in her lap. "All right," she said. She took a deep breath and let it out. "I was standing on the corner of Elm and Vine. At the stoplight."

"Go on." He waved his hand.

"It was crowded. Lots of people waiting for the light so they could cross."

Detective Combs nodded.

"Anyway," she continued, "I was in front of the crowd,

right on the curb. Someone pushed me and—"

He held up his hand. "How do you know you were pushed?" he asked.

"Because I felt it. Hands, shoving me on my upper back. I know what I felt."

He glanced at his notes, even though he hadn't yet written anything since he'd walked in. "In situations like this, where there's an impatient crowd, it's not uncommon for someone to get jostled accidentally."

"This was no accident, Detective," said Aunt Betty. "I was pushed into oncoming traffic, very narrowly escaping being run over. Whoever did this wanted to harm me. Or worse."

He cleared his throat then jotted something on his pad. "All right. I've made note of what you…experienced."

I frowned. Why wasn't he listening to my aunt? If she said it wasn't an accident, I for one, believed her.

Aunt Betty sat up straighter. "I'm telling you the truth, Detective. And right before I was pushed, the person said my name."

Behind Detective Combs, Officer Pike shook his head at my aunt.

I put my hand up to get the detective's attention. "It doesn't seem like you're taking her words very seriously," I said. With that, I also eyed Officer Pike.

"Rest assured I'm looking into everything, Christy," said the detective. "More to the point, Mrs. Hollingsworth is still very much a person of interest in Nan Bittle's murder."

Aunt Betty let out a gasp. "But you have so many other leads. And now this."

I grabbed my aunt's hand again, which had gone ice cold. Turning toward the men, I said, "Like my aunt told you, there are several people who could have killed Nan. Shouldn't the fact that Aunt Betty was out cold across the room at the time we found Nan count for something?"

The detective scratched his chin. "True. But we still have the fact that your aunt had the victim's blood on her hands. And hers were the only prints on the murder weapon. It's difficult to not take those things into strong consideration."

With her chin jutted out, Aunt Betty said, "But I didn't do it. I didn't kill Nan."

Officer Pike smirked. "Those words are uttered all the time by guilty people."

My mouth dropped open. "Hey, that's not—"

A shuffling in the doorway alerted us to Micah's return. When he spotted the policemen, he frowned then glanced at us. "Sorry," he said. "I wanted to get back sooner but had an issue with a patient."

Aunt Betty forced a smile. "It's all right, Micah. I know you're busy."

He eyed my aunt and me. I was sure our expressions didn't register as happy. "Betty, are you doing okay? Lightheaded or experiencing increased pain?"

"I…" She swallowed hard.

Micah's eyebrows lowered as he studied her. He angled to his left. "Detective, I believe my patient needs rest. If you have all the information you need, perhaps you could speak to her at a more appropriate time."

Detective Combs and Officer Pike exchanged a glance. The detective closed his notebook and slid it into his shirt pocket. With a nod to Aunt Betty, he said, "We'll be in touch."

My aunt held perfectly still until the men had left the room. As soon as they were gone, her shoulders slumped.

Micah came closer. "What did they say, Betty?"

She shook her head, as if unable to speak.

I put my arm around her shoulders and looked at Micah. "They didn't seem to believe Betty was pushed," I said. "And they're still keeping her very much in their sights."

Micah moved closer and laid his hand on her shoulder. "Don't worry, Betty. We'll get to the bottom of this." He glanced at me then back at her. "You have a whole team of us who care about you and will keep searching until we find the truth."

CHAPTER TWENTY-TWO

I glanced up at light streaming through the front window. Very bright today. I blinked, my eyes feeling somewhat dry. Also allergy season. Although for me, that was nearly the whole year. Thankfully, one thing I wasn't allergic to was cats. If that happened, I'd have a huge problem. So would Milton and Pearl. And I had a hunch they wouldn't stand for it, no matter how much I might suffer with symptoms. But that was a cat for you. I adored them, but they could be a bit self-centered at times. Not that they'd ever admit it.

When I reached into a back pocket of my purse for eye drops, my fingers brushed against something else. What had I stuck in there?

Frowning, I tugged the object out. It was the bracelet I'd found when Aunt Betty and I had been hanging pictures and moving furniture. I'd forgotten I'd stashed it in my purse after my time with Brutus the guard kitten. When I held the piece of leather up, the bright ray of sun from the window caught something I hadn't noticed before.

There were tiny scratches. No…it was some sort of engraving on the inside, right next to the broken latch, but the writing was mostly scratched out, as if whoever owned it tried to cover up the letters.

I hadn't noticed it before. When I discovered it in our apartment, it had been low lighting beside the woodwork. And the day in the jewelry shop, the lamps she had around the room were dim, at best.

I shrugged. Maybe I could call the shop owner at Sparkly Wearables back and find out if she knew anything about the engravings. Since no one was in the bookstore and Aunt Betty was in the back office, I took the opportunity to get the jewelry store's number online. I punched in the number and waited. It rang six times, and I was about ready to give up when a woman's voice answered.

"Good morning from Sparkly Wearables. How may I assist you today?"

Definitely the same lady from before. I couldn't mistake that voice.

"Hi, I was in your shop recently and asked about receipts for a leather bracelet."

Silence. Was she waiting for me to say more?

"Um," I said, "I showed you the bracelet and you were going to check the receipts for me?"

She was still on the line since I could hear breathing, but she said nothing. It was starting to creep me out.

I cleared my throat and continued, "Anyway, you said you couldn't show the receipts to me, but you'd look and see if you could discover who it might have belonged to." It hadn't been that long since I'd been there. Surely she hadn't forgotten already? I might not know everyone's name yet who frequented the bookstore, but if they asked me about their visit, I could at least remember they'd been there.

Just as I was ready to either hang up or ask if she was still listening, she replied.

"Oh, yes, hello," she said. "You spent time with Brutus, correct?"

So instead of answering my questions, she wanted to talk about her cat? Glad that she at least answered. I nodded then remembered I'd have to speak. "That's right. How is little Brutus doing, anyway?"

"He's a little genius." She let out a satisfied sigh. "Now then, I believe you had a question about the leather bracelet?"

Was I going to have to go through it all again for her? I hoped not. "Yes, that's right," I said. "Since the bracelet was engraved and—"

"As far as the engraving goes, that isn't done here. Each customer has that done at another establishment on their own."

"Could you possibly tell me what that establishment might be?"

"No," she said. "Can't help you. There are too many to count."

In little Green Meadow? "Ah, I was hoping maybe you could at least give me some of the places. Then I could go from there."

"I'm afraid not."

Hmmm. Didn't sound like she was willing to tell me any more. I held in a sigh. "Okay, well, thank you anyway."

"You're quite welcome," she said. "Have a great day."

"You too."

"Did you get that?" she asked.

"Get…"

"I'm helping Brutus wave his tiny paw at you. Are you waving back?"

Feeling silly, I did as she asked. It was easier than lying and saying I had when I hadn't. "Yep, waving right now."

"Perfect." she said.

The line went dead.

I shook my head. What a loon.

"Christy?"

I jumped and turned to find Aunt Betty standing a few feet behind me, her eyebrows raised. "Were you just waving to someone on the phone?"

After stuffing my cell into my pocket, I lifted my hand. "You caught me."

"Who in the world was that?"

"Remember the leather bracelet we found in the living room?" I asked. "And we wondered if it might belong to the murderer?"

"Yes." She tapped her shoe against the floor as she waited for more news.

"That was the lady at Sparkly Wearables. I spoke to her the other day. While I was there, I met her kitten. And she, the lady, wanted me to wave to her cat. Over the phone."

Aunt Betty shook her head. "That woman is crazy."

"That's what I thought too."

Aunt Betty crossed her arms over her chest. "Any leads from her on the bracelet?"

"No," I said. "Well, maybe on a couple of buyers, but no on the scratched-out engraving I just noticed below where the latch was broken."

Her shoulders slumped. "Okay. Thanks for trying. And

for telling me about it. Because you know I want to be kept in the loop, right?"

I winked. "Yes."

The door opened, and Janie entered.

I smiled. "How's it going?"

She shook her head. "Needed a break. Dreamy Sweets has been hopping. Finally slowed down for a bit.

"I came here because I knew you two would let me vent, and then I'd feel a little better."

"Then I'm glad you came here," said Aunt Betty.

I smiled. "Me too."

Aunt Betty pointed to the counter, where she and I had cups of coffee. "Can I get you something to drink? Coffee, tea, soft drink?"

"Coffee would be great," said Janie. "Thanks. Need more to keep me going today."

Aunt Betty tugged a chair over from behind the counter and placed it off to the side then another for Janie. They sat and talked for a few minutes while I gave Milton and Pearl some treats, which, the cats informed me, was long overdue.

Once the cats' tummies were satisfied and they settled in a basket on top of the counter for a nap, I waited on a customer who came in to look at books in our Thrillers section. He found what he needed, checked out, and the three of us were alone again.

Rosey stepped into the bookstore.

I headed toward her. "Hi," I said.

She grimaced.

"Is something the matter?"

Rosey nodded. "I lost track of the days and realized my stupid great-nephew's birthday is tomorrow. If I don't buy him something, he'll have a tantrum. For lack of something better, thought I'd get him the first book in your series."

Gee, what an endorsement about my books. And what a terrible thing to say about her family member. "Um, sure," I said. "Need some help?"

She waved her hand. "No. I know where they are." She glanced toward the counter. "Looks like you're taking a load off over there. You go right ahead."

"Okay. If you're sure. Please let me know if you need

anything."

"Yep," she answered as she headed across the room to where the books were set up on display. I watched for a few seconds, satisfied she didn't need my help at the moment.

I dragged out a third chair and sat beside Aunt Betty.

Janie glanced first at Aunt Betty then at me. "I feel like I've been so busy at work, I might have missed out on something going on with…" She pointed up toward the apartment.

Aunt Betty nodded. "As a matter of fact, Christy was just telling me about something right before you got here."

"Really? Do tell." Janie planted her elbow on the chair arm and her chin on her fist as she settled in for the latest news.

I lifted my chin toward Aunt Betty, indicating she could tell it. Another quick glance across the room at Rosey showed her flipping through the pages of the book, uninterested in our conversation.

Aunt Betty clasped her hands together and said, "In the interest of finding out who killed Nan, Christy took something we found in the apartment to a jewelry store to see who it might belong to."

Janie's eyes widened. "And did you find out?"

I leaned forward. "First of all, it was that store Sparkly Wearables," I said.

"Huh," said Janie. "That lady is certifiable."

I laughed along with Aunt Betty. "Yes," I said, "that's what we said. Anyway, I found a brown leather bracelet we discovered pressed against a baseboard of the same color that we hadn't noticed until we were hanging some shelves up next to the wall."

Janie leaned forward as well. "Did she know who it belonged to?"

"Unfortunately, nothing definite," I answered. "Only a couple of shallow leads."

"Oh, well, that's too bad." Janie shook her head. "It might have helped clear Betty with the police. But you said nothing definite, so maybe there's hope you might still be able to use the information?"

I nodded. "That's my hope. There was something engraved on the inside of the bracelet, and someone tried to scratch it out. But I'm still determined to find out who it belonged to. Even if it means talking to the crazy loon again."

Aunt Betty grinned. "It's good to have something to laugh about right now. Even if it's simply that we all agree the lady is…well, a little nuts."

Rosey rushed toward the counter, glancing down at her watch. "Well," she said, "I've done it this time."

I frowned. "What's wrong? Need to get back to work??"

She tossed her credit card onto the counter. "I have to meet someone at Petals and Stems today. She's supposed to pick up a custom order. And the time is right now. My watch stopped, but I see by your wall clock that I'm running very late. Essie will have my head if she has to deal with it herself. So, if you could hurry?"

"No problem." I put the book in a bag with her receipt and a bookmark. "I hope everything goes well at work."

Without a word, she hurried from the bookstore.

Aunt Betty watched Rosey pass the front window as she headed down the block. "It's too bad Rosey has to put up with such a disagreeable boss."

I squeezed my aunt's hand. "That's why I'm so grateful you and I have each other."

She winked. "Same here, love."

The door opened again. This time it was someone I didn't wish to see. Detective Combs. My heart sped up. Was he here to arrest Aunt Betty? Had he found something he thought linked her further to the murder?

Aunt Betty's face had gone white. I took her hand in mine as we waited.

Detective Combs gave us a nod. "Hello, ladies. I have some information you need to hear."

Was this it? Would he take my poor sweet aunt to jail? Aunt Betty squeezed my hand and swallowed so loud I could hear it.

He approached us, flipped open his ever-present notepad, and looked at something before focusing again on us. He angled his chin toward Janie then said, "Mrs. Hollingsworth, do you have any objection to me speaking freely in front of everyone here?"

"No," said my aunt. "Please continue."

"All right," he said. "Here's what we have. A little while ago, Dennis Paisley was arrested for public intoxication. While lying on the bed in his cell, he mumbled something while he was half asleep and still very intoxicated. The other prisoner, who had sobered up and was ready to be discharged soon, told us what Dennis had said, in hopes of getting his own sentence reduced for the information."

I couldn't stand it anymore. If this was the horrible moment Aunt Betty and I had dreaded, we needed to hear it so we could figure out our next step. "What did Dennis say?" I asked loudly.

Detective Comb's eyebrows rose at my loud exclamation. "He said that he'd come here to find some money hidden someplace before Nan had a chance to get it for herself. He'd known where she'd be because he'd been in the newspaper office to buy a local paper and overheard her say where she was going and when. He stole some papers from her apartment while she was out. Something to do with where the money was hidden. He also said he was glad Nan was dead because that would make it so much easier for him to get the money without her interference."

I gasped. "He's been arrested for Nan's murder?"

The detective raised his hand, palm out. "We still need to check into a few things, but I think it's very likely. Officer Pike is on his way over to Dennis's hotel room to look for any evidence."

And I knew exactly what Officer Pike would find. I let out a huge breath. Aunt Betty sagged against me, a few tears forming on her lower eyelashes.

Detective Combs gave us a nod. "I thought you should know where we are in our investigation. I'm almost one hundred percent certain that Dennis Paisley is our guy." He closed his notebook, turned, and left the bookstore.

I hugged my aunt. Janie wrapped her arms around both of us. It was finally over!

CHAPTER TWENTY-THREE

We'd had a busy day at the bookstore, and Aunt Betty decided we needed a treat. I'd picked up tarts from Dreamy Sweets, strawberry, of course, and had just made it back to the bookstore.

The door squeaked as usual when I opened it. Normally it startled Milton and Pearl, who should have been used to the sound by now but weren't. But they weren't even in the room. Neither was Aunt Betty.

Where was everyone?

A loud hiss and then a growl came from upstairs. That didn't sound good. After placing the sack of pastries on the counter, I hurried up the steps.

The door to the apartment area stood wide open. Leaving it that way was something my aunt didn't ordinarily do.

When I got closer, the first thing I noticed was the tip of a black tail showing over the threshold to the den. What was Milton up to? Usually he was so nosy, he'd be all up in Aunt Betty's business. It wasn't like him, or any cat for that matter, to stand back when there was something interesting to see.

"Milton? What's up, buddy?"

He jumped at my greeting and whipped around, his eyes huge and fur puffed out twice his normal size. Then he darted farther into the room. Something was very wrong.

I stepped through the doorway and into the den.

Pearl was staring at something to my right, but I couldn't see what. Her fur was puffed too, and her thick white tail thrashed side to side.

"Hey, Pearl. What…"

As I moved to stand directly behind her, I nearly collapsed from the sight.

Aunt Betty stood there, her face reddened, and fingers clutched to the other person's arm around her neck. A gun was pressed against her temple. The person holding the weapon was…

"Rosey?" I said, "What are you doing?" I took a step, but she pressed the gun tighter to Aunt Betty's head.

"Don't come any closer. I mean it!" she shouted.

Aunt Betty's eyes watered, and she winced. She moved her lips as if wanting to speak, but nothing came out.

I couldn't take it all in. It made no sense.

I held out my hands, trying to appear nonthreatening so Rosey wouldn't do further damage to my beloved aunt. "Rosey, I don't understand. Why…why are you doing this to Aunt Betty?"

Rosey's eyes narrowed, and her normally grumpy but guileless expression was nowhere to be found. In its place was lips pulled back in a snarl and teeth bared. "You are really an annoyance, Christy."

"What's that supposed to mean?"

"Things were going so well, and then you showed up in town. Why couldn't you have waited? Or better yet, have not come at all?"

"I'm not sure what's going on here," I said. "Uh…maybe you need to talk to someone? See a doctor?" I had no idea if Rosey suffered from any sort of mental illness. Did she normally take medication and had run out? I wanted to believe the best of her, but the scenario before me made that nearly impossible.

"I'm not crazy!" As she shouted the words, spittle flew from her mouth. Pearl, now sitting below them, hissed and took a swipe at Rosey's leg.

Milton, who'd been hiding somewhere to my left, darted out and took his place beside his sister. Shoulder to shoulder, tails lashing in sync. Simultaneous eerie howls rising up from their mouths.

Rosey peered over Aunt Betty's shoulder and down at the cats then said, "What's wrong with those mongrels? Make them shut up."

Rosey kicked her left foot toward the cats, narrowly missing contact with Milton's ear. "Worthless bags of fur."

Aunt Betty's eyes widened, and she gasped.

Pearl crouched down and growled. Milton stayed standing but hunched his back like a buffalo.

When Rosey stomped her foot, making a cracking sound against the floor, both cats darted behind me.

"Please," said Aunt Betty. "Don't hurt the cats. They haven't done anything to you."

Rosey tightened her arm around my aunt. "Be quiet. You don't get a say in this. In any of this."

I took a step closer, relieved that Rosey hadn't seen it. "Why don't you tell me what *this* is, anyway, Rosey?" I asked. "Because I don't understand."

"That's because you're too stupid to live."

I blinked. "What's happened that you're treating us this way?"

"Because your aunt is a traitor," she hissed.

Aunt Betty frowned and squeaked out the word, "*Traitor?*"

Knowing it would cause Rosey to become even angrier if Aunt Betty spoke, I caught my aunt's gaze and gave a brief shake of my head. She blinked slowly, showing she understood.

I crossed my arms over my chest, hoping Rosey wouldn't see my hands tremble. "Wait," I said. "What do you mean by traitor? What has Aunt Betty ever done but be nice to you?"

"Nice?" Rosey screeched. "That's what you call it? Someone who steals from you?"

I tilted my head. "What do you think she's stolen?" I couldn't imagine Aunt Betty ever doing that even unknowingly.

Rosey lifted her chin in defiance. "In a word, Wallace."

My mouth dropped open right as Aunt Betty jerked.

Rosey's eyes gleamed as she stared at me. "I see I have your attention now, Christy. Yes, that's right. I've been in love with Wallace for a very long time."

"Why didn't you ever say so?" I asked. "Especially when Aunt Betty began seeing him?"

"That did throw a wrench in things, I'll admit," she said. "But it was Nan I had to deal with first."

Deep down, I already knew the answer, but I had to ask the question just the same. "You killed Nan?"

"You bet I did. That old bag went to great lengths to get him, but it didn't work. But I overheard Nan when I was in the newspaper office, dropping off Petals and Stems' payment for advertising. The idiot must have been on loudspeaker, because I heard her talking to Betty. Nan had another plan to get him. That she wasn't going to give up. Ever. I had to stop her."

Rosey's arm around Aunt Betty twitched, as if she was weary of holding that position for so long. And since I'd been out getting the pastries for at least twenty minutes before finding them like this, her arm was probably tiring. I chanced another step.

"Stop where you are, Christy."

I held up my hand. "I'm not trying to do anything here, just… It might help all of us if we could sit down together—"

She shook her head vigorously.

"—and talk all of this out. I'm sure you and Aunt Betty could use a change of position. Right?"

On cue, Aunt Betty sagged against Rosey, as if unable to stand up any longer.

As if my suggesting Rosey might be uncomfortable made her realize it, she blinked. "Okay," she said, "I guess. But you don't go near your cell phones or try to yell for help. Got it? I still have this gun, and believe me, I have experience taking someone's life, so I'm not afraid to use it."

Slowly, Rosey loosened her hold on my aunt, who let out a long sigh and rubbed her temple where a red, circular bruise was forming. Rosey glared at her then gave her a small shove toward a couch against the opposite wall.

Aunt Betty sank down into the cushions, grabbing a pillow to clutch against her middle, as if for protection.

Rosey chose to remain standing, but I sat next to Aunt Betty and wrapped my arm around her. I gave her a gentle hug and whispered, "Are you okay?"

She nodded and wiped away a tear from her cheek.

Rosey stomped her foot. "Hey, stop talking to each other over there. Christy, if you want to talk to me, then do it."

I held my aunt for another few seconds then slid my arm away and leaned forward, facing Rosey. "Why are you doing this?"

"Why do you think? I've had enough. It's been so

painful to watch first Nan try to seduce Wallace, and then Betty and Wallace seeing each other. When I heard that he told her he loved her in Perked Up, I nearly lost it. How dare he say that to another woman, especially when he hasn't given me a chance yet."

"All right, Rosey. You've admitted to killing Nan. How do you think you'll get away with it?"

"That's right," she said, "I did kill her. Proud of it too. And would do it again if I had the chance." She whipped the gun around as if it were a sword. "As far as getting away with it, you're watching me do it as we speak."

Suddenly, Aunt Betty clasped my hand. "I'm so sorry, Christy."

"Why would you need to be sorry?" I asked. "You've done nothing wrong."

"I… When Rosey arrived and I saw that weapon, it all came back. How she'd stabbed Nan, right in front of me. And when I screamed and tried to pull her away, she grabbed one of those heavy bookends and hit me. If only I'd remembered sooner, it could have saved all of us so much grief."

Rosey made a tsking sound. "Honestly, Betty, such drama. All your screaming that day. And the crying now. Sometimes emotion has to be set aside in order to get things accomplished."

I glared at her. "Accomplished? You make it sound as if killing Nan was something to check off your list."

"When you put it that way, it was," she said. "I needed to get rid of her, and it needed to happen fast. So yes, it was something I accomplished. And I can say, I'm actually quite proud of how it came about."

Aunt Betty slipped her hand from mine. She straightened her back and stared right at Rosey. "How dare you?"

Rosey glared at her. "Oh, I dared, all right. The only thing that didn't go as planned was you, Betty. I honestly thought I'd killed you. I hit you so hard, I didn't think you'd survive it. Just my dumb luck you didn't succumb. When I saw you were still alive, I was biding my time to see if you remembered or not. When time went on and you hadn't, I assumed the coast was clear for me to carry on as normal and no one would be the wiser."

I shook my head. "Then why are you here now? Threatening Aunt Betty?"

Rosey slashed the gun through the air again. "I'm here now because you, Betty, wouldn't leave Wallace alone. And you got him to say he loved you. How did you accomplish that?"

Aunt Betty's mouth dropped open. "What are you implying?"

"Nan tried to seduce Wallace, and it didn't work. I'm guessing you must have gone the extra mile."

With a gasp, Aunt Betty stood, her hands on her hips. "You're despicable. You wouldn't understand true love if it slapped you across the face."

Rosey's smirk dropped and anger took over. "Now you listen and listen good. I want Wallace, and Wallace I shall have."

I stood as well. "And how do you think you'll do that, Rosey? Wallace loves Aunt Betty. And you won't be around to do anything about it."

"And why is that?" Rosey asked.

"Because you'll be in jail for murdering Nan," I answered.

"Not true. You and your aunty here will be dead, leaving the way for me to have the man I want. Now, hand over your cell phones so you don't get any ideas about calling the police."

I reached into my pocket and took out my phone. If I acted quickly, could I hit 9-1-1 before she saw me? With my thumb hovering over the numbers, I chanced a look up at Rosey.

Faster than I would have thought possible for someone her age, Rosey knocked the phone from my hand then grabbed my aunt's arm, tugging her into the same position they'd been in when I arrived.

"No!" I lunged toward them, but Rosey shoved the gun's barrel hard into Aunt Betty's temple. When a trickle of blood ran down her pale skin, I jerked to a stop.

Rosey winked. "That a girl. Now you're showing some smarts."

I had no doubt Rosey would pull the trigger without a moment's regret. Hadn't she proved herself capable of murder with Nan and attempted murder of my aunt? My phone had slid across the floor and rested right beside an overstuffed chair. Aunt Betty's phone was lying on a table by the far wall. It too was out of reach. By the time I grabbed either one and dialed, it would be too late to save my aunt.

Suddenly, my phone came to life, ringing. I could just make out the number, but there was no name. Who would be calling me? I squinted again at the number. Wait…wasn't that the same number that had popped up on my phone when the nurse had called about Aunt Betty being at the hospital?

Why would they be calling me now? I blinked. Oh, Micah worked there. Was it possible it was him? He'd asked for my number as Betty's emergency contact right before she and I left the hospital. If only I could reach the phone and have him send help!

"Christy."

I turned toward the sound of Rosey's voice. She'd been watching me all that time. My face heated.

Rosey tightened her hold around Aunt Betty's neck, causing my aunt to cough. "Don't even think about going for your phone. It won't do you any good. Time's up for you and your aunt. I'll shoot her first."

I stood up straight, pretending to be brave. "Leaving me to run for help."

Rosey shook her head. "No. You won't. Because you won't know if she's dead or just injured. You'll stay to find out. And then it will be your turn."

I swallowed hard. She was right. No way I'd leave my aunt here with her, no matter the circumstances.

My gaze flew to Aunt Betty's. Was she thinking of Wallace? How their life together was just beginning? He'd be without Aunt Betty if Rosey was successful. And to think I'd once considered him a suspect as the murderer.

My phone rang again. It was then I remembered the message box on my cell was full. Whoever called wouldn't be able to leave a message. My heart sank. Would whoever it was show up in time to save us?

CHAPTER TWENTY-FOUR

If it was Micah trying to call me, maybe he'd eventually come over. Or Janie would. Or Wallace. I'd take anyone right now! But what were the chances someone would just happen to drop by, and in time to save us from crazy Rosey?

My only hope was to keep her talking. If nothing else, it might give someone, anyone, time to come to the bookstore. Even though our business day was over, I was pretty sure I hadn't locked the door when I'd come in after hearing Milton growling in the back room and Aunt Betty nowhere in sight.

"Rosey," I said, "listen, why don't we sit down again? I think Aunt Betty needs a break."

Rosey's laugh was harsh and loud. "Why would I want to give her a break? After she stole my man away from me?"

Aunt Betty struggled beneath Rosey's tight clench then winced when the edge of the gun cut into her skin again. She glanced at me, gave a blink, and relaxed. I took that to mean she was okay for the moment, but don't take too long with whatever my plan was.

Rosey didn't release Aunt Betty completely but loosened her grip and moved the gun away from her head, instead allowing the weapon to hang from her fingers at her side. For a second, I considered diving for the gun, but it might go off and injure my aunt. I couldn't risk that.

At least Aunt Betty didn't have the crazy weapon aimed at her. Now she could move around a little and take breaths without thinking any tiny movement would cause the bullet to go into…

A vivid image of what could happen sat securely in my mind. No. I couldn't think like that. Not if we wanted a chance to escape.

I relaxed my shoulders, hoping some of the tension would ease, but it didn't. If anything, my muscles bunched tighter. How were we going to get out of this alive? After flexing my fingers at my sides, I put my hands on my hips. Maybe a show of bravado would convince Rosey I was brave, even though I wasn't. "Rosey," I said, "you can't seriously think you'll get away with this."

"Of course I will. Didn't I fool both of you and everyone else all this time?"

She had a point, but I wouldn't admit it to her. I had to keep her talking. Time to drag out the nagging questions I'd had ever since the day I'd arrived. "All right. Maybe you'll answer some questions for me."

"Why should I do that?" she asked.

I spread my hands. "You say you're going to kill us. Don't you at least owe Aunt Betty the courtesy of clearing some things up?"

Rosey narrowed her eyes. "What possible reason would I have for doing any favors for her?"

I hardly considered answering questions before murdering someone a favor, but I kept that to myself. "I would think that so many years of knowing each other might be worth at least that."

Rosey gave a beleaguered sigh. "If it will shut you up, all right."

"Okay, then," I said. "I have some things to ask you since Aunt Betty is indisposed at the moment."

A small smile crossed Rosey's lips before disappearing, as if laughing at her former friend's predicament. "Fire away."

Aunt Betty flinched as if shot.

"Oops, maybe bad choice of words?" Rosey chuckled.

I crossed my arms over my chest, hoping to contain the fright building tighter within me as the seconds ticked by. "My first question is, how did she end up with blood on her hands when she hadn't been the one to kill Nan?"

"That's easy. There was quite a bit of bleeding from the stab wound, if I do say so myself. I simply took an old cloth I found in the kitchen drawer and soaked it up then rubbed it all over Betty's palms after I thought I'd killed her."

My mouth dropped open. She was proud of the amount

of blood? But why was I shocked? Any person who could do what she did then hide it and act like nothing had happened was insane.

Rosey winked. "See? Told you it was easy. Anybody could have done it."

"But not everyone would," I said. "Only you."

"Every person is good at something, I guess. Even though I planned on Betty dying, I added in the smeared blood on her hands to incriminate her. She deserved all of that after stealing my man away. Her reputation would suffer along with her. Also, wasn't it clever the way I wore gloves so my fingerprints weren't on the murder weapon?" It at least explained why Aunt Betty's were the only ones on the letter opener.

"Are you the one who pushed Aunt Betty off the curb?" I asked.

"Of course. Quite shrewd of me, wasn't it? I followed her then waited until she stood at a crossing, watching for traffic with several other people. It was crowded enough for me to sneak in close. People don't notice an old woman, so I had no problem doing it. As soon as a car came our way, I gave a hard shove. Easy as pie."

Aunt Betty's jaw muscle formed a hard line. Was she clenching her teeth?

I held out my hands. "Didn't you feel bad, even a little, pushing someone into oncoming traffic?"

"Why would I? I'd hoped her getting hit by a car would have snuffed out her lights permanently, but alas, I had to come over today to finish the job. Like I have time for that."

"Why?" asked Aunt Betty. "You said you thought you were in the clear because I couldn't remember anything."

A slow, evil grin formed on Rosey's lips. "To tell you the truth, I just got plain sick of you and Wallace being all smoochy lovey. I'd had enough. If I could have gotten rid of you quick and easy by you being crushed by a car, I'd have my chance with him sooner rather than later."

I shook my head. This woman who I'd begun to know and like had completely fooled me. But then, she'd done the same to all of Green Meadow, police included. Quite the feat, even though I wouldn't share that with her. It would only make her happy. "And I suppose the leather bracelet we found after the murder belonged to you."

"That's right," said Rosey. "Stupid latch broke, and I didn't know where I lost it. It was only after you'd mentioned it, Christy, that I knew for sure. My mind was on other things the day I killed Nan. Wasn't paying attention to my attire, so to speak. It was you going to the jewelry store to check it out then wanting to know about the engraving that pushed me to come here today."

I shook my head. What a devious person she was. And I'd never suspected a thing.

Rosey went on, "I hid around the corner and waited for you to leave today so I could finish off Betty. But I never guessed you'd be back so soon. I'd hoped you'd go shopping or see that weird friend of yours from Dreamy Sweets for a movie. Too bad for you that you had only gotten pastries and showed back up when you did."

Betty frowned. "But I never saw you wear that bracelet," she said. "Otherwise, I might have put things together before now." Thank goodness some of the shock was wearing off from Aunt Betty and she felt confident enough to talk back to her captor.

Rosey laughed. "You? Put things together? I hardly think so. You'd never seen me wear it because it was new. You're not the only person who can buy pretty things for herself, you know. But enough about the stupid bracelet. My plan was to kill you too. Or at least injure you to the point you would be incapacitated. Neither happened when I struck you, but you didn't remember anything. It was the next best thing."

What a crazy freak. How was her mind so warped to think any of this was okay?

Rosey sighed. "I initially had it engraved with Wallace's name and a heart but decided if you ever did happen to see the bracelet and got a peek at the inside, you'd know the truth. I took a sharp kitchen knife and scratched it out. Nearly killed me to do it." Her eyes squinted in amusement. "Killed? Ha, did it again, didn't I? Keep using these words that might somehow offend your tender ears."

I stomped my foot, enraged at all she'd done. "You also left that threatening note and blacked out the faces of the cats on one of the bookmarks," I said.

"That's right. I was hoping to scare you away, but you were stubborn enough to hang around. My hope was you'd pack up and leave with those mongrels you call pets, leaving Betty alone so I could finish her off without your interference. You showed up in town at the worst time. Very inconvenient, I might add." Rosey shrugged. "I must be getting old. My arm is tired from staying in one position for so long. Arthritis, no doubt."

She gave Aunt Betty a shove. My aunt sprang toward me, her arms out. I caught her before she took a tumble. After giving her the once-over and seeing she wasn't any worse off than before the push, I focused again on Rosey and said, "Maybe you do have a heart after all, giving Aunt Betty a break right now."

Rosey rubbed her wrist of the hand holding the gun. "Just tired. Didn't do it for her. Just me."

Next to me, Aunt Betty let out a harrumph. I was glad to see color had returned to her cheeks and her eyes had regained their luster. Rosey might not have released her for good reasons, but it helped, nonetheless.

Something caught my attention. My phone was still on the floor where it had landed before. Pearl sat next to it, hunched down, staring. What was she doing to it? Her fluffy paw darted out and gave it a poke and a shove. Then another. Was she playing soccer with it like she and Milton did with most anything that happened to fall on the floor?

Milton crouched down a few feet away, watching her. Pearl turned and looked her brother right in the eye and flicked her whiskers twice. Milton sauntered over and pressed his paw against the side of the cell, moving it another couple of inches.

Toward me.

Were they trying to give me access to my phone? Smart kitties!

From where we all stood, Aunt Betty and I could view the cats, but Rosey was facing us, with her back to them.

Having noticed us looking at something behind her, Rosey whipped around and spotted the cats. She gasped. Quickly, she hurried over and kicked the phone all the way beneath the sofa. "Leave that alone, you worthless furballs!" she yelled.

Milton growled and Pearl hissed as they darted beneath a nearby chair. Only their bright-green eyes were visible as they peered out.

Nice try, kitties. Mama appreciates your efforts.

A noise came from down in the bookstore. Had someone finally shown up? I took one step backward, toward the doorway.

Aunt Betty squeaked as Rosey once again grabbed her and pressed the gun to her head. "Go ahead, Christy. Take another step, and your aunt is history. The same thing happens if either of you tries to alert whoever is down there."

I let out a huge breath, exhausted from fear and worry. Now there was possibly someone downstairs who could help with our predicament, but Rosey had the upper hand. As much as I wanted to run downstairs and scream for help, with Aunt Betty back in Rosey's clutches, I couldn't take the chance. Deflated, my shoulders sagged.

Rosey smiled. "That's better. Now we'll just stay right here and—"

A white flash raced past me as Pearl darted across the room and out into the hall. Milton was at her heels, a miniature tuxedo in motion.

Rosey opened her mouth wide as if to yell then snapped her lips closed. Had she realized that raising her voice at the cats would accomplish the very thing she didn't want to happen? That whoever was downstairs would be alerted to trouble in the apartment?

The three of us stood in silence, Aunt Betty and me hoping whoever it was would come to our rescue. Rosey, no doubt, wished they'd go away.

Time seemed to stop. I stood, holding my breath and willing whoever had entered the bookstore to somehow know we needed help. To climb the creaky wooden steps to the apartment and rescue us from Rosey's treachery and malice.

Nothing happened. No footsteps on the stairs. No one calling out our names. Maybe it was just a delivery person dropping off a package or a customer hoping we were still available to sell books today.

My heart sank. Across from me, Aunt Betty's dejected

appearance surely matched my own. What would happen next? Whatever it was, it couldn't be good. I clenched my hands together in front of me, trying to force my brain to come up with a solution. But my thoughts rushed and blurred, nothing coherent coming together to get us out of this terrible fix.

Then, a noise.

I waited, listening. But I knew that sound. It was cat claws against wood. The cats were returning after having checked out the possible delivery person who'd entered. Nothing there to help our situation. Milton popped his head around the corner, and he meowed, loudly. Pearl stood in the doorway, but she wasn't looking at us. Instead, she focused on something behind her I couldn't see.

What was going on?

Footsteps came from the stairs. Not claws this time—actual people feet. My heart leapt. Had help arrived?

"Christy? Betty?" Micah's voice.

As much as I wanted to yell at him that we were in the den, the sight of Rosey's gun stopped me cold. Her eyes now had an evil gleam, worse than before. She wasn't kidding about shooting us. And now, Micah might be in danger too. How could I warn him to be careful, to—

His steps sounded down the hall. He stopped in the doorway next to the cats. His mouth dropped open as he took in the horrid scene. "What's… Rosey!" He took a step.

Rosey clicked the gun. Had she released the safety? "Stop right where you are, Doc. Sorry you happened to interrupt our little soiree. But now that you're here, you can watch me get rid of this traitor."

He spread his hands. "Why? What could she have possibly done to deserve this?" He advanced a half step, slowly. Had Rosey noticed?

"I'll tell you why," said Rosey. "She took away the only man I've ever really loved."

Micah's eyebrows lowered. "Wallace?"

"That's right. If not for her, he and I would be together right this second."

Aunt Betty squeezed her eyes shut. Was she imagining them, Rosey and Wallace, together, Rosey finally pulling the trigger, or both?

After studying Rosey for a few seconds, as if trying to analyze her, Micah gave a nod. Perhaps like he did when a patient came into the ER who he had to figure out how to help. "I'm guessing you feel desperate and alone."

"You got that right."

"But taking someone's life won't change anything," he said.

"It would make me feel a whole lot better."

"No, it won't." He crossed his arms.

"How could you possibly know?" asked Rosey.

He sighed. "Because often, too often, someone comes into the hospital suffering from horrible depression. Many times, it's because of guilt over something they've done. Often to another person. Time and time again I've seen it. Nearly every one of them confesses that they'd give just about anything to go back and undo the damage they've caused."

"Well, that won't be me. I want Wallace, and getting rid of Betty is the way to do that. Just like I got rid of Nan."

Micah blew out a breath. "I figured as much."

"Well, aren't you just a smarty pants doctor?" said Rosey.

Holding his hands out toward Rosey, he said, "Please, I beg you, let Betty go. Take me instead."

My eyes widened. He'd just volunteered his life for Aunt Betty's. What a caring heart he must have. What would Rosey do? Would she—

"No!" Rosey slammed her foot against the floor, the movement causing her arm to tighten around Aunt Betty's throat. My aunt made a choking sound. But then she swallowed and seemed to be able to breathe. Thank goodness.

I caught Micah's gaze, gave him a sad smile I hoped conveyed my thanks for his generous offer, and then faced Rosey. "Please," I said. "This has gone far enough. Let us go. There's no way you can kill us all. Now that Micah's here, you're going to lose control of that gun. Don't you realize that?"

"Don't underestimate me simply because I'm old," scolded Rosey. "I know what I want, and none of you people are going to stop me. Now, Betty, say goodbye to your niece. It's time for you to disappear."

My aunt's eyes closed, and her body went slack. Had

she fainted?

I screamed.

Micah shouted, "No! Stop!"

But the gun didn't go off. Instead, Rosey yelped in pain. Because Pearl and Milton had each climbed one of her legs and sunk their claws in, deep. Bright-red spots of blood bloomed on her pant legs. She dropped the gun, and it clattered onto the floor.

Micah dove for Aunt Betty, scooping her up in his arms as he kicked the gun away from Rosey.

Rosey tried to push away the cats, but they held firm. Their eerie howling duet made my hair bristle.

I ran to Micah's side. "Is Aunt Betty all right?"

As he examined my aunt, using his tender and careful touch, he said, "Yes, she's fine. Just fainted from all the stress. Can't say I blame her." But when he glanced behind me, his eyes widened. "Here, take her. Keep her warm."

"What…" I asked.

The cats, having completed their intended mission, were sitting on the couch, grooming themselves. But that left Rosey free to reclaim her weapon or escape. Micah jumped up, grabbed the gun, and pointed it at Rosey.

With a moan, Rosey collapsed on the floor, sitting in a heap. "Why? Why did you have to show up? It all would have worked out. Wallace would have fallen in love with me. It would have been magical. We would have gotten married."

A rustling sound came from the doorway. Wallace stood there, his eyes wide. "Married?" he said. "To you? Never. Why would you even…" He caught sight of me on the floor, holding Aunt Betty. "What's going on?" He gasped. "Betty!" He attempted to dash across the room but stumbled, caught himself, and finally made it to us. "My darling."

I smiled. "She's okay. Really." Now that I'd stopped thinking Wallace might be guilty of killing Nan, I could see the genuine love and concern in his eyes for my aunt. Thank goodness. Now I could stop thinking he was planning something nefarious for her.

He took Aunt Betty in his arms, and she opened her eyes. "Wallace?" she asked.

"It's all right, my sweet. Everything is fine now."

After retrieving my phone, I called the police. They'd be here in no time, and Rosey would no longer be a threat.

I sighed, relieved that Aunt Betty was safe, relieved that the mystery was solved and we could move on.

When I glanced over to Milton and Pearl, I smiled. They were curled up together in a huge, purring ball of fur.

CHAPTER TWENTY-FIVE

After the police arrived and carted away a screaming Rosey, Aunt Betty and I went down to the bookstore for a change of scenery. We'd be fine going up there later—it wouldn't be like after Nan had been murdered and we kept remembering her in that chair, covered in blood—but for a little while, we needed a breather.

Wallace and Micah stayed as well. Wallace couldn't seem to stop holding Aunt Betty's hand or hugging her. I was so glad it didn't bother me now. That I no longer mistrusted him. My aunt deserved to be happy. And if Wallace was the man for the job, I was thrilled. Hopefully he and Aunt Betty would never know my true feelings from before. I'd do everything in my power to make Wallace feel welcome and to support him and Aunt Betty from now on.

Micah gave me a quick hug and then kept pretty close, seeming not to want me too far away from him. I had to admit, the experience sure had sharpened my senses and made me appreciate what I had. And what wonderful things might be possible for the future.

I shook my head. "I still can't believe it was Rosey. There were several other people I did suspect. But never her."

Micah crossed his arms over his chest. "Honestly, my money had been on Tina, once I heard she'd gotten the job that Nan used to have and then bragged about it to everyone."

Wallace shifted a little to his left, nearly stumbled, but grabbed the edge of the counter before he could fully fall. Aunt Betty reached out quickly to help steady him but said nothing. Then, without even acknowledging it, as if his behavior was nothing of concern, Wallace said, "I thought the murderer was Terrence, until I heard about Tina getting the job. Once that happened, it seemed like he didn't have quite as strong of a reason to kill Nan."

What really was going on with Wallace? I knew now that he was innocent of all I suspected him of, but there was definitely something wrong.

Aunt Betty shook her head. "I wondered seriously about Dennis. Having known him from all those years ago and having liked him, then seeing how he'd changed and drank so much, I'd started to suspect something was up. But when he let it slip to Christy and me that he'd come to town a week before Nan died, we knew he wasn't on the level."

"And then there was Olive," I said. "From what I overheard from her on the phone, she laughed about Nan, saying that now that Nan was out of the way, Olive would now only have to do in her uncle to get her inheritance." I frowned and turned to Aunt Betty. "Olive also told the person on the phone that she'd lost her leather bracelet and wondered if it was here."

Aunt Betty blinked. "Oh! I'd forgotten that part too, I guess, along with Rosey coming here. It was shortly before Rosey showed up that Olive barged into the bookstore. She was trying to get me to give money for something at her grandmother's nursing home."

"But did she follow you up here?" I asked. "To the apartment?"

With a sigh, Aunt Betty said, "Yes, well, I told her no and then assumed she'd leave after that, so I headed up here. But that darned lady had the gall to sneak up the steps after me, right up here to the den! She wouldn't quit hounding me about giving her money. Finally, she left." Aunt Betty rubbed the back of her hair. "Amazing what memories you lose when you've acquired a new lump on your head."

I rubbed my aunt's shoulder. "I guess all of our surmising didn't help though, since the one person none of us ever would have thought capable of the crime was the killer."

Milton and Pearl trotted down the stairs and ran toward us, tails high in the air like furry flag poles. They dove on the counter and sat side by side, wearing what looked to be smirks on their furry faces, with chubby cheeks pushed high into wide smiles.

I reached out with both hands, giving them ear scratches at the same time. I had to be careful with them. Often, they got jealous if one seemed to be getting more attention than the other. I leaned over and kissed first Pearl's head, then Milton's, earning me loud purrs. "You two helped save the day. Thank you for what you did. You were so brave. So smart."

Micah nodded. "They were amazing," he said. "When I came into the bookstore and there was no one around, I was concerned since the door was unlocked. I tried to call you, Christy."

"From the hospital's number? I saw that number come up. But I couldn't get to my phone."

"Yes, I called from my work phone. I can see why now, with Rosey being the center of your attention, that you couldn't answer. Your cats, when they came down the stairs and saw me, ran straight to me, meowing, winding around my legs. I tried to pet them, but they moved away so I couldn't reach them. Then they meowed again. When I tried to touch them, they moved farther away, toward the steps and kept looking back at me. It was like they wanted me to follow them. And I'm so glad I did. They're very smart."

I grinned, a proud cat mom loving the praise for her babies. Because yes, they were very smart indeed.

"And you're right," Micah said. "Because of them clawing at Rosey, the rest of us were able to overpower her and get the gun."

I lightly touched his arm. "No, you were the one who overpowered Rosey. I can't thank you enough."

"Wait," said Aunt Betty. "Wallace gets credit too. He came in at the perfect time to hear what Rosey had been up to and also to cause a disturbance."

I nodded. "True."

Wallace said, "Betty and I were supposed to meet for coffee after the store closed, and I got concerned when she didn't show up. I took a chance that she'd still be here, that maybe some late customers kept her from meeting. No one was around, but I heard a thump from the apartment and wondered if Betty had fallen or was in trouble. That's when I came upstairs and found…"

Aunt Betty's gaze took in Wallace, Micah, and finally

me. "I can't thank you enough, all of you, for what you did for me. For saving me. I have the best family and friends a girl could ever have."

Wallace gave her a wink. "I know when you say family you mean Christy." Milton meowed loudly, making Wallace laugh. "And yes, Milton and Pearl as well. But where do I fit on that spectrum?"

Aunt Betty's face reddened. "I…well…"

He grinned. "Would I be your friend? Or family? Or…" He shrugged.

I glanced at Micah. His eyebrows rose as he looked at me. Was he thinking the same thing I was? That Aunt Betty and Wallace might need some privacy to discuss something personal? When I tilted my head toward the door, indicating it might be time to step outside, he nodded.

I pointed toward the door. "Um, I think we'll just go and…"

"No," said Wallace. "Wait. Please stay."

My aunt's eyebrows lowered. Maybe she was as surprised as I was at Wallace's request.

With a shrug, I said, "Okay, Wallace. We'll stay."

Wallace took Aunt Betty's hand. "What I want to say is this…"

The door opened. Who would be coming in this late after hours? I'd forgotten to lock the door, even when we'd come downstairs after the police had arrested Rosey.

"Hi all." It was Janie. She ran across the room and enveloped me in a huge hug. "Christy. It's so good to see you! Are you doing all right?"

"Thank you. We're all fine now."

Her face fell. "What do you mean, fine now? You weren't fine before? Did something happen?"

I'd assumed her excitement at seeing me had to do with word having gotten out about Rosey and her having us at gunpoint. I might have guessed for Janie it could simply be because it was Tuesday.

Micah gently disentangled Janie from me. She grabbed his hand for support, appearing quite distraught that something had been amiss and she hadn't known about it. Micah took it in stride, surely having dealt with many patients who clung to him from time to time. "Listen," he said, "something has happened that you'll be hearing about around town, and probably soon."

"What? What's happened?" Her eyes grew impossibly big. And she wasn't blinking.

He gave her a kind smile. "Earlier, upstairs, Betty and Christy were in an…altercation with Rosey."

"Rosey? Rosey Davis? What's going on?" Janie yanked his hand so hard he nearly stumbled against her.

"It's okay." I patted Janie's shoulder. "Everything is okay now. It's—"

She gasped. "Tell me. I can't stand not knowing. Anything is better than being kept in the dark."

Micah tugged his hand free and placed his arm around her shoulder. After seeing how gentle he'd been with Aunt Betty in the ER, I could definitely see how his quiet spirit and gentleness would be good at calming someone down. He patted her shoulder lightly. "I know you're scared and confused, but I think if you listen for just a minute, I can clear this all up."

She blinked then nodded.

"Good. Okay." Micah let out a breath. "As I said, there was an altercation with Rosey, Betty, and Christy."

Janie frowned and looked at me.

I nodded. "It's true, Janie. We found out Rosey was the one who—"

"The killer?" she asked.

"That's right."

Janie's hand flew to cover her mouth. She shook her head. "I never dreamed… I mean. Rosey. I never suspected it might be her who'd done all those terrible things. What a shock."

Aunt Betty crossed her arms. "Believe me, I was as surprised as anyone."

Wallace shook his head. "Was all of this mess, the murder, this trouble she caused you, really because she wanted me for herself?"

Aunt Betty shrugged. "Apparently."

"I'm so sorry," he said.

"Wallace, you don't need to apologize for something you didn't do and had no knowledge of. Rosey turned out to be the kind of person none of us ever could have fathomed."

"Still, if I'd known her feelings sooner, maybe I could have stopped her before she went so far as to kill Nan. To nearly kill you." He hugged her again then took her hand. "I have something I need to say."

"Go on." Aunt Betty gave him her complete attention.

"Actually, it's something I want to *ask* you." He gave her a one-sided smile.

Janie hopped up and down "Oh! I bet I know what—"

I grabbed her hand and gave it a tug, stopping her from blowing what I hoped would be a proposal. She gave me a sheepish grin and made an invisible zipper across her lips.

Wallace laughed. "Now that I have everyone's attention, here goes. You see, for those of you who might not know, I suffer from tardive dyskinesia. As I'm sure Micah knows, it's a metabolic disorder. It's a result of having taken antidepressive medication after my wife died. Unfortunately, sometimes it makes me shake and behave in a nervous manner." He looked at me. "That's what happened the first time I met you, Christy, when I nearly knocked you flat outside the bookstore."

I blinked. "Oh." Suddenly feeling small, I clasped my hands together. With my imagination running amok, I'd had him possibly even knocking my aunt down after murdering Nan. The poor man, having to endure something like that, while people like me assumed the worst. "I'm so sorry to hear that," I said.

He waved his hand, which trembled slightly. "I've come to terms with it now. Besides, your aunt is the most loving person I've ever met and doesn't allow me to dwell on it but reminds me daily of my blessings."

Aunt Betty winked at him and said, "It's easy to tell you all of your wonderful qualities, because they're true. You're an easy man to…love." Her cheeks reddened. Was she thinking about the day in the coffee shop when he'd confessed his love for her in front of a crowd of people?

He kissed her cheek. "With that said, I'd like to finish my earlier question."

"Go ahead." Aunt Betty's smile was wide.

Wallace had both of her hands in his. "Will you, Betty Hollingsworth, do me the honor of becoming my wife?"

Janie jumped up and down again. "I knew it!"

With a laugh, my aunt threw her arms around Wallace's neck. "Of course!"

Wow. I wouldn't have dreamed a day that nearly ended with Aunt Betty gone, and possibly me as well, could end up with a marriage proposal. I hugged them both. "Biggest congratulations."

Micah patted Wallace on the shoulder. "Same here."

With a gleam in her eye, Janie said, "I already know what I'll fix for the reception. Let's see, along with a cake, we can have tarts, mints…"

I watched Aunt Betty to make sure Janie wasn't being presumptuous in assuming she'd be the one to cater the reception. If there would even be one. For all I knew, they'd want a simple, private ceremony. They had both been married before. Sometimes people didn't want the same thing the second time around.

But my aunt was beaming at Janie then hugging her. I took that as a yes, Janie was in. She motioned for Janie to follow her and Wallace into the office. "Let's talk about the cake," Aunt Betty said.

Janie squealed like the little girl I remembered. Some things never changed. After they'd left the main area, Micah and I were alone.

"I never got a chance to thank you, Micah, for saving us," I said.

"It was—"

I held up my hand. "If you say it was nothing, I may have to hurt you."

He laughed. "Okay. I won't say it." His smile dropped. "Honestly, I thought…when I walked in and saw…"

"Yeah, I know. It was surreal. And horrible. And scary. But I can only imagine the sorts of things you see in the ER every day. Some of them must be even worse."

"True, but they don't usually happen to people I care about," he said.

Care about?

Micah's phone buzzed, and he frowned. Checking the screen, his frown deepened. "Listen, there's been an accident out on the highway, and I need to get to the ER right away. But I'll call you soon, all right?"

"All right." I watched him go, feeling warm and fuzzy from his "care about" comment. But wait. Was that for me in a possible romantic way? Or as a friend? Or did that include Aunt Betty as a friend as well?

Rats. I truly didn't know. But the fact that he'd call me soon was something. At least that's what I'd tell myself as I'd no doubt constantly check my phone for any missed calls or messages until I heard from him again.

Something whacked my leg. When I looked down, Milton was washing his paw as if he wasn't the guilty party, but he was two inches away, while Pearl was two feet away. "Yeah sure, Milton, nice try."

He meowed pitifully.

"Awww, poor kitty needs a snack? You had a stressful day too, huh?"

Both cats leaped onto the counter mewing and winding around each other as I got a small container I kept under the counter for emergencies. Although anything to do with a cat and his or her tummy was an emergency. At least to them.

As I scattered several pieces of liver-flavored—ick—pellets on the counter, I sighed. "Well, guys, I think the drama is finally over. Now that the police have Rosey and Aunt Betty is no longer a suspect, I guess it will be business as usual from now on and things can get back to normal. No more drama."

Pearl stopped midchew and stared at me, her eyes bigger than I'd ever seen them.

I jerked. "What's that look for?" I asked.

Milton whipped around to face me and let out a screech.

My heartbeat sped up. "Hey, what's going on with you guys? Is something wrong?"

Pearl crouched down beside her brother and tapped her paw against his.. He blinked, twitched his ear, and gave the spot between her ears a single lick. They turned to me at the same time, identical green eyes boring into mine.

It was as if they were trying to tell me something. Like maybe they weren't ready for things to calm down quite so soon and they wanted to continue their obvious interest in sleuthing like their book characters did.

Perhaps we could check into the possible mystery of the John Dillinger money hidden beneath the gazebo out back?

I ran my fingers through their fur. "Okay guys, if you think we're going to make a go of this sleuthing thing for real and not just in your stories, I'm game. How about you?"

I held out my hand, palm toward them. First Milton, then Pearl pressed a paw against mine like a high-five. Now we were a team.

The Milton and Pearl mysteries had officially come to life.

ABOUT THE AUTHOR

Ruth J. Hartman spends her days herding cats and her nights spinning mysterious tales. She, her husband, and their cats love to spend time curled up in their recliners watching old Cary Grant movies. Well, the cats sit in the people's recliners. Not that the cats couldn't get their own furniture. They just choose to shed on someone else's.

Ruth, a left-handed, cat-herding, farmhouse-dwelling writer uses her sense of humor as she writes tales of lovable, klutzy women who seem to find trouble without even trying.

Ruth's husband and best friend, Garry, reads her manuscripts, rolls his eyes at her weird story ideas, and loves her despite her insistence all of her books have at least one cat in them.

To learn more about Ruth, visit her online at:
https://www.ruthjhartman.com/

Made in United States
North Haven, CT
11 March 2023

33912118R00139